Key West Normal
(Bric Wahl Series Book 3)
Thw Whole Ball of Whacks

Wayne Gales

Photography by Tina Reigel

"How to write a book - Jump off a cliff and build your
wings on the way down" Ray Bradbury

Be decisive. Right or wrong, make a decision.
The road of life is paved with flat squirrels who
couldn't make a decision. - Unknown

Wayne Gales

Dedicated To the Lovers, The Dreamers, and Me

Foreword

Well, third time's a charm. I never thought I would write a second book after I wrote the first, and surprised that I've completed number three. I took a few years off between novels. Not writer's block, just that life sometimes gets in the way of living.

You will meet a few new characters in this book, and say a fond "hello" to a few old friends. While "Key West Normal" can stand on its own feet, I strongly recommend you read the first two books, "Treasure Keys" and "Key West Camo" before you tackle this one. It will make more sense for sure.

What's next? Listen to the epilogue. There's a hint.

I hope you enjoy.

Wayne Gales

An Excerpt From Key West Camouflage

The next morning I woke up before Karen made a pot of coffee, poured two cups, and then climbed back up and handed one to her. "So," I started, "a change of heart?" Karen took a long sip of coffee and composed her words. "Started out being one thing, and then became another. That night when that terrible man was pointing a gun at you, I could sense you were thinking of a way to take the bullet so I could get away. If that's not true love, I don't know what is. At the same time, I realized that this may not be over. Running to Oklahoma and moving in with any one of twenty families, all named Murphy, would keep me in danger, and also endanger all of my family. I'm as safe with you and 'your people' as I can be anywhere."

She finished her coffee and handed the cup back to me for a refill. "And?" I offered.

"And, I don't think this adventure is done either. We don't have to worry about work or money. All we have to do is live our lives, and I want that to be with you." She closed her eyes for a moment, deep in thought, then smiled and looked up. "One more thing. Other than the gold you couldn't find, was there anything else on the manifest that you had expected to recover?"

I thought for a minute, and it came to me. "Emeralds. The manifest said there were a hundred and fifty gem-quality emeralds. We never found a single one," my eyes narrowed as I looked into her baby blues. "You're not telling me......"

Karen reached into her purse and pulled out a violet Crown Royal bag. Pulling open the top she turned it over onto the dining table. Small, medium, and large green stones rained out on the counter. "I was going to just throw these in the ocean when we were in Bokellia. The gold has caused so much pain and suffering, I didn't want it to start back up again with emeralds," she scooped them back into the bag and held it out. "Here, they're yours."

I took the bag and poured the stones back on the table. Looking through them, I selected one and held it to the light. It was maybe five carats, nearly crystal clear with no occlusions. "This one I have a plan for," I said, holding the emerald up to the morning sunlight. "The rest let's throw off the Sunshine Skyway Bridge or better yet drop them in a collection plate at some small mission on the road. Maybe all the bad mojo will follow."

Suddenly a light came on in my head. I got up and started a systematic search of the RV. Light fixtures, vents, fans, cupboards. Karen curiously watched me from the cab over, wrapped in a bed sheet. "Ah, there it is, at least, one of them." Under one of the twelve-volt lights was a tiny black dot of a microphone with a wire running through the ceiling. I talked into it. "Hey Tim, just to let you know I found one of your wires. I'm tempted to rip it out, but you probably have five backups, and anyway, you saved our bacon last night. Thank you, I guess. At least, be a gentleman and don't share the sex scenes." I turned to Karen with my eyebrows raised. That was a trick we always had, the ability to almost read each other's minds. She smiled and nodded. "One more thing. Karen needs her new ID also. Since you know where we are, where we will be, and where we're going, I'll trust you to figure out how to rendezvous. Signing off," and I thwacked the mic with my middle finger before closing the light cover. If anyone was actually listening they probably just got a nasty earache.

I got misty-eyed and made a decision. Looking in the cupboard and rummaging through the cans, I found what I was looking for; Dinty Moore beef stew. Grabbing the can, I pulled the ring to open the top and bent the tab back and forth till it came off. Reaching for her hand, I pulled her down from the bed, still sort of wrapped in the sheet, and stood her up. She looked at me like I was an idiot, which at that point, I probably was. When I dropped to one knee, her hands flew up to her face, the sheet fell around her ankles, and she started to cry.

"Karen Murphy, the second I have the chance, I'll get that emerald cut, polished and placed in the finest setting that money can buy, but for now, I hope this will do," and I slipped the pop top on her finger.

"Will you marry me?"

BODIES
FOUND NEAR BOCA
GRANDE IDENTIFIED AS LOCALS

Key West Citizen, Monday, June 2nd.

The bodies of two missing Key West residents were recovered today by the Coast Guard a few miles from the southern end of Boca Grande, some fifteen miles west of Key West, officials announced Key West Native, Russell Bricklin Wahl, 56, and longtime Key West resident, Karen Elizabeth Murphy, 51 have been missing since last Saturday. Florida Fish and Wildlife advise they have not found the boat and assume it has sunk. Wahl and Murphy had both been off-island for over a year on an extended vacation and just recently returned. The deaths appear to have been due to accidental drowning, according to the Monroe County Coroner. Wahl was employed most recently by Tarpon Salvage, the company that recovered a substantial treasure trove from a silver-laden Spanish galleon off Boca Grande two years ago. According to next of kin, both bodies will be cremated. Services have not been announced.

2
I Wish I Didn't Know Now
What I Didn't Know Then

It had been an eventful few weeks. Showdowns and shootings, tearful reunions, and a sad farewell to Key West where I was born and may never see again. Now, maybe it would all calm down. Debts honored, bad guys dead, new identities on the way, and more money in the bank than we could have ever imagined. With little more than a vague idea of what we wanted to do or where we were going, I started up the motorhome, and we eased out on Highway 19, heading north. After I had popped the question, Karen held me tight for a few minutes, wiped off her tears, and got dressed. As we drove off, she sat in the right seat with a quiet smile, but I noticed the temporary ring wasn't on her finger, and I was aware she never actually said "Yes." No biggie on the ring, it probably wasn't that comfortable, but maybe I jumped the gun on the proposal thing. Well, whatever, we're off on an adventure.

It could be worse.

Tim Heminger, my sort of old SEAL buddy, and current CIA spook needed some time to fill out my order to acquire a seaworthy sailboat, and Karen and I needed some "us" time away from all the craziness, so we just drove. We drove north to Tallahassee then hit Interstate 10, heading west through Pensacola, Mobile, and Pascagoula, then took a little detour south to New Orleans for five days. I had been here a few times in the past and considered *Le Vieux Carré* as almost a sister city to Key West. Although firmly part of the good old USA, they both had a noticeable international heritage, a healthy disrespect for proper behavior, and a comfortable ability to blur what other places considered appropriate. We parked the RV by the casino and opted for the comfortable luxury of a suite at the Hotel Monteleone. First things first. I took Karen downstairs to the historic and moderately famous Carousel Bar. Advertised as spinning non-stop for the past sixty-five years, I had climbed on a barstool here on more than one occasion. The round bar makes a revolution about every twenty minutes. The bartop turns but the middle doesn't and it takes a very special bartender to remember who was drinking what since their location was constantly changing. I ordered two Hurricanes and told Karen a funny story.

"The first time I came here I was on leave with a bunch of buddies. All they wanted was to hit the nudie bars so I cut myself out of the pack and eventually wandered into the Monteleone. Sat down at the carousel, ordered a Hurricane, and settled down to enjoy my second most favorite hobby, namely people watching." The bartender heard me start the story and moved nearer, taking a step or two to the left every minute or so to stay in front of us.

"So, in walks this lady and she sat down across from me. Guessing maybe late fifties, around two hundred pounds, big tits, lots of makeup. The bartender," I nodded toward our server, "not you, knew her and poured her a beverage. She struck up a conversation with a guy to her left, and then a couple to her right. With the music, I couldn't hear what she was saying. After a half hour, she worked her way around the rotating bar until there was just a seat between us. She greeted me, and I nodded hello. She told me her name was Anne. I told her mine. She asked where I was from, and I said Key West. She said 'wow what a coincidence' and slid over to the seat next to me. Said she used to live there, worked at Sloppy Joes, knew Captain Tony, and left town in a hurry due to some scandal with a city official. After that, she moved to Chicago and then Las Vegas before ending up in New Orleans. As she told me her life story, she kept getting closer and more touchy. Finally, she asked if I was interested in having some company. I said 'excuse me?' and she reached over and whispered in my ear that she would like to suck my cock, and it would only cost thirty bucks. She was a hooker." The bartender nodded, knowingly. I continued, "An old fat hooker, but a working girl nonetheless. I politely declined the offer. She wasn't offended, finished her drink, and wandered out of the hotel, most likely to change venues in the hope of better targets."

Karen and the bartender both laughed, and I held up my hands. "That's not the end of the story. Seven years later, I was here doing some underwater welding on a dock across the river in Algiers. On my day off, I came into town and walked down Bourbon and Royal

Streets, listening to music and having some drinks. Like I always do, ended up here at the Carousel. I ordered a Hurricane and took in the scenery. Well, guess who walked in? A little older, a little fatter, and a lot more makeup, almost to the point of spackle. I sipped my drink and watched her with amusement while she worked her way around the bar, again without any success, until she got around to me. She introduced herself as Anne again and asked where I was from. I answered 'Oh, here and there.' She asked what I was doing in New Orleans. I was ready for this - 'I'm here for the psychic conference at the Convention Center,' I answered. She replied that the occult and psychic powers fascinated her, and she slid onto the barstool next to me. 'So, tell me about myself' she said. I put my fingers to my temples and acted like I was concentrating. 'You have lived in many places,' I started. She nodded but knew that was pretty generic. I kicked it up a notch. 'I see the ocean. I see an island. I see topless women and lots of beads, but it's not New Orleans.' Her eyebrows came up, but she didn't speak. I continued. 'I also see a windy place and lots of snow, and now you are here.' Now came the punch line. I looked up at her with my eyes wide open. 'I don't understand this part, but, wherever you have lived, I see men, hundreds, no, thousands of men in your life, and for some reason, you called them all John.' With that she nearly fell out of her chair, stammering and backing up until she ran out of the bar and down the street as fast as her chubby little legs could take her. I'm sure she had seen a zillion guys in the seven years since I had first met her, but that was the only old fat hooker that I had ever encountered at the Carousel."

By now we had assembled a pretty good crowd at the bar, and when I finished the story, the whole bar erupted in laughter. I have no doubt it would be shared many times before the night was up.

Using the Monteleone as a base, we enjoyed New Orleans to its fullest, sleeping till noon, drinking beer till dark and rum-filled Hurricanes until midnight, dancing till four, making love until dawn, and rounding out the evenings watching the sun come up over the Mississippi levee at Café Du Monde, sipping Café Au Lait and covering our faces with powdered sugar from eating beignets. There was also a lot of seafood gumbo, etouffee, jambalaya, and more than one oyster roll po'boy on the menu.

After a week of the Big Easy, we drove north past Baton Rouge, then on through Shreveport. We left the main highway and took country roads for almost two days, crossing the Red River and ending up in Marlow Oklahoma, Karen's hometown. We arrived at her aunt Marnie's house and quicker than an instant dance scene in an Elvis movie, a family reunion materialized, complete with chickens on the grill, a fully stocked bar, a keg on ice, fresh apple pies on the window sill and twenty kids underfoot, with about half of them housebroken. Karen was heartily welcomed by all while I was given token but distant acceptance as an out of towner who was undoubtedly defiling their favorite niece's virtues. I kept to my business, drank their beer, ate their chicken, and lurked in the shadows at night till bedtime. Two days later it was time to move on. I started packing with the intent of heading out at oh dark thirty before anyone else was awake for the required forty-five-minute goodbye session. Karen didn't seem to be with the program, and she suddenly appeared to come to a decision.

"Take a walk with me?" she asked.

This is never good.

We strolled down the shady side of the tree-lined street in silence for a few minutes. I knew she would talk when she was ready. She took my hand and stopped.

"I'm going to stay here for a while. I need some time to think, and I'm not in the mood to traipse through national parks with nine hundred Asian tourists taking pictures. You go, take your time, a week, a month, a year. When you're done and want to go sailing, come back by and pick me up."

I can't say I was that surprised. Part of me was disappointed, and part of me felt relieved. Maybe I needed a little quiet time too. After all, it had been a crazy year. I took her hands in mine.

"Okay, beautiful. I'll say so long, adios, au revior, and ciao, but never good-bye. You stay here and hang with your homies, and I'll burn up some highway. Maybe a few weeks, maybe a month, certainly not a year." I let go of her hands and wrapped my arms around her. We just held each other for a while. I felt her quietly sob on my shoulder. After a while we turned and walked silently back to the house, holding hands.

I didn't wait until morning. Karen huddled with her family and gave them the news. They were more than happy, maybe overjoyed that their favorite child was going to stay a while, and even happier that the outsider hoodlum criminal was driving off into the sunset. She gathered her belongings from the motorhome, kissed me on the cheek, and walked back inside without another word. I had nothing else to do but climb into the driver's seat, fire up, and drive away.

I made it clear that Karen gave careful instructions to her family that I *Hadn't Been There.* Honest, hardworking, "good" people these Okies are, I don't have a lot in common with them. Even though I was born and raised in Florida, which is about as south as you can get, and didn't own a pair of socks or underwear or shoes that tied, I was looked upon by them as some sort of "City Slicker Yankee." That, along with an inherent distrust of someone who was shacking up with their baby made me undesirable at best, unwelcome at most, and unacceptable at any time. It was an interesting enough experience, but I was happy to put Marlow, Oklahoma in my rear view mirror. I did learn, however, through overhearing a heated argument at the backyard barbecue, how to put both a gun rack AND lace curtains in the back window of a Ford F-250.

Bless their hearts.

They say if you don't know where you're going, that's where you'll end up. I wasn't aimlessly driving, but I only had a vague game plan. I'd always wanted to see Wyoming, South Dakota, the Black Hills, and Yellowstone, so northwest-ish was more or less my direction. With the motorhome, I didn't need to be surrounded by civilization, just an occasional gas station, nighttime campgrounds, or in a pinch, a truck stop would suffice, and I worked my way north to Salina, Kansas, then due west to Denver. Now there's a boring stretch of road. I felt I could put a brick on the gas pedal, bungee the steering wheel to the seat, and crawl in back for a nap. It made Alligator Alley look like Lombard Street in San Francisco.

Almost.

From Denver, it was a jog north up to Cheyenne, Wyoming, and then west along I-80. I stopped to camp at a rest area about seventy miles from Cheyenne and found a plaque with an interesting story about a little tree that was growing out of a rock. Seems when the Transcontinental Railroad was being built, the construction crews found this tree and were both amazed that it was growing out of a rock, and equally amazed that a tree had managed to grow at all on this barren plain. For that reason, the construction crew decided to detour the railroad around it and for years later, train engineers would stop and water the tree. I never get over being amazed at these little pieces of American history. I sat down near the tree, taking in the vast prairie, and guessed I had to be a thousand miles from any place anyone in my family had ever set foot.

Wayne Gales

Flashback
June 5, 1905, Sixty miles west
of Cheyenne, Wyoming

Twenty-five-year-old Adolphus Wahl stood on a hillside and surveyed the scene below him. Fifty men, mostly German immigrants, and the majority older than him were pulling up rotten railroad ties and replacing them with creosote-soaked fresh timber. They had to work quickly. This was the Transcontinental Railroad, and it was in heavy use. They had six hours to remove and replace the ties on this two hundred feet of track before another westbound train was due. *"Bewegen sich schneller!"* he yelled in German. "Move faster!" *"Ein zug kommt bald!"* "A train comes soon!" A few of the crew glanced up distastefully at the younger man giving orders, but they spoke only German, and Adolph was fluent in both German and English. Born in New Ulm, Minnesota to German immigrants, Adolph was raised in a German-speaking community and went to a German school and a German Lutheran church. He didn't learn English until he was five. His father, Hermann Wahl, worked on this very same span of the railroad in the 1860s when the first Transcontinental Railroad was pushed across America. Adolph, as young as he was, knew how to build railroads and how to lead a crew, and he was tough enough to make the men work, despite the resentment. The few men who tested his authority found out quickly that disrespect resulted in a quick ass-kicking. They would put their heads down and work, or would be quickly sent down the road.

Along with the Germans were a smattering of other nationalities, a few English, two blacks, and a Native American, but they were mostly German, and they were known as the "German Gang." Other crews were one hundred percent Irish. They didn't like each other, and it took more than a little effort to keep them apart in camp.

The first Transcontinental Railroad was built with a thin budget and paid for by the mile completed. Far more effort was put into laying as much track as possible with less than stellar effort in quality. Over two thousand miles of track was laid through some of the most rugged and inhospitable territories imaginable. Native Americans attacked and killed crews frequently, and the weather ranged from hundred-degree-plus summers and winters that could dip below zero for weeks, and snow that could drift up over ten feet. Completed in 1869, the tracks were in dire need of repair by the turn of the century.

This location had some significance, both historically and from family heritage. Adolph's father told him about the little tree growing out of the rock near the railroad right of way. There were so few trees in this part of Wyoming the crews diverted the main line tracks around the rock and the tree. Since then, railroad engineers, usually insensitive with little regard for nature and conservation, would stop their trains and water it whenever they passed by. Adolph stood on the bluff, overlooking the crew and the Tree in the Rock, and remembered his father.

As the afternoon wore on, Adolph joined the crew, bedding in the ties one by one while the rail setters picked up lengths of heavy rail and placed them back on the bed. Using huge sledgehammers, spikes were driven into the ties, and the rails secured. The days were long, the work backbreaking, and at the end of the day, the crews had little to look forward to than a little water to wash their face, a meal consisting of beans and wild meat, venison, antelope or elk, and lonely nights on a dirty mattress, often shared with one or two other workers. Adolph didn't permit alcohol in the camp, and one day and night were pretty much like any other. On Sundays, the crew was permitted to rest, but there wasn't much to do except walk out on the plains and throw rocks at the prairie dogs.

Wayne Gales

3
Suspicious Minds Think Alike

"Come this way often?" a voice asked behind me, and I almost jumped out of my skin.

"Tim, you have to stop testing my heart like that," I said. "Someday I'll just keel over dead from a heart attack. I don't have to ask how you found me; I know the motorhome probably has more bugs than the Executive Lounge at the Hay-Adams Hotel in Washington D.C." I stood up. "But how the hell did you pick this forlorn piece of real estate in the middle of nowhere to pay a visit?"

"Bric my boy, you never stop surprising us. We figured you were good for hanging around the Gulf until we found you a rowboat to go gallivanting off to hell knows where. We didn't have any assets up here in Gawd's country, so I had to commandeer a C-37, that's a Gulfstream to you civilian types, out of Pascagoula and try to intercept you in Cheyenne, but you didn't hang out there any longer than to gas up and buy a six-pack. I finally caught up with you about ten miles back. You pulled into the rest stop, and I figured this was as good a place as any."

"Well, sorry to be so much trouble, but you helped make part of it, so you can deal with it." I sighed. "Okay, you're here; I'm here. What's up?"

"I wanted to fill you in on some details," Tim said. "We killed you both off nice and official like back in Florida. Your kids and Bo Morgan are in on the story. We 'found' you both drowned off Boca Grande. I thought the location was a nice touch. Enough money changed hands so no bodies actually ever existed, which saved me from having to thaw out a John and Jane Doe up in Miami and bring them down to Key West. Services were held at Mallory Square, and your ashes were dumped in the ocean, which I think your kid dug out of a barbecue at Bo's place. Your black cross-dressing friend Scarlet sang a couple of songs accompanied by your kid and your old band. It woulda brought a tear to a glass eye."

He handed me a backpack. "Don't look inside right now, but you will find two passports for Mister Julius Cecil and Ms. Karly Morris, your new I.D.'s, a satphone, and yet another Amex Black card." Tim smiled. "You guys change your names more times than Elizabeth Taylor. Hopefully, this is the last time, but ..."

"But what?" I asked. I didn't like the look in his eyes. Tim shuffled his feet like a schoolboy who'd been caught with the teacher's apple. He sort of changed the subject.

"I parked next to you with a new twenty-nine-foot Fleetwood Class A motorhome. Keys are on the floorboard. When you leave, just grab your things, no food or pots or pans, and drive away. Yes, we have tracking in it too.

"What's the 'but' part of that sentence?" I asked.

He spoke carefully. "There's been some traffic on the internet that makes us think somebody didn't buy off on your 'death.' They are looking around waterfront cities along the Gulf so your change of direction might have turned out to be a good thing. That being said, I think they could eventually find you, so along with your new I.D., so we thought you could use a new vehicle."

I took a deep breath. "Does this ever end? I thought you guys were good at this?" I ventured. "This shit's getting really old. How do we make this trail go cold forever?"

"We are good at this, but these guys are pouring a lot of people and money into finding you, more people and money than we have to keep you off the scope. Hopefully, this is the last time," Tim answered. "The motorhome is trackable but no audio bug so if you need to call me, the number's stored on the phone. I suggest you don't call anyone else but me for the time being."

He smiled. "Now the good news. There's a nice sixty-one-foot Grand Mistral sailing yacht sitting in Mobile Bay at the Buccaneer Yacht Club. A Columbian drug lord was kind enough to donate it to Uncle Sam when his crew got clumsy with a delivery of happy powder earlier this year and was boarded by the Coast Guard. It's got updated nav and radios, and it almost sails itself. The Buccaneer is a private club, and they will have your name at the gate. The boat's stocked with dry goods, so you just need your perishables and a destination. I don't know where you're headed, but if I were you, I'd never set foot in the U.S. again. The boat will be there when you get there."

"Well, you ain't me," I answered. "What do I do with this new motorhome when I get to Mobile?" I asked

"Just leave the keys with the office. We'll take care of it," Tim answered.

"Sounds like you have it all wrapped up," I said. "Guess I'll hit the road." I stuck out my hand, shook Tim's, and turned to walk down the hill to the rig, then stopped with one more question. "What's the name of the schooner?" I asked.

"It doesn't have one right now," Tim answered. "Give me a name and we'll have it registered by the time you get there."

I thought for a second, smiled to myself, and then called out over my shoulder.

"Name it *More Miles to the Galleon*."

Wayne Gales

Flashback
June 25^{th,} 1905 Cheyenne, Wyoming.

Once a month a train came out to the camp, gathered up the crews, and brought them to Cheyenne, where they were housed in the "Big Tent," a portable city under canvas where they were given access to showers, food and drink. They could also take a short walk into downtown Cheyenne and enjoy more physical pleasures. As much as they planned to send money home to their families, they often blew their month's wages over this weekend. As the whole place was run by the railroad, and prices were overinflated, you might say the crews worked for the railroad virtually free.

Adolph stayed much to himself during these breaks. Married with two young children back home in Minnesota, he preferred a steak and a beer by himself rather than partake of evil temptations. As a boss, he didn't have many friends, and despite being a loyal, hardworking professional, his status with the railroad wasn't high enough to give him access to rub elbows with cattle barons and railroad royalty in the prestigious Cheyenne Club. He would complete this project then return home in a year or two, and go back to work for the Burlington Northern Railway in Minnesota. Being younger than much of his crew, there was a lot of resentment, and he didn't want to get involved with a bunch of drunk track layers.

On the last night of their furlough, Adolph ate an early dinner and then cut across the rowdy tent scene to retire in the double-deck rail car used for supervisor quarters. Each deck had a series of rough bunks with a thin mattress. Employees were expected to sleep two to a bunk.

Railroad work at the turn of the century was not glamorous.

As he stepped outside the tent, he saw a movement behind him. His youth and quick reflexes saved his life as the assailant missed his first swing with the handle from a huge sledgehammer. Adolph spun to face him and recognized one of his German crew members. Several others of the crew were standing behind him.

"*Schweinehund!*" The rail worker shouted and continued in German. "No child is going to order me around!"

"You're drunk!"Adolph said. "Go home and sleep it off. I'll

27

forget this stupidity."

"*Nein!*" The German yelled and lunged again with the handle. Adolph easily grabbed the handle, tore it out of his hands, and with a quick swing, hit him squarely on the side of the head. He went down in a heap. Adolph threw the handle on the ground.

One of the other rail workers bent over the limp body. "*Er ist tod!*" "You have killed him! We saw you jump him when he walked out of the tent!"

4
Where's Yogi?

The next city was Laramie, Wyoming, and I stopped for groceries, more alcohol and picked up a Garmin at the Wal-Mart. The gas station also had a Wyoming map, and I started working up my route. I took US 80 west to Rock Springs, then north up a lonely dry stretch of land until the mountains began to rise up and meet me. By the time I got to Jackson Hole, the scenery was beyond spectacular. I spent enough time in Jackson to decide not to spend any more time there. Crowded, touristy, and expensive, it had no interest to me, The Tetons, rising straight out of the valley floor thousands of feet just a few miles away were, however, worth the whole trip. Snow-covered peaks, even in early fall, and the valleys were like driving through a zoo. Elk and deer wandered around wild, and there were warnings that outdoor camping could result in a grizzly bear encounter. I stopped where I pleased, took some pictures, and got some serious de-tuning in place.

I wish Karen was here to share.

I drove the motorhome down a dirt road to the middle of nowhere, took out a camp chair, opened a beer, and just sat there staring at the mountains. The tinnitus in my ears was louder than every other sound in the universe. Then I heard a noise behind me and looked over my shoulder. A bull buffalo about the size of a Volkswagen was standing about ten feet away, giving me the evil eye. Buffalo have bad vision, worse tempers, and have killed more people than Grizzly bears since tourists started driving cars through National Parks a hundred years ago. I eyed the side door of the motorhome and decided that I might have a fifty-fifty chance of beating him to it.

Oh, what the hell. I raised my beer bottle in salute.

"Greetings, Mister Buffalo. I bid you a good day!" And took a big swallow, never taking my eyes off him. He glared at me for a few more moments with one eye, turned, and slowly walked off. I realized that I hadn't breathed for the last minute. I took a big breath and smiled to myself. The world and I were, for the first time in a long time, at peace with each other.

The next two weeks were much the same. I spent several days at Yellowstone Park, where, as Karen had predicted, I was surrounded by thousands of little brown people, all taking pictures of anything that moved or didn't. Woody Guthrie sang, "This land is your land, this land is my land" but nowadays, we sure do seem to be loaning it out to the rest of the world.

After being up to my neck in midgets at Yellowstone, I got to duplicate the experience in Cody, Wyoming, Devils Tower, and, to a lesser degree, Custer State Park. At least, the buffalo outnumbered the tourists there. Since double-decker tour buses wouldn't fit through the tunnels carved in the granite, it was far less crowded.

My only respite was a brief stay in Deadwood, where I abandoned the motorhome for a real bed, a steak dinner, and a constant reminder that Wild Bill Hickok was shot holding aces and eights. I found it amusing that half a dozen bars identified themselves as the Number Nine Saloon, where Hickok bought it when history notes that the real Number Nine burned down eons ago. Well, history rarely gets in the way of the truth anyway. They don't know how many guns killed John Kennedy, and they have *that* murder on film.

After a few weeks, I had my fill of tourist season and decided it was time to collect Karen and get off dry land. I headed back to Oklahoma by way of Denver again. On the way, I passed through Douglas, Wyoming for gas and saw the strangest creature on the planet for sale. A stuffed head of something called a Jackalope. It looked like a rabbit with antlers.

"What the hell is that?" I asked the clerk.

"Well," she drawled. "Rumor has it, the Jackrabbits are so big here in Wyomin. That they have sex with the Antelopes. That there is the result. A genuine Wyomin, Jackalope."

I examined the creature, nicely mounted on a wooden plaque. I pointed to the antlers. "How come if it's called a Jackalope, when it's wearing deer antlers?" I asked.

She looked a little puzzled as if it had never been pointed out to her, but then the light came on, if a little dimly and she responded. "I told ya they was big rabbits!" I just smiled and bought one, then arranged for it to be shipped to Bo Morgan with a note inside for him to figure out a way to get it to the boy. I didn't want it to say Brodie, and I didn't put a return address on it in case somebody was checking his mail.

Other than stopping for gas and an occasional burger, I drove straight through from Wyoming to Oklahoma, pulling up at Karen's aunt's place just two and a half days later. After a big welcome hug and a kiss, she raised her eyes when she noticed the motorhome had strangely changed brands and colors but didn't say anything. We spent the night and quietly slipped out of town early the next morning. Next destination, Mobile, Alabama.

Flashback - Cheyenne, Wyoming, 1905

Adolph hesitated for a moment and realized he was being framed for killing a man in self-defense. Instinctively, he turned and ran toward the tracks, vanishing into the dark in a few moments. Behind him, he heard shouts in German and English "Stop!" "*Halt!*" As he approached the tracks, he was blocked by an eastbound train, moving slowly through the yard. He saw an open boxcar and deftly jumped inside. Crawling to a dark corner, Adolph sat down, pulled his knees up to his chin and waited to see if he had been spotted. Minutes later the freight train slowly started gaining speed and moved off into the night.

Two days later, hungry and parched with thirst, Adolphus Wahl felt the train begin to slow. He stood up and stiffly walked to the open door. Instead of the vast open plains he had seen for days, it was obvious he was approaching a city. He leaned out of the car and looked ahead and the outline of tall brick buildings loomed in the distance. "Saint Louis," he mused to himself. Adolph had been there before on the way to Wyoming. Off to the right, the Mississippi River meandered out of sight. The Saint Louis rail yards were huge, and there would be no tolerance for what they would see as an ordinary hobo, freeloading a ride in a box car. As the train slowed, even more, Adolphus took advantage and eased himself out of the car, rolling in the dust as he lost his footing. He dusted himself off as best he could, and cut away from the direction of the rail yard. A half mile to the south, he crossed a dirt road heading toward town and started walking in the direction of the city.

In 1900, St Louis was the third largest city in the United States with a little more than a half million residents. Recognized for the past one hundred years as the gateway to the West, St Louis was a key shipping and transportation market on the Mississippi River. Trains crossed the Eads Bridge heading east and west, and freight was unloaded from trains and sent down the Mississippi River to New Orleans and the world. Adolph decided a change of transportation mode made sense, and he walked toward the docks, pausing at a public horse trough to wash his face and take a drink.

At the turn of the century, St Louis boasted a row of true

"skyscrapers" along Broadway, including the new Planter's Hotel. He checked his pocketbook and counted one hundred and twenty dollars, plenty of cash to get him fed, clothed and far away from any place people would be looking for him. Regardless, his frugality steered him away from the fancy Planter's Hotel that charged nine dollars a day for a private room. He approached a police officer and inquired about a boarding house. Dirty from his boxcar ride and tumbling out of the car, the officer eyed him up and down.

"Just passing through are ye?" He asked with an Irish brogue.

"Yes, sir. Traveling to New Orleans in a day or two."

The policeman pointed to his left with his nightstick. "There's a respectable boarding house a block away. Two dollars a night to share a room, and there's a café next door." He then pointed his nightstick in the other direction. "That way, about two miles down the road," he said, "is the city limits sign. I'll expect you to be on the other side of it by sundown tomorrow." Adolphus started to bristle at the insulation he was a common hobo, but instead, he tipped his hat, mumbled "yessir" and scurried off toward the boarding house. As promised, it was right around the corner. He opted to pay three dollars for a private room and splurged another dollar and a half for a bath in tepid, twice-used water while the washer lady cleaned and pressed his clothes. Looking and feeling a little more human. He stepped next door to a restaurant for dinner, his first meal in three days. Steak and potatoes, asparagus, and pistachio ice cream for dessert. Total price, one dollar sixty-five cents. He returned to the flophouse and collapsed into a deep sleep.

5
Mobile Bay

After touring God's country, the hop down to Mobile was a breeze. I filled Karen in on the change in vehicles, handed over the new identity, and brought her up to speed on the potential threat. Since the baddies were looking for us along the Gulf, we needed to be a little more careful. With as many cold trails as we had left, I was hopeful nobody could know where we were or where we were headed. For that matter, who the heck would be looking for me? Harry Sykas? I doubt he had that kind of clout or the balls to try anything else. Let's see, who else have I pissed off in the past year? The Russians? Sheesh, get over it. I was tempted to call Tim and ask what he knew, but I was pretty sure he either didn't know, wouldn't tell me, or would just lie. I reached for the phone and almost drove off the highway when it came to life in my hands with a tweet. I answered it.

"You must be reading my mind now," I said. Tim was on the other end.

"No time for chit-chat buddy boy," he said. "As we suspected some bad guys are hanging around the Gulf States looking for you. We don't know what they look like, but we're intercepting a lot of chatter that they are staking out airports, hotels, and marinas all over Florida, Alabama, and Mississippi. I think they have more assets than I have."

My palms started to sweat and what little hair I had on the back of my neck stood up. "Tim, exactly who or what is looking for me?"

"Russians," Tim said. "They are either pissed off and want to nick you because you pinched their prize right out from under their noses, or they think you can tell them where their merchandise went." I considered that for a minute and then thought of something. "Tim, do they know I've got a boat waiting?" His answer was a little too slow for my liking.

"I don't think so. At least, we've heard nothing that says they know. I think you will be able to board and sail away without too much danger, but I wouldn't hang around long."

"Hang on for a second." I put my hand over the satphone and outlined my plan to Karen. Her eyes grew as big as saucers, but she gulped once and nodded. I picked the phone back up. "Ok Tim, here's the deal. We'll be in Mobile tomorrow morning, and we'll load and leave. Just for shits and grins, can your goons stage a little noisy diversion at a different marina nearby? That way you can maybe flush out the baddies before we get there."

"Bric, can you EVER take orders? These people want to KILL you. Can you get that through your thick skull?"

"Must I remind you, Tim, that, without your ongoing 'assistance' over the past year, they wouldn't know me from the Man in the Moon. It's obvious that you still have a few moles in your operation or the Goonies would consider me off the market. For all I know, they've already got a lead on where I'm headed and what I'm going to do before I know what I'm going to do." I took a deep breath and then had a thought. "You want to help? Ok partner, like I suggested, create a diversion. Get a couple of look-alikes to go to a marina other than the Buccaneer and make a ruckus. If nothing happens, we can get out to sea the next afternoon and head to places unknown, even to you. I'll assume you have a GPS finder on that boat. I strongly suggest you not ping on it. You've got more bad guys working for you than you have good guys."

Tim was starting to get ramped up but knew I had him in a corner. His operation was black enough that not a lot of people in the agency knew the deal, but I also was pretty sure he still had counter-intelligence in his midst. I didn't know how embedded they were, but it sure seemed they were always aware of the game plan. I got tired of waiting for a response.

"Either help or don't Tim. I don't care, but I'm going through with my plan either way." And I hung up.

The phone chirped a few seconds later. "You don't leave me a lot of options, Bric," Tim answered. "I'll create your nighttime diversion and tomorrow I'll stake out the marina and try to help you get outta town."

"Okay," I answered. "Thanks, I think," and I pushed the off button again. I turned to Karen. "What I said we are doing and what we're *going* to do is two different things. We're gonna steal our own boat. Use the Garmin to find us a sporting goods store or Wal-Mart. I need two, decent-sized waterproof bags, or, if nothing else, some big trash bags, a roll of duct tape, and some zip ties. I've only got a hundred or so in cash aside from our emergency mad money, and I don't want to use plastic right now. Just a feeling." She nodded.

A box of trash bags was what we ended up with. While I drove to Mobile, Karen sorted our stuff into what stayed and what went and started creating two waterproof kits, leaving enough air in them so they could be used as floats. When she was done, our whole life was bundled up in two ten-pound black pouches. She showed me her work. "Great job," I responded. "Use the duct tape to make some loops so they can be towed."

"Do you think we need to do it this way?" Karen asked.

"Maybe not, but I didn't get to be this old by trusting everyone. I think Tim's people have been compromised by bad guys. It happened to me once, and I think it's happened again. Either way, let's just call it good insurance." Karen came back up to the front of the motorhome and sat down in the passenger seat. She was quiet for a few minutes, and then spoke, choosing her words carefully. "Bric, I was just planning on this sailing trip as part of our extended vacation. I don't want to run and hide for the rest of my life."

"I don't either," I reassured her. "I want this to calm down and blow over. I think we can take this little voyage, maybe Mexico, maybe Central America, and be able to come back to the States and live in peace, hopefully in Florida. Eventually, I think they will give up."

At least, I hoped so.

The Garmin directed us to the Buccaneer Yacht Club on Mobile Bay. We arrived a little before dark and parked across the inlet on Bayfront Road, looking all in the world like normal people setting up camp to do some night fishing. I looked across the inlet and spotted what had to be our boat. I went over the plan one more time with Karen, and then we just holed up and waited. Nothing looked suspicious, and I was probably a little over-cautious, or even over-dramatic. At midnight, I started making a third package up, stripping down to my shorts, and putting my shoes, shirt, the backpack Tim had given me with the keys to the sailboat, and a flashlight inside. I started to close it up and Karen said: "Wait." She handed me her shoes, hesitated for a moment then took her shorts, hoodie, and top off, leaving nothing on but her tighty whities. She explained, "I don't have that much clothing, no sense leaving it here, and no sense getting it wet. I didn't pack much because I was planning on a shopping spree before we sailed. Guess that will have to wait for a while."

I love a girl that's comfortable in her skin.

A few minutes before one, I started to turn out the lights and then hesitated. "Let's leave the lights on, music on, and generator running. Anyone watching will just assume we're still inside." I stepped outside the motorhome, walking out to the point to see if the 'diversion' might be visible someplace on Mobile Bay. Suddenly a few miles to the south, I heard a few pops, and then more, and then in the distance, the glow of a fire. A minute later, the whine of a police siren could be heard in the distance. I trotted back to the Fleetwood, and quietly said to Karen, "Showtime." She came outside, carrying one bundle, and reached back inside for the other two. There was no moon, and I didn't want to risk a flashlight, so we had to rely on the lights from the windows. I just hoped we wouldn't step on a beer bottle on the way to the water. I quietly slipped into Mobile Bay, and I could hear Karen catch her breath as she eased into the cold water. It was only a few hundred feet across the inlet, and ten minutes later we were underneath the stern of the sailboat. I checked the name on the stern and grunted with confirmation – the name *More Miles to the Galleon* was fresh in gold leaf on her tail. As I expected, there was a small dive step on the stern, and we hoisted our 'luggage' on the step, and then pulled ourselves up. Step one complete. The police sirens were still sounding in the far distance, and hopefully, if someone was watching *this* place, they were distracted by the commotion in *that* place. Karen climbed the ladder and shivered while I handed her the three bundles. She hastily started opening up the small package and got her top, hoodie, and shorts back on. She handed me the keys, and I opened the cabin. Inside, I used the flashlight and looked around, opening a few cupboards to confirm they were full of canned goods. I went back topside and put the keys in the dash. "Cast off," I whispered to Karen. This would be tricky, driving a large, unfamiliar boat out of a small harbor I had never seen in the dark without any lights. I was happy the night was moonless but knew it made it that much tougher. Karen came back to the console and nodded that we were free. It was an outbound tide and the boat already started moving away from the slip. It was now or never. I flipped on the key and happily other than the dash lights, nothing else came on with the battery power. I turned the key one click further, and the diesel engine came to life. It was a quiet engine but in the nighttime silence, it sounded like I was revving a dragster. Committed now, I eased it into reverse and backed the sixty-one-foot boat slowly out. Clear of the slip, I put it in forward and then idled out into the bay.

So far, so good.

I just drove straight out toward the middle of Mobile Bay. I couldn't see any other boats in the area, so I kept the '*Miles*' dark. No sense in drawing attention. Again, I thought to myself that it was unlikely they could have people watching every single marina in four states, not to mention airports and heaven knows what else. I started to relax a bit, realizing I was probably being an over-cautious fool. Now that we were a little ways from shore, I looked to the south to see if I could get a visual on Tim's diversion. It was a mile or two away, but there were obviously several police cars, maybe a fire truck or two, and a visible fire. Wow, that was quite a diversion. I looked back toward the Buccaneer Marina, and it was still peacefully quiet and dark. I flipped a few more lights on the console and started up the Marine Garman GPS. It came to life, thought for a second, and then figured out where 'here' was. I had never been in Mobile Bay in my life and knew that sailing around in pitch dark in unfamiliar waters was stupid. I decided to make my way toward the far side of Gaillard Island, drop anchor, and wait till sunrise. Karen had been keeping watch on the bow for a while but now came back to me and wrapped her arms around me in the cool air. "So we escaped," she said. "Now what? Do you think there was a real danger, or did you just want to see how hard sixty-degree water made my nipples?" I chuckled and ran my hand under her hoodie. "Maybe a little of both," I answered, "but yes, I think we are safe, yes, I always think there's danger, and, now that we're out here in the middle of Mobile Bay, yes, maybe I overreacted. I'm sure we could have cuddled in that motorhome all night," I pointed back toward the Fleetwood, "and got up in the morning, walked onto this little dinghy with loaded suitcases, bags of groceries, dry feet, and……"

My sentence was cut off by a flash of white light streaking in from the left. The motorhome erupted in a huge ball of flame and explosion, going nearly thirty feet into the air and falling upside down into the bay in a mass of flames.

Flashback
St Louis, Missouri, June 20, 1905

The next morning, Adolphus left the boarding house and walked two blocks to the docks. There were a number of paddlewheel riverboats tied up. He chose one, aptly named *America* and walked up the gangplank. A purser was standing at the top of the ramp.

"May I help you sir?" he inquired.

"Are you going to New Orleans?" Adolphus asked.

"Vicksburg" he responded He pointed to another sternwheeler. "If you desire New Orleans you can catch the *Orleans* over there. I can take you to Vicksburg for twelve dollars, steerage. I suspect the *Orleans* is twice as much."

Adolph didn't know where he wanted to go. Vicksburg is as good as anyplace. "I'll ride with you." He handed the purser a ten-dollar gold piece and two silver dollars and walked aboard.

It was a little over five hundred miles from St Louis to Vicksburg. Traveling downstream with the current, Mississippi paddle wheelers could reach a speed of speed, eight to ten knots. With a full moon, they might cruise at night, but most often came ashore at a river town, where passengers and crew disembarked, ate, drank, and spent money in many other ways. There were ten paying passengers aboard the sternwheeler, a cargo of construction materials packed in wooden barrels, sixteen milk cows in a pen on the forward deck, and two hundred burlap bags of wheat. There was no real assigned bed with a steerage ticket, but the quarters below decks were stifling and smelly, so Adolph spent most of the time sitting on the wheat on the deck, watching the shoreline drift by. He made casual acquaintances with some of the other passengers and was surprised when one of them had a German accent. "Sprichst du Deutsch?" He asked. "Ja!" And they became instant friends. Joseph Muller was an immigrant from Munich, arriving in the US only five years earlier. To Adolph's delight, Joseph was also a railroad worker, most recently on the Baltimore and Ohio Railroad, where he worked on a repair crew.

"What brings you to Mississippi?" Adolph asked.

"I rode a boat down the Ohio River to Cairo, where I boarded the *America*. I'll get off in Vicksburg and catch a train to St. Augustine Florida. From there I plan to get work on the Florida East Coast Railway. They are building a magnificent railroad all the way to Key West." Joseph reached into his coat pocket and pulled out a well-worn flyer, which he carefully unfolded and handed to Adolph. It was an ad soliciting railroad workers from all over to work on Henry Flagler's railroad to Key West. The pay was almost double regular railroad construction pay. Sixty dollars a month.

"I plan to stay in St Augustine for the summer and then go to work on the railroad," Joseph said.

"*Wunderbar!*" Exclaimed Adolph. "I'm sure they need supervisors too, and that will pay even more!" Adolph went on to tell Joseph about his experiences in Wyoming, along with his father's legacy as a worker on the Transcontinental Railroad. He pulled out his father's presentation pocket watch and showed it to Joseph, opening the back and showing him the inscription.

"Presented to Herman Adolphus Wahl for 25 years of loyal service. The Union Pacific Railroad Company. January 25, 1889."

"Your father would be proud of you," said Joseph, nodding. "His son follows in his footsteps."

On the evening of the fourth day, the bluffs of Vicksburg Mississippi came into view, and the America tied up on the busy dock. The two burly Germans left the wharf and made their way to the train station in the middle of town. Post-Civil War Vicksburg was a bustling community, shipping cotton and tobacco north, east, and south to New Orleans by steamship and rail. Passenger trains left daily to the southeast, going to Mobile, Tallahassee, Jacksonville, and eventually, St Augustine, where the Florida East Coast Railway connected to points south. They inquired about ticket prices and decided to find an open boxcar instead for the trip east. Joseph and Adolph chatted as they rode alone, sitting with their feet hanging over the side of the open boxcar. It was hot and humid, and the breeze felt good. Adolph felt Joseph was almost too inquisitive about his past. He finally stood up and said.

Enough questions! I'm tired of talking. I'm going to sleep." And he crawled to a straw-filled corner and closed his eyes.

Wayne Gales

6
Sailing

We stood there transfixed for a moment, and then I reacted. Pushing the throttle forward, I urged the little diesel engine to its best speed of about five knots and aimed for the back of the island, knowing that the next RPG could very well be aimed at my head. Leaving the lights off, I trusted the Marine Garmin to keep enough ocean under us to clear the bottom until we were out of sight. It took fifteen minutes, but it felt like hours before the glow of the motorhome, along with all the fire trucks and police lights, vanished behind Gaillard Island. My plans to drop anchor till dawn went out the window with that explosion. I powered down and let the schooner drift for a moment to gather my wits. Eventually, I had to light up the boat. The Coasties or any number of law enforcement would fuss if they caught us cruising dark in the bay. Hoping the Garmin charts were up to date, I aimed for the mouth of the bay.

Approaching the Mobile Bay Lighthouse, I turned on the navigational beacons and made us look legit. This far offshore, we were just one of another dozen craft in the bay heading out for a day of fishing. The next spot to clear was the mouth of the bay, and it was just starting to get light in the east when we passed Fort Gaines to the port and Fort Morgan to starboard. I half expected a go-fast to head our way by now, and I didn't have anything bigger than a flare gun to defend ourselves with, but maybe the Ruskies thought they blew us up in the motorhome. With the sun up and a decent quartering breeze, I unfurled the mainsail and jib, shut the motor off, and flipped the electronic switch to hoist the sails. As big as the schooner was, it was easily operated with a two-person crew, and both Karen and I were expert sailors. We could relax now.

I think

"Where to?" Karen asked. She had hardly said a word all night, but out on the water, she looked happier. The early fall sun was warm, and it didn't take long before she was back down to her skivvies, soaking up the sun.

"Don't know for sure," I answered. "Mexico or someplace in Central America, eventually, but we need supplies and some distance from this neck of the woods. What do you say to someplace along the Texas coast?"

"Good by me," she smiled thinly. "Alabama seems to have worn out its welcome."

"Okay. Take the wheel while I go over the charts," I answered. "Head south until we get beyond the delta, and then we'll figure out what port in Texas to aim for."

Karen brought the bow of the *'Miles* around to one hundred eighty degrees to steer clear of the Mississippi Delta and the busy shipping lanes while I poured over the charts. The breeze stayed a brisk twelve knots out of the east, and the sleek schooner slid along with little or no input. Comfortable for the moment, Karen locked down the autopilot and joined me below deck. "Where to, Skipper?" Karen ventured. She looked happier than she had since we were reunited in Key West. I quietly shook my head. What seemed like ages ago, was only about a month past. On top of the charts, I had a good old fashioned road map of the U.S. "Let's look at it this way," I started. "Farther from here, the better, but I want it to be still in the good old U.S. of A when we stop for supplies." I stabbed my finger on the far edge of Texas. "I vote for South Padre."

Karen grinned. "Perfect! Been there. There's a lovely marina right at the entrance to the bay, and across the bridge in Port Isabel, there's stores, including a Wal-Mart and more. Let's go."

"I've been there too," I answered. "I was based in Brownsville for a while when I was in the Navy." I gave a thumbs up. "Ok, game on." I picked up my calculator. "Let's see, five hundred fifty miles, speed, six knots or so. Three days, give or take." We went topside and punched in the destination on the Garman. It more or less agreed with my calculations. We would arrive at South Padre Island, sometime in the morning, three days from now.

I needed to do one more thing that I didn't relish. Reluctantly taking the satphone out of the backpack, I turned it on, waited until it got a handshake from space, and dialed the one saved number. It rang twice, and the answer had little formality. Tim spoke without saying "hello."

"The paramedics didn't find any bodies in the motorhome, so I guessed you left it as a decoy," Tim said. "I have to hand it to you my friend; you called this one better than me. That little 'diversion' we staged at Mobile Bay Marina ended up in a full-fledged firefight. They lost four, we lost one and some Arab's fancy hundred and fifty-foot luxury yacht is currently smoldering in its slip with about five mil damage." Tim went on. "I was pretty pissed you did a change-up on me, but I guess it worked out. It bought you some time and got you outta sight. Where are you headed?"

"I would guess," I started, "that you probably know where I am. Where I'm going is, at this point, mine to keep to myself. Did you figure out who your new mole was?"

"Yep, that's how the motorhome got whacked. I told five agents five different stories, and like a half dozen minutes later an RPG hit the RV. That freaked me out. I figured there was plenty of time to figure out who knew what. You were lucky to be away when you were."

"So, you think that's the end of the leaks?" I asked.

"Doesn't matter," Tim answered. "Our unit has been dissolved as of this morning. The Agency decided to go limp on the bad guys, figuring that makes just me responsible for where you are and what you are doing, getting you set up with the witness protection program, one more time, I must point out, and then quietly fade into the sunset. You got a boat, your money, and the whole world to run and hide to. I'm sure the baddies already know that nobody was in that motorhome, so you are still high up on their shit list."

"We shall see Tim, we shall see. In the meantime, I'll shut this phone off, and I won't plan to use it unless I see aliens or three wise men on camels and a star in the east. Keep the black card solvent and for the time being, forget about us."

"Happy to do that sir, but do me a favor, touch base every month or so, just to keep tabs. I don't care where you are, but we do need to stay in touch. You are, you know, still an asset. I don't need to tell you that any destination with the word 'Florida' in it is off limits."

"I'll think about that, Tim." And with that, I pushed the red 'off' button. It was so tempting to see how many times I could make it skip across the water.

We sail on.

As planned, we docked shortly after dawn at South Padre, caught a cab to the Walmart, and were back in open ocean by one o'clock, refueled, with fresh water, a freezer full, a supply of fresh fruit and vegetables, and an ample supply of adult beverages. The sails went up not long after I cleared the harbor entrance and we set a course to the southeast. I locked down the autopilot again and then sat down with Karen to plot our destination. We were very aware this was peak hurricane season and kept close attention to the NOAA radio. The gulf was quiet and smooth; for the moment, other than the expected afternoon thunderstorms, the weather wasn't a problem.

"I'll say it again," said Karen, "Where to, Skipper?"

"Here's what I'm thinking," I said. "Let's head for the Yucatan peninsula, cruise down past Cozumel, Cancun, Isla Mujeres, and places south, and maybe end up in Belize City where we can find a slip, hook up to power and catch our breath for a few weeks. After that, I think it might be a good idea to change oceans for a little while."

"Change oceans?" she asked. "Like where?"

"What do you think about scooting across the Panama Canal into the Pacific? I can't believe anyone would look for us there," I answered. "There's a place I got pretty close to when I was racing in Baja that I've heard a lot about. It might be a fun place to hang out for a while."

"And where is that?" she asked.

"Cabo San Lucas," I answered. "From what I hear, it has good fishing, sunny weather, cold beer, noisy bars, and loud music. It's time to start living again."

"Sounds to me like a very short timeline for planning forever," Karen said, "But I've heard worse ideas. I guess it will have to do for now. Cabo it is."

Sailing free in the open ocean was just what the doctor ordered. The wind stayed steady between ten and fifteen knots, and the sky was so blue it hurt your eyes. During the day, Karen wore a shoestring thong bottom and SPF thirty block (or even less), and at night, lying on the deck with sails furled and a light blanket around us, you could lose count somewhere past a zillion stars. On more than one night, I would idly find Pegasus and Cassiopeia, draw an imaginary line between them, and find Andromeda, our nearest neighbor galaxy, some two million light years away. It never failed to amaze me that a speck of light you could hardly perceive with binoculars in the city with all the light pollution, you could clearly pick out in the night sky with unaided eyes out here. Andromeda has an estimated one hundred billion stars in it, and scientists believe there are over a hundred and forty *billion* galaxies in the known universe. It's almost for sure one of them has a star with a planet circling it with two little green creatures lying on a boat in a liquid nitrogen ocean, holding flippers and wondering if there was any intelligent life in that other galaxy, a question I'm still not sure I know the answer to. The Milky Way was so bright you could read by it, the moon looked close enough to touch, and we ran out of wishes before we ran out of shooting stars. I couldn't do this forever – I would quickly go nuts, but for a while, it was an amazing way to de-tune.

What could have been accomplished in five days, we took two weeks, sailing lazily, finally docking at a marina in Belize City. Belize City is the largest city in Central America - a pirate town that never became civilized. The waterfront is crawling with the shallow end of the gene pool. I suppose the unattentive, unarmed, unassuming tourist is fair game for the thieves, street hawkers, pickpockets, and hookers that mob you when you walk off the boat. Karen and I are a little savvier than the average flatlander and I could more often than not make a thug veer away with nothing more than a stern glance. Heck, I saw darn near as many Americans as I did Latinos. The cost of living was cheap, the weather amazing and the fishing better than average. As a home away from home, it will have to do for a while. The dock master met me at the head of the marina, and we agreed on a fee. He had a rather unusual suggestion.

"Senior, a beautiful boat like that, I theenk you should hire a guard to watch it." He paused for a moment and then added, "And also another *hombre* to watch the watchman." I considered this for a moment. "And which position would you be qualified for?" I asked.

"Oh, senor, I would be most pleased to offer my services for either, or both," he said with a toothy, gold-grilled smile. I laughed and a few more dollars changed hands. We walked onto terra firma.

My first project was not one I approached with any joy. If I was ever going to be able to take my shirt off again, I had to get rid of my SEAL tattoo. People that know what that artwork means would ask too many questions, or tell too many stories, and it's a pretty exclusive club. I had to change more than just my name. After a stop at the bank to pull some cash out with my Amex Black, we cruised the city and had no problem finding a half dozen tattoo parlors. I picked one at random, casually walked in, and started perusing the sample books. 'Uno momento, por favor," a voice called from the back. "No problema," I replied. I expected some overweight, hairy Latino with full-sleeve tats and maybe a pierced nose to walk out from behind the curtain, but I was surprised when a trim, good-looking guy around fifty years old with a well-groomed mustache and goatee emerged.

"Ola señor, como esta?"

"Bien, bien, y tu? Comprende Ingeles?" I asked. My Spanish would likely just get me in trouble.

"Yes, I speak English he replied with hardly an accent. How may I help you?" He stuck out his hand. "My name is Fernando."

"Julius" I stammered and shook his hand. I had almost forgotten what my name was supposed to be. "I have a need. Can you cover up an old tattoo with a new one?"

"Of course, I would be happy to do that. Show me what you want me to fix. It's your ex-wife, yes?" He said with a smile.

"No," I answered, "just a distant memory that I need to forget." I rolled up the sleeve of my rash guard for him to see. I looked carefully into his eyes to see if he knew what that eagle and anchor emblem meant, but if he recognized it, he did a good job of hiding his knowledge.

"It is a busy tattoo," Fernando said. "We will need something vivid. Do you have a preference?"

"Not really," I answered. "Give me some suggestions." Fernando started thumbing through the catalogs on the desk, stopping and looking back at the SEAL tattoo a few times. He stopped. "Here. This might work. The eagle talons could become the dragon talons, and then, I would have the dragon holding a viper." He grabbed a sketch pad, expertly drew the existing art, and then fleshed in a dragon to cover it. "Like this señor," and he handed it to me. I hated the thought of covering it up, but I guess there was no way around it.

"How much?" I asked.

"Maybe five hundred Belize. That's two hundred fifty, U.S. señor. It will take much of an afternoon to complete." I nodded, and he motioned me to a chair. It was only the second time I had done this – the first time in Key West so many years ago. Pain is only in the mind, and the bottle of tequila and the little clay shot glass helped keep me distracted. Four hours later, I reached in my pocket and peeled off five, one hundred Belize dollar notes, and handed them to him, then counted out ten more.

"Señor?" Fernando looked confused.

"Five for the work, and ten more to forget you ever did it."

Fernando gave a big toothy smile. "Si, si, señor. I have already forgotten. An Americano? No, no. I have never covered up a tattoo on a Gringo!"

I mused for a moment. I had to ask.

"Fernando, you speak English better than I do. How?"

He smiled for a moment, considered how to answer then decided. "My father is Lebanese and my mother is German. I have a college degree from the university in Cologne, Germany and I speak six languages."

"So how did you end up running a tattoo shop in Belize?" I asked.

Fernando smiled again. "Where else could I make a thousand bucks covering up a Navy SEAL tattoo on an American Hero?"

I raised my eyes in surprise, took the hint, peeled off another five hundred Belize, shook his hand again, and walked out the door.

One more link to my past broken.

El Arco – Cabo San Lucas, Baja California

7
The Far Side of The World

The days passed pleasantly, if a little boring. We took walks through town and found shady cantinas for afternoon beverages and waterfront restaurants for dinner and music. It was warm, pleasant and romantic. And two more weeks of this I would climb up a church steeple with a thirty-ought-six and start thinning out the neighborhood.

"Time to sail" I blurted out to Karen over a margarita. She smiled and didn't even ask why or when.

"Let's go," She answered, almost to herself.

I could feel her energy, "You know," I mused. "Given my 'druthers' I'd rather just cast off, sail right to Key West, pull up at Mallory Square, and yell 'April Fools, we were just kidding' to everyone." I sighed. "But, that's probably not that smart of an idea."

Karen sighed too. "I know. Wish we could go back and just get a do-over. Forget the gold, forget everything else and just go back to our normal dysfunctional relationship." She turned toward me, took my head in her hands, and gave me a kiss on the forehead. "Like you said, I wish we could just go back to Key West Normal."

"Well," I answered, kissing her back on the lips. "That's not in the cards, at least not in that fashion."

"When do we leave?" She asked.

"Sunrise tomorrow morning, weather permitting. Let's stock up on provisions."

We negotiated with a cab driver to commandeer his services for the afternoon, hit the local grocery stores for fresh fruit, frozen steaks, dry goods, and alcohol, and then returned to the boat to top off the fuel and water tanks, dump the biffy and go over the current Caribbean weather. There was nothing of concern beyond a tropical wave south of Puerto Rico that was not expected to develop.

All good.

The next morning "weather permitting" decided not to permit. Dawn greeted us with a sunrise squall and enough thunder and lightning to delay departure for at least a few hours. We hailed a taxi and went into town for a last breakfast and to wait out the storm, watching the rain over *huevos rancheros con frijoles y chorizo* strong Columbian coffee, and a glass of fresh-squeezed orange juice. Unless it's a tropical system, storms in this part of the world never last more than an hour or so, and by the time we finished breakfast the rain was gone and the sun was out. "Let's walk back to the boat," Karen said. "Gonna be a few days before we can walk anywhere." I nodded, and we strolled back to the dock hand in hand, in silence. When we got back to the '*Miles*, I scooped Karen up in my arms. "I never carried you over the threshold," I said.

"It's because I haven't said 'yes' yet," Karen answered and planted a kiss on me with her arms around my neck. I kissed her back and put her down. This boat was big enough to call for a crew of four, but Karen was as expert a deck hand as any, and we easily cast off, crabbed the boat about-face in the marina, and motored past the breakwater. Clear of land, we hoisted sail, shut off the engine, and became our version of modern-day pirates, cruising the ocean blue, looking for adventure in every port.

Next stop, Panama.

A week later, we were anchored at Bahia de Manzanillo in the busy harbor at the eastern terminus of the Panama Canal, just off the city of Colon. We were dwarfed on all sides by giant Panamax container ships and colorful cruise liners, all queued up to transit the canal. A little sailboat like ours had no status among the big cargo ships. We were paid a visit by a harbormaster, where twelve hundred bucks in cash changed hands. The harbormaster consulted his clipboard, re-boarded his orange boat, and got on the radio. He shouted out the window. "Eleven a.m. tomorrow morning. Stage your craft by Fuerte Sherman," he pointed north. "You will meet up with one other yacht there and proceed to Panama Lock. You start transit at one p.m." He confirmed the radio frequencies, fired up, and left.

The next day, we cruised over to Fort Sherman and hung out in front of the yacht harbor. An eighty-four-foot Altura Yacht cruised out of the harbor and the skipper waved at us. Our schooner was a small fry compared to this big boy. I eased around to the stern of the big boat to see who I was hooked up with, but the name was in a Middle Eastern language. This would be my first canal transit so

I obediently motioned him to proceed and I took up the rear and followed him to the entrance to the canal. We furled the sails as we approached the entrance. We would be under motor power from here. Entering the canal from the Atlantic side you go through two locks, then a longish cruise through Gatun Lake, and then three more locks on the other side before emerging into the Pacific. Total distance, forty-eight miles. Elapsed time, is about seven hours.

Container ships, cruise ships, and other various vessels, all much larger than me, were everywhere, and I had to be on my toes. Sailboat or not, I was under power, so we had no right of way like we would if we were under sail. It wasn't quite as bad as driving the houseboat to Tarpon Springs, but I had quite a knot between my shoulders by the time we were clear of the canal entrance and out into the Pacific. It was an uneventful transit other than one moment when we went under the Bridge of the Americas at the Pacific entrance/exit. Two people were standing on the bridge as we passed under it, a man and a woman, and the man was staring intently at us through some serious binoculars. No big deal except I saw a couple that looked just like those two when we went under the Centennial Bridge six miles behind us.

It had to be a coincidence. Didn't it?

Once clear of the bay, we hoisted sail, turned northwest, and the '*Miles* bent nicely into a quartering breeze. I dialed the Garmin Marine for the tip of Baja California.

Next stop, Cabo San Lucas, twenty-two hundred miles away. No, not non-stop. We hit port in Puntarenas, Costa Rica and Salina Cruz, Mexico. No rush. The weather stayed nice, and the people were friendly. Yankee dollars were always welcome. We averaged a little more than a hundred miles a day, and three weeks later, the postcard image of El Arco (the arch) showed up just off the starboard bow. I had never been to Cabo San Lucas before but knew lots of people that had. The cool thing about this harbor was that it's virtually in the middle of town. Walk off the boat and you're two minutes from dozens of bars and restaurants, and for that matter, massage parlors, strip clubs, and pharmacies where you can buy every drug, pain killer, antibiotic, and "male enhancement" product known to man. Cabo is, by its own definition, the "Land of the

Happy Ending." I planned to stock up on some of the former, and I had no need, thankfully, for any of the latter. We hailed the harbormaster who pointed us to a berth at dock "M" alongside some pretty serious yachts from all over the world. The dock was secured by a locked gate and a watchman, which meant, this time, I wouldn't have to hire someone to watch the boat and someone else to watch the watchman. After five weeks at sea since Belize, we needed clean laundry and some dry land, not that we wore very much on the water, but you still needed to launder delicates. Karen gathered a pillowcase full of clothes and an overnight bag, and we walked ashore. There's a big Wyndham Resort right at the harbor, and we checked in for a little R&R.

After a forty-five-minute shower, with copious amounts of soap and shampoo, we dressed and checked out the town. From what I have been told, Cabo underwent two huge changes since the seventies. Once, when Howard Hughes built an international airport in nearby San Jose del Cabo in the mid-seventies, and then again when cruise ships started coming twenty years later. Like Key West, the cruise ships were a big boon to the tee-shirt shops, bars, and so-called pharmacies and a complete disaster to the ambiance of this beautiful desert town surrounded by water.

Karen and I walked out of the hotel and took a leisurely stroll. A few minutes later we were munching chips and salsa at Sammy Hagar's Cabo Wabo Bar and getting outside of a bucket of ice-cold Pacifico Sun beers. We were surrounded by cruise people, all decked out in the same attire they wore when ashore in Key West; Aloha shirt, shorts, white socks, orthopedic walking shoes, high-water Capri pants, and sunglasses crusted in rhinestones that came to a point on both sides of the eyes. All extremities were lobster-red except for the nose, which was covered in a gooey mass of zinc oxide. I need to subscribe to "cruise ship quarterly" to see where this required wardrobe was listed. I chuckled to myself.

"What's so funny?" Karen asked.

"Look around," I pointed out. "All the tourists think we're locals, all the locals know we are not from here. We're not blending in very well."

"Well, at least for the first time in a while," Karen observed, "I think we are someplace that nobody would think to look for us."

"Why do you think I suggested this place?" I answered. "Mexico is a place where even the bad guys that are chasing us are out-gunned."

"Where from here?" She asked. "Up the California coast?"

I thought for a moment. "We could," I considered, "but my thoughts are to hang here for a month or so, and then head back through the canal and..." I hesitated for dramatic effect.

"And?"

"Go home."

And that's what we did. After a few days at the Wyndham, we moved back to the 'Miles where we could enjoy privacy and sleep in our own bed. The weather was pleasant, and there were countless places to eat and drink. We settled on a few locations that became our favorite, Cabo Wabo when the cruise ships weren't in port, and the Giggling Marlin, where breakfast, lunch, and dinner were cheap and tasty. They actually created homemade salsa right at your table, custom-made to your taste and served with fresh chips. Nothing like good huevos rancheros with hot frijoles, spicy chorizo sausage, and a glass of fresh-squeezed orange juice to start your day.

I did have one goal before we left this town. In my life I have caught just about every kind of gamefish in the water, mahi, permit, cobia, sailfish, tarpon, marlin, wahoo, tuna, and more, not to mention largemouth bass on Lake Tojo in Saint Cloud and monster rainbow trout in the mountains of Utah. There's a fish in these waters you don't see in the Atlantic, and they are on every serious fisherman's bucket list. So early one morning, well before sunrise, while Karen slept in, I quietly sneaked out and walked a few dozen yards to the other side of the dock where the charter boat guides hung out. They were likely always booked solid on weekends, but on a Tuesday morning, you had your pick of the litter. They descended on me like ants at a picnic. "Hola, señor, we go out for beeg marlin! Lots of marlin being caught! Señor, we catch Dorado! You catch, we cook for you!" I ignored them all and then spoke up to the crowd. "Little boat, close to shore. I want to catch one kind of fish and nothing else." A young Mexican, maybe twenty years old stepped up. "Señor, My name is Juan. What do you want to catch? Lots of Spanish Mackerel near shore. Come with me, we get mackerel." I shook his hand. "Juan, you can put me over a boatload of Spanish Mackerel, and I wouldn't be interested, but if I can catch just one fish today, I'll give you a big tip."

"What do you want to catch señor?"

"Roosterfish."

The Roosterfish, *Nematistius Pectoralis* is a gamefish found only in the warm Pacific waters from Baja California to as far south as the Galapagos Islands. They are uniquely distinct with their seven huge "rooster comb" spines of their dorsal fin. They are also famous for being one of the hardest-fighting fishes in the ocean. I always wanted to catch one. When I said Roosterfish, Juan, who was only about five foot three to start with, shrunk a little more. "Oh, señor, not many Roosterfish are being caught right now. I theenk you will have more luck fishing for Spanish Mackerel. We caught a thirty-pound mackerel yesterday." I smiled to put him at ease. "Juan, let's try. If we don't catch one, I won't blame you. If we do, I will be a very happy gringo."

Juan saw my determination and nodded. "Ogay, señor, we go try to catch you a rooster." He led me to his pride and joy, a little sixteen-foot wooden boat with an outboard, a red canvas shade, and a plastic Walmart chair bolted to a swivel that served as a crude fighting chair. We cruised out of Cabo harbor and stopped for a moment to pick up some live bait, seven little Jack Crevalle about eight inches long. I expected a half hour, maybe forty-five-minute boat ride, but we were hardly out of the harbor before Juan pointed the little craft toward the shore. Sensing that I knew my way around a boat, he asked me to take the wheel while he readied the gear. He put a bait on one rod and ran the line up an outrigger and the other line he strung out the back of the boat. Idling down to just a few knots we worked our way along the beach, hardly a hundred feet from shore. On the shore were tourists, horses, dogs, and girls in bikinis. This was the strangest kind of fishing I had ever encountered.

We trolled back and forth for a half hour with no action before Juan asked if I was hungry. "I could eat," I said. "What do you have?" Juan opened a bag pulled out something in foil and handed it to me. "Burrito, señor," he said. I unwrapped it and found a cold chorizo sausage and scrambled egg burrito. Spicy and tasty. Holding my rod in one hand with the drag off and my thumb on the reel, I started to take another bite, when Juan said excitedly. "Rooster!" He pointed behind the boat, and I briefly saw the unmistakable spines of a roosterfish come up behind my line. I dropped the burrito and prepared for the strike. He crashed the bait but took it deftly off the hook without getting snagged. One bait down. We re-baited and kept trolling. I threw the burrito mess into the water, and Juan handed me another. This time, I hardly had it unwrapped when the spool on my reel started moving. I tossed the burrito down again and let the line run out. "Easy, easy, NOW!" Juan shouted. I lifted the pole and felt the satisfying tug of a fish. "It's a mackerel, señor," Juan announced. Agreeably, the fight wasn't what I was expecting, but a fish is a fish, and I worked it toward the boat. Then the fish apparently saw the boat and the pole bent nearly down to the water. Now I had a fight. I sat in the "fighting chair" and worked the fish carefully. In a minute, we saw color. "It *is* a Rooster!" Juan exclaimed. I worked the fish alongside the boat, and after a few more runs, Juan reached down and captured the fish by the tail. "No too big, but nice, señor! Maybe eighteen, twenty pounds!" He handed the fish to me, and I admired the creature. Zebra stripes on its sides and the unmistakable rooster comb dorsal fin. I looked it over for a few more minutes and then eased it back into the sea. I was happy. I had my rooster. However, I was still looking for breakfast. Juan looked in his sack and handed me one last burrito. I opened it up and took a bite while he re-baited and let the line out. This time, the line was hardly out before I had a second fish on. The foil-wrapped burrito hit the deck while I concentrated on getting the fish to the boat. A little smaller than the first, it was nonetheless a second roosterfish. I returned it to the Sea of Cortez and looked at Juan expectedly. He was busy putting the poles away, apparently getting ready to head back to the marina.

"What's the matter, Juan, are we out of bait?" I asked.

"No señor," Juan grinned. "We're out of burritos."

8
I'm Glad We Left a Trail of Breadcrumbs

Three weeks later we started getting our provisions together for the voyage back to the Atlantic. This time, we planned on no ports of call between Cabo San Lucas and the little yacht harbor at Shelter Bay on the Atlantic Side of the Panama Canal. We would sail during the day, find a sheltered cove at night, and catch fresh fish when the opportunity arose. I was enjoying the adventure but wanted to figure out a way to sneak back into the keys. It was probably a dream, but we both missed that rock. It was against everything the Witness Protection Program proscribed, but it wasn't like we were going to parade down Duval Street with a sign on our backs.

We motored out of the Cabo marina shortly after sunrise, cleared El Arco, and hoisted sail. The *More Miles to the Galleon* heeled into a brisk west wind. I dialed in the Garmin and pointed the bow toward our first waypoint, the sheltered bay at Puerto Vallarta. Tempting as it was to stop and play, we stuck to our plan, leisurely sailing down the coast. Eventually, the coast turned us due east, and finally, south and even a little west as you enter the Panama Canal on the Pacific side you are almost west of the Atlantic exit. We were old hands at this now and crossed back over to the other side with no issue. From there, I pointed us to old Fort Sherman and Shelter Bay. There's not a lot here, which made it perfect, and no way to get there except by boat made it even better. All we needed was a little fresh water, diesel for the motor, dump the head, and add a few fresh vegetables. The store at the marina didn't have a lot, and what they had was expensive, but I was growing just a little weary of fresh fish for dinner every night. A steak sounded good. We laid in for four days, and we chose our next port. I spread a map of the Caribbean out on the deck in front of the wheel and looked it over. Karen sat down beside me. I traced the coast with my index finger.

"I say we head for Cartagena, Columbia, and then work our way along the coast to Aruba, Curacao, and Bonaire." I pointed to the map. "From there, around the tip of Puerto Rico, hit San Juan, then slide into a port in the Middle Keys, maybe Faro Blanco Marina in Marathon." I looked at Karen. "Work for you?" She smiled and put her arms around me, kissing my neck. "Love it. Let's get this tub moving, Now."

"Before we cast off, let me double-check that all is secure below decks," she said. She started down the steps into the cabin and suddenly stopped and slowly backed out. "Bric?" She said slowly. I turned and saw the barrel of a Russian Makarov pistol coming up the steps. I instantly recognized the woman before she spoke.

"Yes, please, Karen, come into the cabin and make sure all is ready. We have places to go."

Karen looked at me, wide-eyed. I just closed my eyes for a second. This day just went to Hell in a handbasket.

"Karen, please permit me to introduce Ilenia Teranarmov, Russian spy, slimeball bitch cunt. Ilenia, Karen."

Ilenia and I were "old" acquaintances. A double agent for Tim and the Russians, she was supposed to be my travel partner and so-called bodyguard while I toured Europe hiding from people who wanted me dead. As it turned out, Ilenia was one of those people. She nearly got me in a Paris hotel. Looking back, I guess I should have punched her ticket then instead of staring at her tits.

"You want to take a cruise?" I pointed across the bay. "That NCL mega-ship over there would be a lot more comfortable, and they even have live music and free vodka. Hey, I'll be happy to drop you off."

She wasn't smiling. "Just complete your preparations and get underway," she said. "Leonid and I will keep your wife company downstairs. Don't do stupid things. I think you understand."

Leonid? Sheesh. Two of them. I still didn't have any serious weapons on the boat and, with Karen at gunpoint, all I could do was shut up and cooperate. I spoke.

"Ilenia, what do you want? I don't have any more info now than I did before. I told you. I dove, snagged the package, attached it to a boomer, and headed back to the mother ship which you conveniently blew up over me. End, No more, Fini." She looked disgusted.

"Mister Brickwall, if that's your name, this is not about the Russian Government. I work for other people, and you cost them hundreds of millions of dollars. They don't want any information that I agree you do not have. They want to piss on your cold, lifeless body. It is my job to bring it to them, but I don't know how to drive a boat like this so I will arrange that you deliver yourself to them. As long as I keep your wife hostage, you will do what I say, no?"

"She's not my wife."

"I'm not his wife."

This made Ilenia almost smile. "Then you do not mind if I shoot her and throw her over the side."

I closed my eyes and counted to five. "Where are we going?"

"Set your course for Santiago De Cuba," she said. I have been told that a good sailor can get us there in five days. I will give you six, or I will kill this woman, whatever she is to you."

I raised my arms. "Look, no weapons. Let me go to the console and check. I dialed Santiago de Cuba into my GPS and whistled. "Eight hundred sixty-four miles. Figure seven knots max under sail. That's about 125 hours non-stop. It will take every bit of five days and how am I gonna stay awake for five days non-stop? And besides, I'm flying an American flag on the back of this boat. Last I heard Cubans didn't welcome Americans sailing into their ports with open arms."

"We have friends there, and they will be more than happy to let you dock there so they can keep your sailboat. Leonid and I will take turns watching you. You are wasting time. Leave now. The woman will stay downstairs with us."

"It's not downstairs, it's below decks and the 'woman' needs to help me get this yacht out of the harbor or we will run into something sharp and sink before we pass the breakwater."

Ilenia thought for a second and slipped the Makarov into her belt. She waved at Karen with her hand. "Go. Do what you need to do. If you jump, I will shoot your hus…boyfriend."

Karen shrugged and looked at me. I smiled and winked, then started the motor. "Cast off the bowlines!" Karen walked towards the bow and Ilenia followed closely. I walked to the stern to slip that line off. "Clear!" Karen said from fifty feet away. I eased the boat into gear, and we quietly slid out of the slip and into the bay. It took nearly an hour to work our way down the river through the anchored cargo ships and into the main bay. We cleared the point, and it was time to be a sailboat. Like the expert she was, Karen unfurled the foresail and mainsail. With a flip of a switch, both sails climbed the masts and caught the breeze. I shut the auxiliary motor down, and we were sailing. It crossed my mind that I could probably do a quick tack and bat this Russian bitch fifty yards out into the ocean, but there was still an as-of-yet unknown goon below decks that might not take that well. Anyway, just as I was formulating a plan Leonid emerged from below carrying a Heckler & Koch HK 417 Sniper Rifle. Handy if I was a hundred yards away but a little cumbersome for close-order combat. Either way, nothing to be trivial with. Big guy, older with a big white bushy mustache. He could have tied for third place in a Wilford Brimley look-alike contest. He had more hair on the back of his palms than I did on my head. He raised his voice and spoke to Ilenia in Russian, and she answered. She didn't bother with introductions.

"You must be Leonid," I said. Any more like you at home? I bet your ancestors didn't evolve an opposable thumb till like three or four generations ago."

"Da. Leonid" he answered. And that was all.

"He only speaks Russian," she said. He sat down on the top step, laid the gun across his lap, and lit a cigarette.

"Hey, this is a non-smoking boat you weasel-eyed little fuck. *Ne kurit.*" And I waved to indicate he throw the cigarette overboard.

Leonid didn't know what I said but was pretty sure it wasn't a compliment. He took another long drag, and with the cigarette in his mouth, jacked a round into the Heckler, brought it to his shoulder, and aimed it right at my forehead. I just stood there and looked at him. Ilenia said something in Russian and Leonid shrugged and fished a pair of handcuffs out of his jacket pocket. With the gun still pointed at me, Ilenia walked over and cuffed my left hand to the wheel.

"Gonna get a little stinky around here in six days," I said.

"You will have time to use the toilet," Ilenia said. "But now no chance of you playing tricks."

I glared at Leonid. Paybacks will be a bitch you little commie prick, I thought to myself. After a moment, he gave a little smile put the gun back in his lap, and kept smoking. I could see his eyes narrow a bit under the unibrow, as he probably wondered to himself just how much Russian I knew. Like most languages, I could find a beer and a bathroom in Russian, say hello, goodbye, thank you, and a few swear words, but that was about all. Not enough to know when that blonde bitch was going to tell him to put a bullet through my temple. I guessed that they were under orders to bring me back alive, but I was also very aware that if they were successful, the eventual outcome wouldn't be optimistic.

I needed a plan. One solution was very close, but I wasn't sure how to do anything with it. There was an inconspicuous plastic box sitting behind the main mast. Inside was the satphone, our passports, a dive knife, and twenty thousand in cash. It's my "crash box", waterproof and designed to float even if the boat sinks. I've always had a version of that on every boat, although none of them previously had a satphone or more than twenty bucks. I would have put my wallet with the Amex card in it, but we were rather unceremoniously welcomed when we boarded. There was also a K-Bar knife in a sheath right below me on the console plus a very sharp pocket knife, and I might put them to work if the opportunity arose.

In the meantime, we sail east.

The Ruskies didn't know much about sailboats, especially big ones like the *Miles*. I could have dialed in the destination, and it would have more or less sailed herself there, but I didn't want it to look that easy or I would have found myself hogtied to the mast for the next five days. Ilenia knew I was dangerous and even with the handcuffs, one of them had a gun trained on me all the time. After we got underway, they took Karen downstairs and probably tied her up. I warned Ilenia that no harm would come to her, or they would have to kill me and learn how to sail on their own. Weasel Eyes made some sort of snide comment when she translated, but her response sounded like a warning. I heard *"Pechat"* which means seal in Russian. He looked at me after that with a little different level of caution and made double-sure there was a round in the chamber.

This went on for three days. They let Karen come up and give me a chance to catch a nap a couple of times, but mostly it was me behind the wheel. An occasional baloney sandwich and a Gatorade pretty well summed up my life. No pee pee breaks and I just had to aim left and hope the pump was still strong enough to keep the deck dry.

They had removed the mic from the radio and tossed it overboard so I couldn't call for help, but I was able to listen, and from the chatter, it appeared that little tropical low was gathering strength and headed more or less this way. It sounded like it would be someplace around the Caymans about the time we got to the bottom end of Cuba. Both locations were in very close proximity. I started to formulate a plan.

Day four dawned gray and whitecaps were starting to grow. The wind was dead out of the east, and I had to take a southerly tack to make any progress. A little southerly direction fit my game plan. Leonid showed up wearing one of my rain jackets which didn't fit him, and I pointed at it and motioned that I wanted one too. He just lit another cigarette and ignored me. I cranked the wheel hard right and he had to duck to avoid the mainmast. He yelled at me and pointed the gun my way. I flipped him the bird and spun the wheel back the other way. He lost his balance and tumbled down the steps into the cabin. Ilenia came up the steps with the pistol.

"No funny stuff Brickwall!" She said above the rising wind.

"What?" I answered. "It's rough. Weasel Face doesn't have his sea legs yet. Anyway, while you're up here, I need some foul-weather gear and food. Can you send Karen up?"

She hesitated for a moment and spoke down the steps in Russian. Ten minutes later Karen emerged with a yellow jacket and pants. "Just the jacket for now," I told her. I pointed to the handcuffs and Ilenia yelled down the hatch for the handcuff key. Leonid handed it up, and she gave it to Karen to unlock the cuffs, pointing the pistol at her all the time. "Too warm for slicker pants. Hold the wheel while I get this jacket on. She took over while I spent way too much time struggling into the jacket, dropping my hat in the process. When I stooped down to pick up the hat I reached into the cabinet and grabbed the pocket knife whispering. *"Storm coming. Gonna run the boat into the Caymans. Be ready."* And I slipped the knife into her pocket. She nodded, but other than that just looked ahead without expression. I took the wheel back, closed the cuffs myself, kissed her on the cheek, and whispered one last word into her ear. *"Geronimo."*

The *More Miles to the Galleon* porpoised into the leaden sea in ever-increasing darkness. The wind had changed to dead out of the north now which meant the storm was directly in front of us. I would guess the wind was up to forty knots with some higher gusts, and it was getting close to the point where we needed to turn and run with the wind. The main sails were furled and I was operating with just a flying jib and the diesel motor. A good skipper can minimize the rocking with good maneuvering, but I wanted it rough, the rougher, the better. I hadn't seen either crook for quite a while, and I would guess they were getting a little green around the gills by now. Good. The weather overlay on the GPS indicated we were only a few hours away from some bad shit, and I needed to play my hand soon. I changed the destination to Georgetown, Grand Cayman on the GPS and I grunted with satisfaction that it was exactly due south.

Showtime.

I cranked the wheel hard to starboard and the turbulence immediately eased up as we ran with the increasing winds. Ilenia immediately came up. The blonde beauty now looked like a sick puppy. The front of her shirt was a mess, and her hair was matted down.

"What are you doing?" she yelled above the wind.

"Running from the storm!" I yelled back. "We need to find shelter behind the Cayman Islands or we will sink, and I need Karen up here to help me. Now!"

Ilenia hesitated and then went below. Karen came back up a moment later with her foul weather gear on, followed by Ilenia, gun in hand. I pointed toward the stern.

"Check the boom," I instructed. "I think it's still tied down."

Karen gave me a puzzled look. In this kind of weather, you definitely want that boom tied and tight. She hesitated. I pointed with my free hand. "Just go back there and keep an eye on it until I tell you." And winked. She nodded and made her way to the stern. I turned to Ilenia. "Close the hatch! Too much water is getting into the cabin!"

"I don't know how!" she yelled.

70

"Just stand on top of the cabin and pull the door forward. You just have to unlatch it. Hurry! I'll run with the waves so you won't fall."

Ilenia looked unhappy but she put the gun in her belt, climbed up on top of the cabin, and stood up. Now was the time. "Geronimo!" I yelled to Karen. She unsnapped the boom and it slid to the left in the wind. As I had hoped, she had already loosened all the rigging. The boom arced out over the water, and I whipped the wheel hard to port. Karen dropped to the deck as the boom came rushing back. I ducked my head but Ilenia never knew what happened, and it caught her right in the face, spanking her thirty feet into the ocean, likely unconscious and probably dead.

One down. Suddenly Leonid appeared from below, rifle in hand and already raising it in my direction. No time to be civil. I reached down, opened the cabinet, grabbed the K-Bar knife, and threw it in one motion. The Heckler stitched ten rounds into the deck right in front of me as Leonid's eyes went wide with surprise, the K-Bar stuck squarely in his sternum. He tumbled into the cabin.

Checkmate.

"Karen, close the hatch and secure! I don't want that goon waking up." She ran past me to the cabin hatch, slid it shut, and latched it from the outside. "I think I got him but need to make sure." Now I needed to get myself free. I could probably break the wheel, but then I couldn't steer the boat. First things first. I glanced at the GPS, and we were maybe three miles from Rum Point. The boom served me well, but now it was banging back and forth in the wind. I tried the auto trim, but the lines had been loosened too much. Oh well, twenty more minutes and we would be ashore. Rum Point has a south-facing harbor, and if we could make the breakwater, it just might be possible that we could walk away from this. I wasn't exactly sure if I wanted to tie up safely. With my luck, the dock master would have a Russian accent. I came to a decision. Locking the steering into autopilot, I kicked the wheel two or three times. No joy. Why couldn't Tim have acquired a cheesy boat instead of this well-made yacht?

"Karen, unlock the hatch and take a peek downstairs. Need to see if Leonid is asleep."

71

"Why?" she asked. "Leave him there."

"I think he has the key to these handcuffs, and if I don't get unhooked in a few minutes, I'm going down with the ship."

Karen unlocked the hatch and slid the door back, then peered carefully down the steps. She looked up at me. "He's at the bottom of the stairs. Not moving!" She went gingerly down the steps. It seemed like an hour, but it was more like five minutes when she emerged.

"No key!" Great, it was probably still in Ilenia's pocket.

I looked at the GPS. We were in twenty-five feet of water, half a mile from shore in a driving wind.

Think, Bric.

"Open the toolbox in the galley. Bring whatever is big and heavy. Hurry!" Just then the boat shuddered and lurched to one side. The centerboard caught on a piece of coral and then went free again. Running out of time. Karen emerged again with a crowbar. I wedged it into the handcuff that was hooked to the wheel and started twisting. The wheel held but the cheap Russian handcuffs didn't. They popped with a clink. Free.

Even with the autopilot, the sailboat was struggling in the waves. I wanted to get as close to shore as possible but didn't want to be in the middle of a wrecking sailboat in the process. Suddenly the keel caught on something hard, and the 'Miles lurched over, tossing both of us over the side. I'm an expert swimmer, and Karen taught the fish, but we were breathing more water than air. I could see lights on the beach and I yelled to her and pointed. We swam for our lives.

Literally.

9

Cayman Dreaming

I was lying in the warm sun, dozing, with the sound of gentle waves in the distance, and seagulls calling overhead. Thirsty. I raised my hand to see if I might catch the attention of the cabana boy. An ice-cold Corona sounded good. Where's Karen? I bet she would like a beer too. I tried to call her name, but it just came out a croak. Where's that cabana boy? Suddenly there was a searing pain in my left big toe. I sat up and opened my eyes. A big land crab was latched on and starting to work his way around to the tender meat. I yelled (croaked) and jumped up. The crab, rather disgusted that his victim wasn't as dead as he thought, glared at me and scuttled off sideways for something a little deader.

Then I remembered. Swimming. Drowning. Storm. The storm was gone, and the sun was rising over a clear blue sky. Karen. Where's Karen? I looked up and down the beach. There was the *More Miles to the Galleon* lying on her side like a beached whale, mast gone and the hull torn open. I started walking toward the wreck. There was a lot of trash on the beach, some from the boat and lots of just normal storm flotsam. I caught a glimpse of yellow under some seaweed. It was the Pelican "crash box" still safely closed and watertight. I picked it up and kept walking toward the boat. No sign of Karen. I climbed onto the boat and peered into the cabin. Everything was trashed and waterlogged, but there was no sign of Leonid. I crawled down through the hatch and opened the fridge. In the jumbled mess were a couple of bottles of water. I opened one and drained it in ten seconds. I wanted the second one but put it in my pocket for Karen. I crawled out of the hatch and stood on top of the boat, looking up and down the shore. I saw something in the distance. The green jacket and what looked like blonde hair meant it was likely Ilenia. I jumped off and trotted up the beach toward the body. It was definitely the Russian and the night's voyage had not been kind. The unnatural way her head was tilted meant the mast had broken her neck.

Serves her right.

I rummaged through her pockets, found the handcuff keys, and unlatched the broken pieces from my wrist, then got an idea, opened the Pelican box, and took the Amex Black card out, slipping it into her back pocket. I was pretty sure they didn't have any kind of I.D. on them so a little identity switch might go a long way toward misdirection.

Couldn't hurt.

Still no Karen.

There was nothing else I could do but look for some help. Sad, I walked off the beach and saw a sign for the Wreck Bar at Rum Point. I doubted there would be anyone there after the storm, even if it was just a strong tropical storm and not a hurricane. None of the houses I walked by looked occupied and I didn't see any sign of power, but when I approached the bar, I could hear a radio playing island music and the hum of a generator running in the distance. I rounded the corner, and the outdoor bar had a half dozen locals doing what Caymanians did before, during, and after a storm, namely drink rum. I looked like last night's washed-up road kill, but the locals didn't look that much better. "Join us, mon!" a boatman motioned me over. "A rum drink for our friend. It's not cold, but it's wet." I nodded thanks, took a long pull, and turned to the gang to speak. "I need help," I said. "We wrecked off the point last night, and I'm missing someone." Suddenly a pair of small hands covered my eyes from behind. I spun around on the stool, spilled my drink, and put my arms around Karen. "Are you okay?" I asked.

"She's fine, mon," one of the locals said. "We just found her wandering up the beach before sunrise, outa her mind and naked as the day she was born. Didn't even know her own name." I untangled myself from her and noticed she was wearing a big floppy tank top and dirty shorts. Her hair was a seaweed-tangled mess, and she had a noticeable lump on her forehead.

"Can you talk?" I asked.

She smiled. "Yes, but these guys think they have to talk for me. I've inherited at least three black families since sunrise. I think I took a pretty good shot on the noggin. I don't remember anything after we were thrown from the boat, and I hadn't even thought about you until you walked in here. I'm sorry."

"No worries. Just a little concussion I suspect. You're a tough gal."

I picked my cup up and handed it back to the bartender. "Guess I spilled my drink. I'd love a replacement."

"Sure my friend, but I'm not da bartender. I'm just old Ray. Nobody here when we showed this mornin, so we volunteered to open the place up for tourism. Call me crazy but looky here, you two showed up!"

"I don't think we qualify as tourists. In fact, there are a couple of bodies over on the beach that we need to contact the authorities about." I suddenly got an idea. "Well, at least one body, but I think you will find a second. We were just passengers on the sailboat." Karen raised her eyebrows a smidgen, but she kept focused on her beverage.

"Da nearest constable might be at Old Man Bay or maybe Breakers." He held up his cell phone. "Phone tower must be outta order. Finish ya drink and I'll run you over dat way."

Ten minutes later we were bouncing down the two-lane road in a beat-up 1983 rust-covered Toyota pickup, crammed into the seat alongside two hundred and fifty pounds of hygienically challenged native. Grand Cayman doesn't have a lot of square miles, but it's got a big lagoon in the middle of it, and getting from Point A to Point B usually meant some sort of roundabout route. Aside from the capital city, Georgetown, what passes for towns on the rest of the island look more like wide spots in the road with a gas station, a convenience store, and a four-way stop. We got to Old Man Bay, and Ray pulled into the gas station.

"Seen Constable Barnes?" Ray yelled. "Not this morning!" was the response, and we drove on toward The Breakers. A few miles down the road we passed a patrol car going the other way. Ray laid on his horn and the car stopped and backed up. Ray explained our story briefly to the young black officer. "Two bodies?" Barnes said. "Let me call the station so they can send the coroner out. He's had a busy day. Pontoon boat capsized in the storm off East End, and everyone drowned. Stupid assed tourists think they can have a storm party in the middle of a real storm." He reached over and opened the back passenger door. "Hop in and I'll run you into Georgetown. I'll need to take a statement at the station then we will find you accommodations. I'm afraid you will have to stick around for a few days."

We climbed into the back seat of the patrol car. "No problem, sir. We have no place else to go and no way to get there anyway."

Forty-five minutes later we were sitting at the police station in Georgetown. Officer Barnes and an older grey-haired gentleman sat across from us. He took out a pencil and a legal pad.

"Name?"

"Russell Phillips and this is my wife Jane. Sorry, she got a bad bump on the head when the boat sank and isn't talking much right now." Karen looked properly forlorn and kept quiet. It would be a heck of a lot easier for one person to spin this yarn than two. We were walking on dangerous turf.

"Address?" Think fast Bric

"Well, actually we don't have one right now sir. Sold our house in Memphis last year, cashed in the retirement, and had been gallivanting the world since." I faked my best cough. "See, I've got lung cancer, and we don't know how much time we have together." I coughed again for effect.

"I'm sorry Mr. Phillips. I understand." His next question came out of the blue. "Have you ever been in the Florida Keys?"

Why the hell would he ask that?

N...No, we've never been down there. I've heard it's really pretty. Why do you ask?"

His answer put me back at ease. "My great-grandfather worked there on the railroad. He lived in Islamorada in the twenties. I was just curious if you had been there." He pronounced it 'eesla morada'.

He motioned toward the box in my lap.

"What's in the little box?"

I acted like I was just going to hand it to him and then pulled it back, opening it with the lid facing them. "Just a little cash and some hotel receipts. I sure wish we had put our passports in there too, but we didn't know we were going to be in a shipwreck."

"What were the names of the deceased?" he asked.

"Julius Cecil and Karly Morris, at least, that's the names they gave us."

"Where did you meet them?"

"In Belize. We were there renting a condo and met them in a bar. Friendly couple, and attractive. We hit it off and met for drinks and dancing a few times, and other stuff." I looked a little sheepish and grinned. Caymans are notoriously straight-laced and the hint of anything off-color would make him change the subject. It worked.

"Go on"

"They said they were going to sail their yacht to Jamaica and then on to the east coast and invited us. We said yes. That was a week ago. The storm came, the boat sank and here we are."

The elderly man made more notes. "The territorial medical examiner is on his way to Rum Point to pick up the bodies. I got word they found the other one, but he's been the subject of some predation. I'm sure there will be no issue in letting you go, but he will want to examine the bodies. Where are you staying?"

I looked uncomfortable. "Not a clue, sir," I started. "We don't have any identification or credit cards." (Sort of true. My wallet was in my jacket pocket, but it had names that weren't mine anymore.) It's going to be a few days before I can get replacements."

He turned to Barnes. "Take them to the Holiday Inn and let the manager know I'll guarantee payment until their replacement documents arrive."

I thanked him, and a half hour later we were checked into the Holiday Inn Resort Georgetown. Nice, clean, and quiet. Constable Barnes got us checked in and let us know he would be in touch. The door closed, and I looked at Karen's eyes for the first time in hours. She had played her part well and did little more than mumble thanks when the constable left. She sat down on the bed and started to cry.

"I can't do this anymore Bric," she sobbed. "This is fucking insane. Guns, mobsters, tied up, shipwrecks. Do you realize what I have been through? AGAIN?"

I sat down next to her and took her hands in mine. "Baby, I so agree. That's why I just 'killed' us one more time. Maybe they will think we finally bought the farm." I stood up and walked over to the little Pelican box, opening it. "First things first." I turned on the satphone and waited for it to find a signal, then auto-dialed the only number in the directory. It rang three times. A familiar voice picked up.

"What are you a fucking cat?" Tim started. "How many goddamn lives do you have?"

"Thanks to you Tim, if I were a cat I would be about four lives in the hole," I answered. "What do you know?" I asked.

"All I know is that the direction finder on the sailboat stopped working about three a.m. this morning, just about the time the locator said you were a hundred yards off the shore of Grand Cayman Island in the middle of what was nearly a hurricane. I got a satellite image handed to me two hours ago, and your pretty little sailboat was scattered over half the north shore. We don't have assets on that island to check it out, so I just was guessing you finally bought the farm." He paused, "What the hell were you doing sailing into the middle of a storm? You have good nav equipment and radios. Didn't you know what was in front of you? Death wish?"

"To make it short Hemminger, I was handcuffed to the wheel of the yacht by your old girlfriend, Ilenia at gunpoint, who was in the process of taking me to Cuba so I could be drawn and quartered by the Russian Mob. HOW'S THAT WORKIN FOR YA?"

Dead silence on the other end. When he spoke, he was down a notch or two.

"Where are they now? Is Karen okay?"

"Karen's fine but pretty well up to here with this spy shit, as am I. Again, no thanks to you and the agency, I managed to dispatch both of them, break the handcuffs, and swim ashore through a couple of hundred yards of eight-foot seas. Just a regular dance in the daisies."

"I….."

"Let me stop you right there," I interrupted. "I just swapped identifications with the dead Ruskies. Bodies are fairly unrecognizable unless the coroner gets really snoopy. Karen and Ileana are both blondes and the Ilenia doesn't have a face left to identify. As far as Leonid goes, he has a knife hole in his chest, but that could have been caused by lots of things, and I understand he has body parts missing, thanks to the un-discretionary dining habits of the local fauna. As it is, the coroner's a busy boy with lots of dead people to deal with so, he will likely be happy with two names and two bodies. You need to make sure those I.D. 's are untraceable, so it's enough of a dead end that they just put them in a box and plant them." I thought for a moment and then continued.

"As for us, I had to think fast so now we are officially Russell and Jane Phillips, formerly of Memphis Tennessee, traveling the world while I die of lung cancer. Can you make that happen in like the next three minutes and FedEx me some new docs?"

"Bric, I have gone through more names with you two than the whole rest of the agency combined in the last twelve months. I'm going to need to walk this upstairs."

"You do that Tim, and while you're at it, tell who the fuck is 'upstairs' that you have two resources in the Caymans that will spill their guts on CNN tomorrow morning about you, the agency, and their involvement in all the shit I have been put through in the last year or so. That will put us in jail for a decade or so, but I'll have the satisfaction of having adjoining cells with you."

A pause and a deep sigh on the other end of the phone. Tim finally spoke, "Where are you staying?"

"Holiday Inn Georgetown, Grand Cayman."

"Ok," Tim said. "Let me get to work."

I just hung up.

"Now what?" Karen asked.

"First things first," I answered. "We both need some clothes, you more than I. Probably tourist stuff if that's ok. We don't look presentable enough to walk into a real clothing store."

"And then?"

"Figure out how to get out of here. Providing Tim comes through, we just buy a ticket, get on an airplane, and fly out of here."

"Where to?"

"Florida"

10
Just Click your Heels

Our shopping spree was a short one. Karen normally loves to re-wardrobe, but this time, she was almost mechanical, picking out shorts, a tropical top, some Crocs, a pair of Ray-Bans, and a visor. I did the same with a Field and Stream olive fishing shirt, cargo shorts, Reef flip-flops, a baseball cap, and Riva sunglasses. Reading will be a challenge until I can get my prescription refilled. We also ripped the ID Pages out of our passports and ditched the books in a dumpster. A block down the street someone was burning trash in an old oil drum, and I walked by and dropped in the photo ID pages.

Goodbye, Julius and Karly.

We found lunch, and I realized that I was completely exhausted. "I need a nap," I said.

"I need to walk and think" answered Karen. "I'll see you back at the hotel." We kissed, and she walked away without saying another word. I felt terrible, how much I had put her through, and not one bit of it was her fault. Karen's a trooper, but I think she was getting close to the breaking point.

I had hardly fallen asleep when there was a knock on the door. "Don't need any towels!" I yelled.

"Mister Phillips? It's Adam Cooper from the Cayman Compass. Could I have a word with you?"

Oh crap, the newspaper.

"One moment" I answered. I threw on my clothes and opened the door a crack with the safety chain still hooked.

"What do you want?" I asked, rather abruptly.

"We understand from Constable Barnes that you were in the shipwreck off Rum Point last night. I'm doing a story for the Compass. Can I ask a few questions? Just one or two."

I would have rather kissed a cobra, but I undid the chain and opened the door. "Just a few", I answered. "I'm tired and very sore," and I sat down on the edge of the bed. He asked my name where I was from and all the usual stuff, and I regurgitated the made-up information without embellishment. Then he asked about the dead people. "I can't tell you much more than I told the cops," I answered. "Well, one other thing. The guy had this tattoo on his arm. Like a big dragon. Lots of colors. It looked really fresh." Thankfully I had bought a long-sleeve fishing shirt as I was describing the new tat on my upper arm. I stood up.

"I'm sorry to cut this short, but I'm exhausted. If you'll forgive me, I need to rest." And I walked him to the door, then stripped and went back to bed. It wasn't three minutes later there was another knock. Shit. So much for rest. "I don't need towels!" I yelled at the door.

"It's me!" was the answer. Karen. I forgot they only gave me one key.

I got up and opened the door, nude and she burst in and jumped up, wrapping her arms and legs around me, kissing me. "I found a way home!" She exclaimed. I put her down, and she danced a happy dance all around the room. "It's just perfect!" and she came back to me and kissed me again. I stood there with my arms folded and smiled. This was the "old Karen" that I hadn't seen for ages. I just enjoyed the moment. She would give me details shortly. Finally, she stopped in front of me and took my hands. She said just one more word.

"Home!"

"OK, so I click my heels? Where is the balloon that lets us leave Oz or do I just clap my hands for Tinkerbell?" I asked.

She stopped a moment to catch her breath. "Well," she started. "I was walking down by the docks, just strolling, and walked past a big cabin cruiser fishing boat. The kind that goes out for a week or two. She was parked stern-first, and I saw the name. Fish Buster, Key West!" She started to dance around again. She finally settled down a little and sat on the side of the bed. "So I started chatting with the deckhand who was washing the boat. Seems they just bought it here in Georgetown, painted a new name on it, and plan to leave in a week for Key West. The Skipper's name is Ted Brown, but everyone calls him Buster."

"I never heard that name on the rock," I said

"That's what makes it perfect. They aren't from Key West. He's from Maryland. Sold his house, bought this boat, and is moving to Key West to go into the charter business." She jumped up again. "And here's the cool part. We can hitch a ride back if we throw in five hundred bucks for fuel!"

I smiled. "That does solve a problem. We can more or less sneak out of Georgetown without a soul knowing how, when, or where we're going." I gave her a big hug. "Great job Karen, or should I say Jane."

Three days later Constable Barnes knocked on the door and told us were free to go, and the day after that, a Federal Express package arrived at the front desk with two passports and and another Amex Black card. We were officially Mr. and Mrs. Phillips. Married at last, even if we weren't. The following morning, we cruised out of Georgetown Harbor looking like no more than a husband and wife going out for a day of deep sea fishing.

We took a week, caught up on our sleep, and started thinking about the future. I was growing facial hair and didn't look much like my old self. Karen was more challenged, and there was just so much you could do with big sunglasses and a floppy hat. We decided that permanent residency should be someplace in the middle keys at best, maybe even Key Largo, but I was more inclined to settle in Islamorada or Marathon.

The ride back was long but uneventful. Stops in Montego Bay, Port Au Prince Haiti, and George Town in the Exumas. A few hours out of the Exumas, I reached into the dry box and took out the satphone.

"You gonna call Tim from here?" Karen asked.

"Nope," and I heaved the phone as far as I could into the ocean into four hundred feet of water. "That phone and all it means is now behind us."

From the Exhumas, it was a long run to Conch Marina on Stock Island. We arrived late on Tuesday afternoon, landing as if we boarded that morning, just another couple walking off a boat after a long day of fishing. A Pink Cab was parked in what little shade was available with the driver sound asleep. I kicked a tire to wake him up, and he bolted upright and grabbed the steering wheel. We didn't wait for an invitation and climbed into the back seat.

"Where to?" Asked the driver.

I opened the Pelican box and threw him two one-hundred-dollar bills.

"Faro Blanco, Marathon, if you think this bucket of bolts will get us there, and you back." He examined the bills carefully, radioed his dispatch for permission, confirmed the two Ben Franklins were in his hands and off we went.

We took a one-bedroom suite at Faro Blanco. Built in the 1950's, Faro Blanco was wrecked by Hurricane Georges. It just re-opened as a Hyatt Place and the only thing remaining from the original place is the landmark lighthouse at the marina. For us, it was the perfect place to hide until we decided what we wanted to do when we grew up. I took a room for a month and would extend it as needed. The resort also had two pools, a super nice Tiki bar, a restaurant, and a big marina where you could rent sailboats, and watercraft or charter a fishing trip. Lots of diversions if you wanted and lots of quiet if you didn't.

After all the time on the water, you would think a little stint on terra firma would have been on my shortlist, but I'm always happier in, or on the sea, so I booked a fishing trip for a day of flats fishing. Fishing in October meant fewer crowds, rougher water, and the chance to nail some pretty decent fish if you are patient. I'm normally a committed "catch and filet" kind of guy, but wasn't in the mood to stink up our little hotel room with fish smells, so I opted for a day of sport. The middle keys are the tarpon capital of the planet, and Captain Mike took little time in getting me over some fish. I'm not a fly fisherman and prefer live bait, so we brought a selection of little blue crabs to tempt the silver kings. Mike eased the flats boat over the shallows toward a deeper channel. You could see the glint of several tarpon lazing in an eddy. Mike pointed, but I was ready. I cast a little above the current, and the crab drifted down toward the tarpon, presented like a normal meal in the current. Almost instantly the line went tight. Contrary to what you often see on ESPN, you don't jerk the pole straight up to set the hook. Just lift. I was rewarded with a hundred-plus pounds of tail-walking monster. Tarpon, especially in skinny water, are among the most acrobatic of fish, and this one didn't disappoint one, two, three times in the air, and then he threw the hook. Captain Mike was an expert guide, and it didn't take me long to hook up again. We hooked five, touched, and released two. By late afternoon I was an exhausted but happy fisherman.

When I got back, I walked a few hundred feet to the room to find a construction site. Karen had set up a large table in the middle of the room and was surrounded by yards of material. She was focused on a sewing machine and didn't even hear me come in.

"Whatcha making?" I asked.

"The perfect disguise," she answered, not looking up. "Did you happen to look at a calendar? Know what next week is?"

"Ah, Halloween?" I questioned. "Ain't we a bit old to go trick or treating?"

"Think a little harder, Einstein," she answered. "Next week in Key West."

"Fantasy Fest? You want to go to Fantasy Fest?" I asked.

"What other time would we be able to walk freely all over town and have nobody recognize us?" she answered.

"Hey, don't get me wrong, I love Fantasy Fest," I replied, "Just didn't know you liked it."

"I don't, but it's just a great excuse to get out. I'm tired of hiding."

"OK, game on. Let me see if there are any rooms available. I'll go naked on roller skates."

"What kind of costume is that?" she asked.

"Pull toy,"

"Very funny, but I already have your costume done. Sorry if it's not quite as exotic as your idea, but it's a good way to go incognito."

"And for you?" I asked. "Care to give me a preview? And where did the table and sewing machine come from?"

"No, and they are rentals," she answered. They have to go back tomorrow, so if you'll excuse me, I have work to do. Get us a room. Preferably on Duval Street."

"Yes, Dear." And I scuttled off. Since tossing the satphone into the Atlantic, we have been without electronic communication, which is not all that bad unless you need to do something like book a hotel room. The hotel has a business center, and I resorted to surfing the web. As expected, rates were eye-popping and availability almost nil, but surprisingly, the Crowne Plaza La

Concha on Duval had one room at a heart-attack rate, and I dutifully snatched it up. Another ten minutes and we had a rental car booked for the week.

Key West here we come.

11
Come As You Aren't….Again

It probably wasn't a good idea since we had "died" more times than Cher has retired, but the urge to haunt the old haunts and the guaranteed opportunity that Karen and I could sneak in and out of town without a ghost of a chance of being recognized was just too tantalizing to turn down.   Fantasy Fest week in Key West gives everyone an equal chance of either being conspicuously invisible or blatantly, ah, over exposed.   Over the years, the public nudity ordinance in the official Duval Street Fantasy Fest Zone had relaxed to the point that the annual sales for Mardi Gras beads, items used to coax women to expose their breasts, had gone from a price-gouging seller's market several years ago to nearly non-existent and totally unnecessary. There were far too many willing subjects that needed no swag to expose their breasts or for that matter numerous other body parts.

Karen and I were fit but were still people "of a certain age" who weren't interested in going naked in public, and besides, the goal was to blend in, not stand out.

Depending on when the first cold front comes through, late October can be as hot as a pizza oven or sweater weather. This year it was about the middle and Karen's choice of outfits fit my mood if not my personality. Covered from head to foot in a brown monk's robe with a pair of mirror Costas covering my eyes, my mother wouldn't have recognized me.

Karen took a similar direction with a little twist. As a parochial school-educated Irish Catholic, she chose to dress from head to toe as a nun, from black robe to headdress, and aside from an out-of-character pair of white Ray-bans to hide behind, she was quite convincing.

From the front.

From the other side, it was a very different story. The entire back of the outfit had been replaced with sheer red lace, and Karen didn't have a stitch on, aside from a little piece of dental floss that she wore as underwear to create some sense of false modesty.

The first cruise down Duval Street was eerie. The local street vendors, Rotarians, charities, and other service organizations were selling food and adult beverages, and every other person would have recognized Karen or me in an instant instead of the names on our passports, Mr. & Mrs. Russell Phillips.

On command, Karen would turn her backside to cameras for photo ops as I solemnly worked my rosary beads and blessed the moment.

Once we got over the heebie-jeebies of feeling like we were the invisible man and woman, we started to enjoy the afternoon. It was good to be in a temporary state of Key West Normal. Karen's outfit, while arrestable attire on a Halloween night in downtown Cleveland, hardly got a second glance on Duval Street in Fantasy Fest. It was definitely a target-rich environment, and, with my Costas on, I could get my voyeur fix a dozen times over every two blocks.

We cruised from event to event over the next few days, staying in the same outfit, and occasionally looking out of place, especially while dropping into the Lazy Geko to spectate the Redneck Party and the Toga party at Sloppy Joes. There aren't a lot of rules, and we even managed to fit a little into the erotic ball at the 801 with Karen's outfit, (as long as she walked backward.) We were staying at the La Concha, paying an arm and a leg every night, but my Amex Black wasn't even breathing hard. Most of the food was room service, and our ventures were normally after dark. We made it all the way to Friday night where we hung around the outside of Pat Croce's Rum Barrel and watched lots of people we know go inside for the Pirate Bash. Pirates both in heart and heritage, I would have given my left nut to dress up in Buccaneer apparel and mingle with the gang. Perhaps another day but tonight we just had to watch from across the street. As we turned to walk back up Front Street, I heard an all too familiar voice behind me.

"Right height, right limp, wrong glasses, but it was that click in your right knee that gave you away." The voice was unmistakable.

Rumpy

"Ah, señor, ju must bee meestook." I said, keeping my back to him and uselessly disguising my voice with my terrible Spanglish accent. "That person ju mention, he is muy muerto." Karen didn't know what to do, turn around and face Rumpy, or keep her bare ass exposed to someone she knew. She resigned to the inevitable and turned to hug my friend. Rumpy kind of gave a half hug from the wrists up, not knowing how to embrace Karen without touching a lot of nearly bare skin. I shrugged my shoulders and also turned and gave him a big man-hug, then put my finger to my lips. "Shhhh! I whispered. That's Russell and Jane Phillips to you, Rump."

Rumpy, who was in full regalia, all the way down to a patch over one eye and a gold earring, grinned from ear to ear. True to pirate spirit he was also obviously outside of a moderate portion of Captain Morgan's finest. 'Subtle' did not appear to be within his grasp.

"Pal, I went to your funerals! Shed a tear even. This story I've got to hear!"

I lowered my voice to make it clear. "This for sure ain't the place, my friend. Tell you what, we'll make our way out to your place on Saturday morning, no, afternoon. You will need to sleep off your character a bit I think."

"Make it Sunday," he answered. "I hope to be face down in some pirate wench before the night is over. I may not make it home till then."

"More likely face down in the gutter, but ok, Sunday it is. See you then." I responded, and we walked away. Being Friday night at Fantasy Fest, we would have enjoyed nothing more than drop in at the Pimp and Ho event at the Bottle Cap, but the monk costume would have just stood out a little too much so we opted for a stroll through the crowds down Duval Street and back to La Concha. Being Fantasy Fest, we were lucky to get a room there on short notice, but they had a last-minute cancelation, and most people would have choked on the eight hundred bucks a night I was being banged for the street side room with balcony. That's the hottest spot in town on Saturday night during the parade, provided you don't want to sleep much. For us, it would be perfect. We could take in the show, drink our fill, and not have to risk being identified. Getting caught once was enough, and we were lucky it was the Rumpster.

The big event at Fantasy Fest is the Captain Morgan parade on Saturday night. It's probably the only parade in the world where the spectators wear less than the participants. With a balcony room at the La Concha, we had the best seats in the house. In years gone by, occupants on the balconies would throw beads to ladies in exchange for a titty flash, but it was fait accompli in this day and age. It was amateur night everywhere you looked. We hung out on the balcony and waited for the parade, which, as normal, was running a few hours late. Alcohol was flowing freely down below and I was pleased not to be in that mix. We had changed into "normal" clothes, comfortably obscure in the darkness. Eventually, the floats came and went, each a little gaudier than the one before it. Fantasy Fest is fun, but after five days it's like eating your way to the bottom of a fifty-five-gallon drum of Neapolitan ice cream.

Eventually, it gets old.

The following day we checked out and motored up to Big Coppit Key. Like always, I ignored the front door or doorbell and walked around back, opening the sliding door. The *Wave Whacker* was there but no Rumpy. Assuming he was sound asleep, I elected to make a pot of coffee. "See if his highness is among the living," I said to Karen. She wandered into his bedroom and returned, wide-eyed. "Sound asleep, naked, on top of the sheets, face up. I may be blinded for life and will undoubtedly need therapy," she said.

I was tempted to grab a big stew pot and a wooden spoon but elected to let the coffee do its job. We flipped on his flat-screen TV and found an old James Cagney cops and robbers movie. Either the coffee or the gunfire roused Rumpy, and he stumbled out into the living room, thankfully wearing a pair of fishing shorts, dangling an unlit cigarette from his lips.

"I heard gunfire and just assumed you were in the neighborhood, Mister Wahl."

"Not I, sir, I've given up wanton killing for Lent," I said.

"A noble gesture," he said, "but likely not plausible. Mayhem seems to find you."

We sat and drank coffee, and I filled him in on recent events, the Readers Digest version. I intentionally left out all the dead people, based on his smart-assed comments.

Too close to the truth.

"Mobile, Belize, Cabo, Panama, the Caymans, shipwreck, jeez, can't you just go to Disneyland or SeaWorld like normal people do? Did you forget the part where the flying monkeys picked you up and hauled you to the wicked witches' castle?"

"As they say, Rumpy if you ain't livin, your dyin." I stood up. "Time to burn some road. Got to turn in this POS Hyundai or it turns into a pumpkin after dark."

"Where are you burning the road to?"

"We're hiding out at Faro Blanco. Nice place where nobody knows our faces."

"Yeah, nice place," said Rumpy. "Killer ceviche at the Lighthouse Grill."

With that, we all hugged goodbye and headed up the road

Flashback –
July 3rd, 1905, Miami Florida

The German stepped out of the passenger car in Miami, Florida. His application for employment at the Flagler offices in St Augustine rewarded him with twelve dollars, enough for a ride south in a seat instead of an empty boxcar. The ride south from St Augustine to Miami was like nothing he had ever seen before. In the beginning, the route stopped at several settlements, Palatka, Ormond, Daytona, New Smyrna, Titusville, Rockledge, and then over a hundred miles through swamps, coastal inlets, and slow-moving rivers before stopping in Palm Beach. From Palm Beach, more wilderness until the Florida East Coast Railway terminated in the village of Miami. Asking directions from the Stationmaster, he was directed toward an office just across the tracks. The sign above the door, *"Florida East Coast Railway - Offices"* confirmed he was in the right place. He knocked, and someone inside said in a loud voice. "Door's open." Stepping inside, he removed his hat and stood at the door, facing a half dozen men at various tasks. After a moment, one put his pencil down, took his glasses off, and faced the German. "Well, are you just going to stand there? What do you want?"

He shuffled his feet and replied in an awkward stammer, "I was sent here from Saint Augustine. To work. On the railroad to Key West. I have experience."

The man put his glasses back on and eyed him up and down. "Experience do you?" he started. "Do you have experience with vermin and insects so thick you can't breathe? Alligators that can eat a man whole and poisonous reptiles? With malaria and dysentery, yellow fever, and typhoid? This ain't a job for the faint of heart, and no place for some kid who thinks he can swing a hammer." He stood up and looked the German over one more time. Broad shoulders and rough hands hinted he could at least possibly work.

"What's your name?"

"Adolph Wahl," he said. "I was a line foreman for the Central

Pacific."

"I don't care if you were the King of Prussia. On this railroad, you will work on the road gang. This is like no job you have ever known." He nodded toward the south. "Before you can build the railroad, you have to create dry land out of a swamp. It's too thick to drink, too shallow to swim in, and too wet to plow. We have over a thousand men working twenty-four hours a day, six days a week. We don't have many Germans, mostly colored from the Bahamas and the Cayman Islands, and useless riffraff from the north, most of which don't last a month. Dollar fifty a day, plus room and board." He pointed toward the door. "Walk down the tracks a hundred feet. Three sleeper cars will be heading toward the railhead forty miles to the south. The foreman will get you situated." With that, he put his glasses back on and went back to his journal. Adolph was a little stunned at the abrupt nature. He never learned the man's name. He guessed he wasn't important enough to need to know it.

12

Faro Blanco Resort, Marathon Florida

97

Twin One

Faro Blanco was a good compromise It's still the keys with brilliant blue skies, amazing sunsets, and sand between your toes, with a little less craziness and only a small chance of an accidental recognition. It will have to do for now.

Back from Key West after Fantasy Fest, we decided to keep the suite for at least another month. I spent my days either on the flats with a local guide trying to coax bonefish, tarpon, redfish, or permit to take the bait, or sitting with Karen at Sombrero Beach, watching the sunrise and soaking up rays while sipping mimosas. We often spent our evenings at the Lighthouse Grill. Drinks were cold, the air was warm and, more often than not, people-watching was, if nothing else, entertaining. This night was no different. Karen was off someplace, so I admired the tourist talent behind my shades from a neutral corner while sipping a Tito's and cranberry. It never failed to amaze me how relaxed and downright daring ladies would get after a few days of being off the chain, and outside of a decent volume of distilled spirits. My agenda wasn't conquest, but voyeurism, and I enjoyed the non-stop chicken dances that moved around the pool and the bar. Young ladies inviting young guys in rut to "look but don't touch," and borderline senior citizen cougar wannabes eyeing those same young men with the intent of offering "touch but don't look."

You could sell tickets to this show.

In the middle of this Friday night summer meat market sat a visual anomaly. Looking more in place sitting in a bookstore in Seattle, I sat back and casually evaluated her. Late twenties, early thirties, long print sleeveless dress that went to her ankles with a white sweater over it, overdressed to heat stroke level in this ninety-degree, hundred percent keys humidity. Birkenstocks on her feet, and, of course, white ankle socks. Short cropped blonde hair that would have looked cute in a pixie cut but just made her look all the more frumpy. Black horn-rimmed glasses perched halfway down her nose. Her tits were smaller than my man-boobs, but from what I could tell through the clothing layers, she was either wearing a long-line Maiden form bra, or she was expecting a flack attack from an anti-aircraft artillery battery at any moment.

I bet she hoards cats.

And, *she was looking at me*, or at least furtively in my direction. Sipping on an iced tea, this nervous Nelly kept throwing sidelong glances at me, and I felt she was trying to get up the nerve to approach me. Slightly amused and more than a little curious now, I flashed her my best come hither smile just to see what kind of reaction it would generate. She suddenly appeared to make up her mind, carefully placed a napkin over her iced tea, undoubtedly to ward off the chance some studley with poor vision and a death wish would slip a roofie in it, and walked up to my barstool, standing rigidly at attention. I got a little amused by just ignoring her. After thirty seconds it was apparent, she wasn't going to make the first move. I just wasn't rude enough to make her stand and squirm, so I spun around in my seat, and lifted my drink, "A beautiful good evening to you," I said. She looked terrified but determined to get through the moment, and she opened her mouth to speak. Out of any thousand pickup lines, charity solicitations, paternity accusations, and lame "sure is hot outside today." Her first words nearly knocked me off my chair.

"You're Bric Wahl."

I froze for a moment, and then carefully considered my options. One. Stand up, run like hell, catch a cab to Miami, and fly to China, or Two, Reach out and snap her homely little neck. With us being surrounded by two dozen tourists in broad twilight, that option would probably cause a little too much consternation amongst the patrons. Or three, find out how she knew, and what she knew. Three seemed like the best option for the moment; I could always revert to one or two should the answers be the wrong ones. That being said, she didn't look much like a Greek assassin or a Russian nuclear weapons dealer, so, yes, it was going to be option three.

"You asking me or telling me?" was the best snappy answer I could muster.

"You are him, aren't you?" Couldn't tell if that was "him" or "Him" from her tone of voice.

I responded. "That depends on who is asking, why she is asking, and how she knew to ask."

She chewed on her answer for a few seconds. I could tell she knew how to answer, but knew what she said in the first sentence was going to determine how long I would be in sight. She hesitated for a few more seconds.

"Let me start this," I said, leaning right into her face. "Who the fuck are you?" I thought she might faint right there after I used the 'f' word, but the answer was almost as surprising as the first thing she said before. Almost in a whisper, she said, "My name is Mary Elizabeth Sawyer."

Sawyer? My, my. A Conch and likely an in-law. That's the last thing I expected. Well, at least, we're getting somewhere. "And, Mary Elizabeth Sawyer, what made you think I'm who you think I am, and," to paraphrase Bogie in Casablanca, "of all the gin joints, in all the towns, in all the world, why did you walk into this one?"

Her answer was so low I had to lean over to hear her answer. "Because," she said, "A friend of a friend of a friend told me you might be here. I sat in the bar for a while, and you looked, well, different, so I figured it had to be you." She was so relieved to get that sentence out that she plopped down on the stool next to me in relief and wiped her brow with a napkin. I motioned to Cheddar the bartender to fetch Mary's tea. She nodded gratefully, took a long drink, and held the glass to her forehead. She was pouring sweat, half from nerves and half from being dressed for an Everest assault.

"Girl, you got way too many clothes on for this neck of the woods. Other than your name, I would venture to guess you ain't from around these parts." She took another sip and nodded again. "I was born twenty miles from here. My dad died when I was four and we moved to San Francisco. Mother died last year, and I just got back a few weeks ago for my great-grandfather's funeral."

Ah. I recalled. Johnny Sawyer, Wendy's great uncle, died at the ripe old age of ninety-seven in Islamorada recently. I saw it in the papers. "So, if I am who you say I am, then you are my late wife's great niece. That would make me Uncle Bric if that's who I am." I got weary of the ifs and came out. "And, yes, I am Bric, but I don't use that name anymore, and you won't either if you want to live. I knew your mom too, and I sort of remember you as a little

100

girl. That was the most miserable woman to walk the face of the earth, and I dare say she did a good job of wrecking you too. Do you know why your dad died? Because he *wanted* to. Now you need to tell me who that friend of a friend of a friend is so I can put him on the wrong side of the lawn."

That was almost too much for her, and she started to hyperventilate. I started to motion to Cheddar the bartender to get me a paper bag for her to breathe into, and then realized how inappropriate it might be. After all, I'm pretty sure it wouldn't be the first time a guy wanted to put a paper bag over her head. I softened my voice. "Look," I said, with a smile. "I'm just kidding. I'm not gonna hurt anyone, it's just that nobody in the world is supposed to even know I'm alive, even family. It's not safe to know me." With that, she relaxed a little and even cracked a tiny smile. That smile changed her and even reminded me a little of Wendy. If she could loosen up a little and get that cob out of her ass, she might even look halfway decent, but I doubt even then I could drink her up much past a "two." I spoke.

"Ok, you found me. To what occasion honors me with your presence?"

She sat her purse, slightly smaller than an army duffel bag, on the bar top and started rummaging around in it. "I have something to show you," she said. She dug out an extra sweater, a pair of winter gloves, a stocking cap, and wool socks and sat them on the counter, then continued rummaging around in the bag for another minute. "I inherited only one thing from great-grandfather," she said and finally pulled out a small cloth bag. She dug something wrapped in an old newspaper out of the bag, and then held it in her hands for a moment, cherishing it. Looking up at me she explained. "It's wrapped in a copy of the Fort Lauderdale Daily News from September 1935." And she handed it to me. I unfolded the paper, and a gold pocket watch and a large gold coin dropped out on the counter. I picked up the watch and gave it a quick going over. It was a gold Burlington Railroad Watch, well-worn with a scratched crystal. The face was stained like it had been in the water. Nothing spectacular, just an old watch, other than it was apparently made of gold or, at least, gold plate. I picked up the coin and turned it over.

A well-worn gold Double Eagle. You could hardly read the date, but I made out 1861 after holding it up to the light.

"Read the article," she said.

I put the watch down and unfolded the paper. Glancing at the headlines, I nodded. I knew this story well. It was two pages, the front page and a smaller clipping from somewhere else in the paper. The front page described the Labor Day hurricane of 1935, one of the strongest storms ever recorded. A small storm, it hit the middle keys with as much as a 20-foot storm surge and killed over seven hundred people, while the citizens in Key West hardly knew there was a storm. Many of the dead were former World War One veterans who had been brought down to the keys to work on the overseas highway as part of the Depression WPP program. A train had been dispatched from Miami to rescue the workers and evacuate the citizens, but it was delayed in leaving and ended up caught in the storm. Everything but the locomotive, along with a sizeable stretch of railroad track was washed away. It signaled the end of Flagler's Florida Keys Railroad, a venture that operated for two dozen years and never made a profit.

The second page of newsprint showed dozens of bodies being burned in a huge bonfire. Many of the dead had their clothes literally stripped of their bodies from the wind and water, and hundreds were never identified. Mary pointed to a boy in the picture. That's my great grandfather" she said, "and he took that watch from one of the bodies."

"A touching story, but what does it have to do with me and the price of tea in China?" I asked.

Mary dug back into her purse and pulled out a small book, water-stained with the cover missing. "It's great great grandma Sawyer's diary. My mother had it," she said and opened it to a bookmarked page. "I'll read it to you. Dated September 10, 1935.

Today, Johnny and Thomas helped with the burning of many more storm victims, a terrible task for a ten-year-old boy. The bodies were so bloated and unrecognizable. The stench was horrible. Some were from the Russell family, some Army veterans, and four other men. I know one of them was Al. Johnny will never know who his father was now, and I will take Al's secret to my grave.

Johnny found a watch and a gold coin on the body and gave them to me for safekeeping. I shall cherish them forever."

"Ok. Thanks. That's Brodie and Grace's family, and I appreciate the research. Over a hundred Russells were living in Islamorada before the hurricane, and less than a dozen survived the storm. It still doesn't explain why you broke my cover." I sighed. "Look, I've had enough cloak-and-dagger stuff over the last few years to last a lifetime. If you have some reason for this to be of interest to me, let's lay all the cards face up. Now."

She smiled again and reached for the watch. "Let me open the back cover of the watch. I want you to read something." She pried open the case and handed it to me. "Mary, my reading glasses are sitting on my dresser in the room." I pushed it back. "Please"

She pushed the glasses back off her nose and held the case in the light of a candle on the bar, reading slowly.

"Presented to Herman Adolphus Wahl for 25 years of loyal service. The Union Pacific Railroad Company. January 25, 1889."

I almost fell off the barstool. My great, great grandfather's name, who was born in Minnesota over a hundred and fifty years ago, was inscribed on a watch taken off a drowned railroad worker in Islamorada in 1935. A body that was possibly my wife's great-great-grandfather.

Holy shit I married my cousin.

I sat for a few minutes took it all in, and then turned to Mary. "I vaguely remember that my great grandfather Wahl vanished around the turn of the century, supposedly on the run from the law for killing someone in Wyoming." I searched my memory a little more. "That's really about all I know other than he worked on a railroad like his father did." Mary looked disappointed. "I was hoping you knew more," she said. "And I'm also hoping you can help me with something else."

Ah, here comes the hook. Beware of Conchs bearing gifts, even homely ones.

"Not sure where your sources are Mary, but any rumors of my wealth are rather unfounded. I found a couple of gold bars and used that money to put my kid through college, buy a sailboat which is currently a washed-up wreck on an island in the Caribbean, and take a little vacation from my life. I'll likely have to go back to work pretty soon. (That was a bit of a fib, but I thought it best to see how good her source was, and for that matter, figure out WHO it was).

She looked like a lost puppy. "Oh, sir, I don't want your money," she said. "My late stepfather left my mother with some money and it was put in a trust fund for my sister and me." (Jeez, another guy that figured the only way out from misery was the grave)

"I've decided to move back to the keys. I want to trace my family heritage, starting with this watch, and I want to go to work down here. I need help meeting the right people."

I can't stand a trembling lip, so I softened up a little. "OK Mary, I don't think I can personally help you too much as officially I'm pushing up daisies, but I'll see what I can do to help."

"Where will I find you?" She asked.

"You just did. I'm around here almost every night. Now skedaddle along so I can finish my adult beverage in peace." She gathered up her bag and loose items and stuck out a limp hand for me to shake. "I'm sure you think I am some sort of miserable shut-in. I want you to know I have a Masters in Journalism from UC Berkley with a minor in creative writing." And with that, she bolted across the pool deck and out of sight up the beach.

As so often happens, I turned back to my drink, and Karen was sitting in the chair next to me. I nearly jumped out of my skin. "How do you do that?" I asked. "Farming a little below your age ceiling, aren't you?" she quipped. "Who, or should I ask, What the hell was THAT? You usually go for something a little closer to the deep end of the gene pool."

I was a little amused that Karen thought I was making time with Mary. Smart-assed answers flew through my head until I remembered just how uncomfortable that chaise lounge was on the hotel patio.

"That," I answered, "might be your next project."

Flashback
December 1905 south of Homestead Florida

Six months later, Adolph found himself shoveling coal into the boiler of a huge steam dredge. The smothering humidity was doubled by the open door of the boiler. If there was any small solace to working this fiery Hell, it was that the coal smoke seemed to keep the marauding mosquitos at bay. There were dredges on both sides of the roadbed, scooping up muck and piling it between them. Alligators managed to keep out of the way, but water snakes, including poisonous water moccasins, were frequently scooped up and dumped onto the pile, where they angrily slithered off the side, and often up onto the dredge.

Adolph stopped counting at a dozen snakes, both poisonous and nonpoisonous that had been chopped in two and either thrown off the side or shoveled into the furnace, along with the next scoop of coal. After the raised ground was allowed to dry some, loads of gravel, hauled to Miami from the Northeast by ship, then trundled by rail to the railhead were added to the roadbed and smoothed by hand. It wasn't until after all of these steps were taken could a single rail could be laid. They inched along a few feet at a time working on what would later be called the Seventeen Mile Stretch toward the first of over thirty bridges between Homestead and Key West. At Jewfish Creek, crews, using barges that had been towed up the creek, were already working on the bridge, driving huge oak pilings into the muck, sometimes as much as forty feet trying to find solid ground.

Later on, when the railroad was closer to open ocean, most of the crew would be housed in huge floating barracks, but this segment, far from navigable waters, meant the crews were shuttled back and forth to dry land near Homestead or housed in huge multi-story bunkhouse railcars. Experienced or not, Adolph only rarely got to use his railway skills. It wasn't until early in 1906 before the rails crossed Jewfish Creek, and approached Key Largo, only to be surprised when they encountered a previously unknown lake right in their path. They named it Lake Surprise, and again brought the dredges forward, digging up the gritty marl from the ocean bottom miles away, and dumping it into the mile-long right of way. The marl dried into a hard substance nearly as resilient as concrete, and by late 1906 the crew was rewarded with the relative luxury of hacking their way through miles of mosquito-infested mangrove forest as they graded and laid the track down the spine of Key Largo to Rock Harbor. Now into the keys proper, Henry Flagler's company brought all resources forward, expecting to finish the railroad to Key West in less than three years.

Mother Nature had different plans.

Statistically, the Florida Keys are the most hurricane-prone places in the western hemisphere, if not the world. Tropical storms come in cycles. Decades can come and go without a single storm, and then it seems like they come one after another. A case in point was the storm-free period between Hurricane Donna in 1960 and Hurricane Georges in 1998. Even Andrew in 1992, which devastated Miami, hardly touched the keys, but after Georges, the gates opened. Mitch followed Georges, then Irene in 1998, then Debbie and Grace, and finally Wilma in 2005 that put much of the lower keys under water. This cycle is caused by several factors, including the cyclic El Nino and La Nina conditions in the Pacific, where water temperature affects currents, the wind, moisture, and the jet stream. After a fairly quiet period in the keys after the turn of the century, the pattern shifted back to more tropical activity. The result had a devastating effect on Mister Flagler's goal.

By October 1906, Adolph was finally able to become again at true railroad worker, supervising a crew of thirty, mostly black Bahamians, Hattians, and crews from the Cayman Islands, smoothing gravel roadbeds, laying huge oak ties, and placing rails. His pay had increased to two dollars, twenty-five cents a day for a twelve-hour, six-day week. Working year-round through hurricane season, the relentless mosquitoes made a difficult job almost intolerable. Adolph and all the workers were relegated to working in ninety-five-plus degree weather covered from head to foot wearing hats draped in copper screens, long-sleeved shirts, gloves covered in oil, carrying palm leaf switches to drive the insects away, all while shoveling earth, dragging wooden ties and mainline rails that ran up to a hundred pounds a yard.

Weather forecasting in the early nineteen hundreds was haphazard at best. With little or no communication coming from the Caribbean Islands, storm warnings were rare or nonexistent. Even though barometers had existed for centuries, there were few of those among the railroad crews. At best, supervisors kept a tube of water with a few wisps of weed lying on the bottom. Theoretically, if the weed floated to the top, the air pressure was falling, and a storm may be imminent.   For the locals, there were many other clues that generations of island life, first in the Bahamas and later in the keys had trained them to know a storm may be in the area. First, before a storm, the dome of high pressure that rides above the cyclone, results in sweltering humidity, light winds, if any, and a sky so blue it would blend with the sea. Birds would suddenly become absent as low pressure made flying difficult, and sunrises would greet the day with incredible colors. As winds began to pick up and high cirrus clouds announced the approaching storm, wind direction could determine the storm track.

On October 15, 1906, supervisors noted those wisps of weed were indeed floating at the top of the tube, and they ordered all loose items secured. By now there were crews strung up and down the keys, from Key Largo to Long Key, working on bridges and clearing the roadbed. Crews were housed in huge barracks built on barges, along with mobile kitchens.

A storm that was first documented hitting the Windward Islands a week earlier crossed Cuba, hammering Havana, turning due north toward the middle keys.

Adolph Wahl was housed in one of those floating barracks, along with one hundred fifty other men, anchored haphazardly in Hawk's Channel, just offshore from Long Key, near present-day mile marker sixty-seven, close to the northern terminus of the Long Key Viaduct. Adolph woke at six a.m. on the morning of October 17 to the sound of screaming winds, the big houseboat rocking in the waves, and already taking on water.   An hour later, the houseboat gave a sudden turn sideways, broke its moorings, and started drifting southwest, away from any land and out into the Gulf.

The lumbering houseboat was designed to be towed slowly in calm seas, and couldn't cope with wind and waves, and it slowly began to fall apart in the storm. Only a handful of workers could swim, and all were doomed to drown in the maelstrom. Grabbing a floating piece of wood, Adolph jumped into the churning seas and kicked away from the disintegrating barge. Waves constantly pounded him, and it took all of this strength to hang on.

As the storm subsided, rescue ships were summoned to the area to search for survivors. Among them, an Austro-Hungarian steamer, the *Jenny*, found Adolph, barely conscious from the pounding, and brought him aboard. Most of the crew spoke German and gave Adolph comfort, warm clothes, and a hot meal. The following day, Adolph along with forty-nine other survivors were returned to the remains of the camp at the North end of Long Key, where he joined the survivors to access the damage. Over a hundred twenty-five workers had perished, and months of construction on the overseas railway and more than sixteen miles of track was wiped out in a single day.

While many survivors fled the keys back to the North, Adolph chose to stay, and his dedication earned him a foreman's position. It took over a year to get the project back to where it was before the storm, only to be hammered again in 1908 by another storm. By this time, all the crews were housed in more substantial quarters on dry land, and while the hurricanes caused localized damage, it was far less devastating than the 1906 event.

By late 1908, Adolph saw the fifteen thousand foot Long Key Viaduct finished and the Florida East Coast Railway was complete all the way through Key Vaca, now called Marathon. Scheduled rail service began between Miami and Knights Key, the northern terminus of the Seven Mile bridge, but events in Washington DC may have spelled the end of the dream for Henry Flagler right there.

Wayne Gales

13
Twin Two
I know what I'm dreaming, but what the
Hell am I thinking?

Three days later I was back on my favorite stool at the Lighthouse, and I noticed a familiar face across the bar. The face may have been familiar, but nothing else was. The mousy Mary Elizabeth Sawyer had undergone an amazing transformation.

Looking more in place walking down Deco Drive than sitting at a bar in Marathon, I casually evaluated her. Amazingly short white terry shorts almost not covering a pair of shapely and nicely tanned legs, wedge heels that meant she definitely didn't come by way of the beach, a teal-blue Island Jay "Girls Just Want to Have Sun" tank top, cut around the bottom to expose a lot of midriff, somewhat concealed by a long sleeve, oversized white cotton blouse, unbuttoned, and tied at the waist, flaunting an unencumbered storebought, d-cup rack that must have been bound by duct tape the first time we met. Short cropped blonde hair in that pixie cut and oversized Gucci sunglasses that probably cost more than my last car.

In five minutes she had successfully derailed the agenda of every other female in sight, young or old, and jeopardized countless pairs of male eyes which were approaching permanent damage from not blinking.

And she knew it.

What the Hell happened to Mary Elizabeth?

I picked up my drink, walked over and slid into the seat next to her. "You" I announced, "look like what started the riot. Was the other day just an act, or did the caterpillar become a butterfly?"

She didn't look amused. "Do I know you?" she asked.

Now I'm confused. "We met three days ago. You don't remember me?" She put her finger to the bottom of her chin in mock deep concentration.

"Well, let's see, I don't work as a candy striper in the old folks home, so no, I don't think we've met."

"Ok, I get it, Mary Elizabeth Sawyer fell down, hit her head on a rock, got amnesia, and came back to life as the hottest trick in

Marathon."

Her face bloomed in a bright smile that probably cost more than the sunglasses. "Now I get it," she said, "You met Mary." She stood up and extended a hand. "Whoever you are, my name is Alexis Sawyer. Mary Elizabeth is my twin sister. Call me Lex." I shook her hand and then hesitated. Do I out myself one more time, even to family? And do I want this vision to know she's family? Bric! Stop thinking with the little head. "Russell," I replied, taking her hand. I thought I would let it go at half a truth for a moment.

She looked me up and down for a moment swirled her perfectly manicured finger in her Long Island Iced Tea and licked it in a way that just about resulted in premature ejaculation, and spoke again. "I can't wait to hear what my sister had in common with you that caused you to meet."

She had me in check. I had to spill at least part of the story to her now. I sighed. "My name is Russell Bricklin Wahl, Bric for short. Your mother and my late wife were sisters." There, it was out.

Her eyes grew wide and she carefully re-appraised me. "So, you're Uncle Bric. Sis told me she hunted you down. Ok, I know the rest of the story. Gawd I hope your wife was nicer than my mother. She ran me off before I was sixteen and I never saw her again."

"Wendy was a good person and an amazing mother," I answered. "I was the bad fit in that relationship. Just couldn't figure out ways to stay home and make a living, or maybe just couldn't find a way to stay home. I don't know," and I looked away for a moment. We sat in awkward silence for a moment. Then she leaned forward, maybe to make her point, and maybe to give me a better shot of her ample boobilage.

"So I'm sure Mary shared the reason for looking you up," Lex ventured.

"Sort of," I replied. "Just hinted that she needed help to find a job." I sighed, "I'm not sure I can help her. I don't know if you know the story, but I sort of don't exist, and it would be dangerous to blow my cover, but I might be able to point her in the right direction. Then I thought of something. "That explains why she came here. What's your story?" She shrugged and twirled her finger in her drink again.

"I don't know. Bored I guess. She wanted to come to Florida, and I wasn't sure she could cross the street without me holding her hand, so I just came along for the adventure." She leaned over a little farther so I could almost see her navel. "And I was worn-out the last sugar daddy." She tipped the sunglasses down below her eyes and looked at me with an even stare. "Are you looking for something to cuddle up with? Rumor has it you might be able to afford a crib mate."

I spit half my drink over the table. That was about as subtle as a fart in church. I blushed and took a moment to wipe the table while I got my composure back. I spoke.

"Don't beat around the bush Lex, why don't you just come out and say what you mean," I ordered a replacement drink. "For one thing, I'm very happy in a relationship, (Who would be dragging me down the path by the balls about now if she was around) and you're also young enough to be my granddaughter. Almost. If you want to play that kind of game, I suggest you pack up and head back to the West Coast."

That took her down a notch. She tossed her head back with a chuckle.

"Just kidding, Unc. I don't really mean it. Like you said, family and all that, even though I've dated older than you." She smiled, and then looked at me like a hunk of meat, "but not many better looking." She motioned to Cheddar for a refill. "I've only seen this part of the keys, and it's about as exciting as watching a paint-drying contest. If I'm gonna stay, I think Key West will be more suitable for my style."

Whatever style that was, I thought to myself.

"Mary said you two had an inheritance. Key West isn't a cheap place to live, you know. Most people down there either have two roommates and three jobs, or three roommates and two jobs."

She chuckled again.

"Inheritance? It's a measly structured stipend. Hardly covers my shoe budget. I'll need to do better than that, and without roommates. I love my sis, but we are oil and water. She's the

115

water."

"How do you plan to do that?"

"It's not that hard," she said. (*Speak for yourself girl*) "I did very well in San Francisco as a dancer." She pressed her boobs together with both hands, so they nearly popped out of the tank top. "Just keep these tanned and," pointing to her head "keep this blonde, and I'll never starve to death." She leaned back triumphantly, tipped her sunglasses back down her nose again to let me look at those stunning blue eyes, and sipped her drink.

"Most of those girls dance on their feet but make their money on their backs," I said, recalling some of the action I saw when I was on Duval Street a few weeks ago.

"Never," she said. "I don't sell it, and I don't give it away. I put out for sport, or on occasion, a sports car." She sat her drink down and looked at me, seriously for once. "Uncle Bric, I like to flirt and I live my life like every day is the last, but I'm not a hooker, and I'm not a slut. I'm just a good old-fashioned American girl living the dream."

I kept silent for a minute and then made up my mind. "Listen, meet Karen and me down the street at the Sunset Grill around six tomorrow evening. Bring your sister. Between the two of us, we might be able to help her get started and give her some ideas on finding her roots. It looks like you already have a plan."

And with that, she unfolded herself from the chair like a boneless leopard and took a few steps away, then stopped and turned, almost in the exact same spot her twin did three days earlier. "I'm sure you think I'm a dumb blonde little tart." She flashed that smile again. "My friends know I'm not dumb," and she started to walk away again, then paused and looked over her shoulder. "And my *really* good friends also know I'm not blonde."

With that, she strolled across the pool deck and out of sight around the buildings. It was at that point I realized that every conversation at the Lighthouse Grill had stopped until she rounded the corner.

Maybe I'm a little bored, maybe a little intrigued, and maybe I'm just a little attracted to this vision of beauty. I said to myself "Dear Saint Jude, the Patron Saint of lost causes, why are you sitting

116

on my shoulder tonight. The last thing I need is a couple of lost sheep to herd."

But maybe…

The next night, without giving Karen too many details, I convinced her to join me, and we caught a cab to the Sunset Grill. Built a few years ago, the Sunset is one of Marathon's newest party places. It's on Knights Key and was built over the location of the dock that was used during the building of the Seven Mile Bridge back at the turn of the century. I remember years ago parking near this spot to watch the sunset when it was just a big vacant lot and found a big concrete pad with what looked like the foundation for a crane or derrick in the middle.

I envisioned railroad crews living here for months while they built one of the longest bridges in the world at the time. But now it's a party bar with a pool, live music, and a killer sunset view. We took a table away from the combo on the stage so we could talk, and ordered beverages. Karen was still a little distant and had been busying herself during the day perusing stores, beach walking, and hanging out at the pool.

A little before sunset the twins showed up, Mary in a paisley hippie maxi-skirt, floppy hat, and black tennis shoes and Lex in an off-the-shoulder bright orange micro mini-dress and three-inch beige wedge sandals. Karen looked at her, then looked at me, then looked back at her, folded her arms, and began a slow simmer. We exchanged introductions, which went over like a lead balloon. They sat down across from us, and if Lex caught the icicles, she didn't show it. I started the conversation, looking at Karen.

"The Sawyer sisters are my late wife's nieces" I started. "And believe it or not, they also might be mine." With that, Karen raised an incredulous eyebrow. "As family, they are asking me for a little help getting them acclimated and possibly employed. I would be grateful if you could help them get schooled to the keys way of life."

I handed Lex a piece of paper. "Here's a name I got from my friend Rumpy this morning." I noticed her eyes came up when I mentioned Rumpy's name. Strange. "Go by Teasers on Duval and ask for Joey. He's always looking for fresh talent." Karen rolled her eyes looked away for a moment, and then turned back.

"If I'm going to get involved with this, you two are going to have to meet in the middle a little," Karen started. "Mary, you need to go to charm school, change what you wear and grow some *cojones*. We've been sitting here for ten minutes, and you haven't said a word." Mary covered her mouth with her fist in horror. "And you," Karen nodded toward Lex, "need to take your chicken dance down a notch or nobody will ever take you seriously."

"What's wrong with my appearance?" Lex sniffed.

"Well, for one thing, while we have been sitting here, I have noticed you possess neither panties nor pubic hair. I think that's a bit more information a casual acquaintance should need to know."

Lex seemed to ponder this for a moment, then swiveled her chair more in my direction and slowly uncrossed and crossed her legs in such a way that I too was aware that Karen's observation was clearly accurate. She turned to Karen. "As you people in the South say, you catch more flies with honey than vinegar."

Karen tossed her beer down and got up. "That's all of this farce I'm willing to tolerate," she said, looking at me. "If you want to play grab-ass with that slut go right ahead. I'm going for a walk."

And she left, walking up US-1. Mary gathered up her bag and scuttled off behind her.

Well, that went rather well.

Lex pulled out a petite cigar, offered one to me, which I declined, ordered another drink, and lit the cigar, relaxing back in her chair with legs crossed, looking at me in the eyes with a half-smile. Awkward moment. I swirled the ice in my drink and pondered. Karen misunderstood the dynamic. I don't want to get in this little girl's knickers, I just want to do something interesting. I've been busy with work, family, and just life since I was a kid, living hand to mouth, paycheck to paycheck. I make a piss-poor domestic poodle, and all this money is starting to make me feel useless. I have no intention of slowing down, and I need a distraction, and helping this miss-matched pair of siblings get pointed in the right direction fits the bill.

I need me some Key West Normal.

Then again, she's got one helluva pair of wheels. Long silence.

"So" she started, "Uncle Bric, where do we go from here?"

"It's your plan," I answered. "Get your ass on the Rock and get moving. I'm just a mentor, for more reasons than one. Remember, I'm dead." I took a sip of my Titos and cran. "I do have a couple of questions. Your sister is afraid of her own shadow. You just seem to overpower her. I can't even see how you two are sisters."

Lex rolled her eyes a little. "Sis and I are total opposites except for one thing. We're smart. Get through her façade, and you will find one helluva shrewd business manager and a very good journalist. Just wind her up and get the fuck out of the way. You might be surprised."

I took it all in and decided to change the subject. "Do you know about your side of the family and the watch?" I asked.

"Oh yes," she answered. "That's what got us looking for you. We thought with family connections on both sides, you might be able to help her solve the mystery. It's more important to her, but I think it will be fun to find out the truth, and who better to get help from, you being a kissing cousin and all."

"Let's get this clear, Lex" I interrupted. "We're not 'kissing', and for that matter, I'm even not one hundred percent convinced were cousins. Something just doesn't play right, but that's another story." I leaned toward her to make a point. "And while we're on the subject, Karen has a valid observation. Heaven knows I'm a sucker for a pretty girl, and you are surely that, but from a personal aspect, this ain't Madison Avenue, and as many doors may be slammed in your face as your appearance may open. You are who you are, but you might take it down a notch. On the stage, you can be as slutty as you want for tips, but on Duval Street, you will need to be a bit more discrete, or everyone in this town will shun you. I've known more than one stripper in town and even a few ladies of the evening, and when they are off the clock, they usually put a lot of effort into blending in. A little Key West Camouflage might do you good when you're not working."

Lex quietly puffed on her cigar for a moment, stubbed it out in her drink, and seemed to come to a conclusion. "Ok, Unc. I got it. I'll tone down a little and you keep Karen off my ass. Deal?"

"Well, I'm not in charge of Karen, and you will have to deal with that as it comes, but if you become a little less intimidating, she might meet you half way. In the meantime, you're gonna need to head to Key West sooner than later. I'm ready for a little change of pace here too. What say I hitch a ride with you and your sister down to the rock tomorrow?"

"Mary has her own car, and besides, mine only seats two. I'll pick you up at eight in the lobby," she answered.

I agreed and left the Sunset Grill for Faro. Karen was not in the room. No note, but it looked like she had packed a few things and left. Not forever, but probably for a few days. That's Karen. She will be back.

Flashback –
1909, near present-day Marathon

Since his days as a principal of Standard Oil Company, Henry Flagler had staged a running gun battle with Teddy Roosevelt. Roosevelt, whom Flagler once supported in his bid for Governor of New York, had put tremendous effort toward breaking up the huge "Robber Baron" companies like Standard Oil, run by Flagler and John D Rockefeller.

As Flagler began to prepare for the complete terminus in Key West, he ordered Key West harbor to be dredged deep enough to accommodate ships that would haul cargo from the rail head through the new Panama Canal to the West Coast. Suddenly, the US Navy ordered the dredging stopped for no reason. Undaunted, Flagler announced the railway would end at Night's Key, and he ordered the area in front of the key be dredged in preparation for building piers. It was disastrous news for Key West and exciting times for residents of the middle Keys. With no railroad, and the prospect of Key Vaca becoming the biggest city in South Florida, Key West would be relegated to a backwater fishing village of little consequence.

After some weeks, the Navy relented, opening the doors for the railroad to be completed across the ocean all the way to Key West. The island celebrated, and Flagler's company embarked on the most challenging part of the railroad, the bridge spanning over seven miles of ocean between Knights Key and Little Duck Key, with only one tiny dot of land between, Pigeon Key. As they prepared to start, Adolph and the other foremen were gathered so they could help envision the task before them.

"This viaduct will require no less than two hundred eighty-six thousand barrels of cement, much of it imported from Germany, Adolph." He nodded toward the burly foreman, who smiled in acknowledgment. "It's a special kind of concrete that hardens even underwater." He went on, "We're also importing a hundred seventy-seven thousand cubic yards of crushed rock that will stand on over six hundred thousand feet of pilings, each pounded into the mud until they find hard bottom. It will take over two and a half million board feet of timber just to build the forms."

Adolph also knew this meant he wasn't a railroad worker again for the next several months. With such a huge turnover ratio, Adolph, who had now been on the project for nearly five years, was recognized as one of the hardest working, capable, and loyal employees. His pay had been raised to a lofty sum of eighty dollars a month, approaching that of some of the management who were paid one hundred twenty-five dollars a month. The construction engineers put him in charge of a crew as they followed the pile drivers with wooden forms, pouring waterproof concrete around the bottom to seal the structure, more concrete to create the sides of the hollow arch, gravel to fill, and a third pour to finish the arch. Each arch took over five days from start to finish, and nearly two weeks to harden. This step was repeated one hundred eighty times to create the bridge. Adolph overheard one of the crew announce, "This project is a true marathon." The name stuck and the village of Key Vaca was renamed Marathon shortly after completion.

Despite another hurricane in 1909, with winds over 125 miles per hour and costing nearly two hundred thousand dollars in damages, the Seven Mile Bridge was completed by the end of that year. The odds of a repeat storm the following year were small, but another strong hurricane did hit the lower keys in October 1910, this time wiping out the roadbed from Bahia Honda through Spanish Harbor, Big Pine, and Ramrod Key, adding, at least, another year to the planned completion date. Not that building every mile of the railroad wasn't a superhuman task, there remained one last major obstacle before the railroad to Key West could be completed. The bridge across Bahia Honda. Unlike all the other bridges, which had to be built over fairly shallow inlets in calm seas and light currents, Bahia Honda was a deep water channel, over thirty-five feet deep in many places, and swift. The concrete arches that comprised most of the railroad bridges would only work at the ends of the bridge, the middle span would much more resemble a traditional railroad bridge, with girders and arches. Adolph thought the result was one of the most beautiful and picturesque structures in the entire hundred forty miles, something that could only be seen by boat, or by the Bahia Honda auto bridge that wasn't built until over seventy years later.

Completion of the Bahia Honda bridge didn't mean the railroad was finished; there were still thirty miles of swamp, mangroves, and muddy waterways to get to Key West, but by January of 1912 Adolph witnessed the ceremonial last spike driven at Knights Key. Ten days later, as a loyal worker, he was invited to join the entourage in Key West to watch Henry Flagler, blind and feeble, climb out of the first official arrival by train into that city. Adolph pulled out his gold watch and noted the time, ten thirty-four a.m. Flagler had spent thirty million dollars (1912 dollars at that) to build what was called at the time "Flagler's Folly." Unlike most of the twenty-five hundred or more men who labored on the overseas railway, Adolph saw his employer on that day, even though he was over a hundred feet away.

After the celebration, Adolph wandered into downtown Key West and found a bar on Caroline Street, where he ordered a beer. He assumed he was out of work now, and contemplated his future. A man in a dark suit, bowler hat, white shirt, and tie sat down next to him. Adolph immediately stood up. It was Johnathan Jacob Weeks, the man who hired him back in Miami those seven long years ago.

"Sit down, Mister Wahl, and let me buy you that beer," he motioned with his hand. Slowly Adolph sat back down and nodded thanks. Weeks ordered a beer and one for himself. He stood and addressed the patrons. "A toast to Mister Henry Flagler and to the future of this fine town, and a toast to my best worker, Adolph Wahl." He lifted his glass and the men in the bar cheered. He sat back down to Adolph.

"Well, was it as tough as I described it to you back those seven years ago?" Weeks asked.

"Honestly, sir, if you hadn't sugar-coated it like you did that day, I would have probably run away north and would still be running today." They both laughed.

"What are your plans, Wahl? Back home to your family? Do you have family in America?" he asked.

Adolph chose his words carefully. "No, no family. I have no plans." He paused for a moment and took another pull from his mug.

"You might think me crazy, but I like it here. I might seek employment someplace in the keys."

Weeks looked at him for a moment and then spoke. "I may have just such a job, Wahl. Because the railroad is built, it doesn't mean there isn't any work. I will have a minimum of five full-time section gangs between Miami and Key West, working the line, doing repairs and upkeep. I will pay you eighty-five dollars a month, and provide room and board, either in Key West, Summerland, Pigeon Key, Islamorada, or in Homestead if you will be foreman for one of those crews." He reached into his pocket and tossed Adolph a large coin, which he caught in the air. "There's a double eagle for your hard work. I'll give you a second one if you sign on."

Adolph pocketed the twenty-dollar gold piece and stuck out his hand. "I'll take that job. I'm thirty-two years old and I don't want to work this hard for the rest of my life, but I'll give you a few years before moving on. Pigeon Key will be just fine."

Weeks shook hands and gave Adolph the second gold coin. "I'll send a message to the Station Agent at Pigeon Key and let him know to make a bunk available for you. Take a week off, spend those double eagles, and enjoy Key West." Weeks consulted his pocket watch and stood. "The train to Miami leaves in fifteen minutes with the old man. I'll be accompanying him to his home in Palm Beach to go over some plans with the company. We need to start filling these boxcars so Mister Flagler can recoup his investment."

14
A Girl Named Lex
in a Car Named Porsche

The next morning I wrote a note to Karen and left it on the dresser.

Off to the rock for a week or two. I'm sorry for the dust-up. It's not what you think. I'll be at the La Concha, yes, by myself. If you want to come down, I'd love to take you on a sunset sail. Love, Bric.

I went to the reception desk and advised I was leaving for a few days but to keep our room. Karen had a key and besides I just wanted to bring a few things with me. I waited out front, and a few minutes later a classic, white, 1985 Porsche 911 Carrera Targa convertible pulled up with a screech. "Told you it was a two-seater," she said. "Let's roll!"

She popped the hood latch, and I dropped my overnight bag in the bonnet. Strange there wasn't as much as a makeup bag in there. I would have expected a forty-foot semi in tow with enough luggage to dress a Fifth Avenue fashion show. "Traveling light?" I ventured. "Mary has my luggage in her practical white P.O.S. Chevy Impala. Besides, if I'm going to take your advice, I don't have much to bring. Shopping time!" she said with apparent glee, and with that she dropped the Targa into first and dumped the clutch.

With a chirp of rubber, we bounced out of the hotel onto the Overseas Highway. I figured she would hit ninety by the time we crossed the Seven Mile Bridge and be in the Monroe County Jail before we got to Bahia Honda, with me explaining who I was and how I got here, but she settled down to a moderate fifty-five and we flew under the radar. Seven Mile Bridge, Bahia Honda, Spanish Harbor, and down to forty-five to cruise through the Key Deer zone on Big Pine. Back up to speed through Summerland. I was sorely tempted to ask for a detour to the swimming hole except I didn't know if the Porsche could navigate the potholes, and was more concerned that Lex didn't have a swimsuit and would love the opportunity not to wear one. Temptation enough, despite the somewhat toned-down choice of wardrobe, skin-tight day-glow orange capri pants, wedge sandals, and a long-sleeved white blouse,

129

unbuttoned and tied at the waist with a sheer electric blue tube top underneath.

For Lex, that was a nun's habit.

With the top down, it was too noisy to make small talk, and that was a blessing because I'm not much for idle chatter. I wanted a little time to think anyway. Was I running *to* something or running *from* something? Relative or not, was some little voice inside of me thinking of Lex as a potential sportfuck? No, I needed to get that thought out of my brain. My love for Karen was real, but she needed to understand that I can never be someone's lap dog.

I just need a little change of scenery.

My story and I'm sticking to it.

Twenty minutes later we were on Big Coppit Key, and I motioned to Lex to turn down Emerald Drive. "I want you to drop me off at a friend's place," I said. "I'll catch up with you later. Where will I find you?" I asked.

"I'm not sure yet," she answered over the wind and motor noise. "Where can we meet?"

I thought for a second. "Meet me at Schooner Wharf on Saturday, say about two," I answered and started to motion for her to pull over at Rumpy's house, but she had already started to slow down. "You know where I'm going?" I asked.

"How do you think we found you?" she said with a smile.

I'll be damned.

I retrieved my bag, making sure Rumpy's Forerunner was in the driveway, and waived to Lex. I didn't bother with the front door but just walked around back to the patio. Ah, the Wavewhacker was gone, which meant so was Rumpy. The back sliding door is never locked, so I went inside and fetched a bottle of Absolut vodka from the counter and a can of grapefruit juice from the fridge. Filling a glass with ice, I went back out to the patio, made a beverage, and waited.

Rumpy had some explaining to do.

I was dozing in the shade an hour later when I heard the soft rumble of the *Wavewhacker* idling up the canal. Rumpy was at the wheel, and two mature, well-nourished, milfy-ish redheads were lounging on the bow. Obviously, a secluded island, clothing optional beach day as there wasn't a fishing rod in sight, and no swimsuit under the loose tank top on redhead number one. I stepped off the porch and looped the line over a cleat, drawing him into the seawall. The women looked neither interested in nor sober enough to assist. With the boat secured, I helped the girls off the boat, catching a downblouse peek at a no-tan-line chest while Rumpy handed their beach bags up to them. One of them smiled at me over her sunglasses, dug in her bag for keys, and they both wobbled off around the side of the house.

"You gonna let them drive like that?" I asked.

"Why not?" He answered. "They were hammered when they got here this morning. Amy probably doesn't know how to drive sober. Anyway if they get pulled over, I'm sure they will be able to work out some sort of mutually beneficial arrangement with Monroe County's finest."

"Good point," I agreed.

Rumpy shut the *Whacker'* down, and we walked back to the shade of the porch for another afternoon boat drink. We clicked cups and drank in silence for a moment. He lit a cigarette and spoke. "What brings you down to the rock my friend? Last I heard you were holed up at the Faro Blanco."

I hesitated a moment for dramatic effect. "What brought me here? How about a blonde in a white Targa. Rumor has it, she's someone you have made an acquaintance with." And I pulled my glasses down and looked into his eyes. Rumpy looked away and swallowed hard.

"Ah, yes, we've met. Nice car, and for that matter, nice legs too."

"Rumpy, you know, telling the world how to find me will get at least me killed, likely Karen, and probably you too, which would be fitting at this point." I frowned.

"I didn't tell the world, just that cute little blonde," he answered. "Her story was compelling, her smile inviting and her body irresistible." He held his thumb and index finger about two inches apart. "Honest, I only was gonna put it in that far, or at worst, just borrow her throat for a minute, but alas, it was all flirt and no payoff. Once I told her where her long-lost uncle might be, she climbed off my lap, kissed me on the forehead, and drove off into the sunset."

"Not like you to let a short skirt betray your best friend," I growled.

"Bric, she was family, and the story sounded legit. She's your late wife's niece. And honestly, I was just joking about trying to get in her pants. Well, sort of." He took a sip of his drink. "It seemed innocent at the time." He bowed his head. "Sorry, pal."

I softened up. "As it turns out Rump, no harm, no foul. Yes, they are family, and no, they won't rat to the commies. No worries. All forgiven." I stood up. "Tell you what, give me a ride into town and I'll buy you dinner at Conch Republic Seafood." I smiled, "on the way, I'll tell you about her twin sister."

"She's got a twin?" Rumpy asked, looking up hopefully. "Oh yeah," I answered, trying not to smile. "Hot little number you know. Name's Mary. She makes Lex look like the Church Lady. I'll see if I can set you up on a blind date."

I slapped him on the back, and we walked out to his car.

Flashback - January 1912, Key West

Adolph watched his boss leave and turned back to his beer. A week without work almost felt like a guilty pleasure to him, but with forty extra dollars in his pocket and nearly two hundred more saved up, a few days of indulgence wouldn't hurt. His first stop was the First National Bank, an impressive multi-colored brick building at the corner of Duval and Front Street, where he opened a savings account and deposited most of his cash. He hesitated at the teller window and decided to keep one of the Double Eagles as a souvenir good-luck piece. Working the line from Pigeon Key to Key West meant frequent visits to this town and access to his savings. Stop number two was a stroll down Caroline Street to visit one of Key West's dozen brothels. Although worldly pleasures were available up the keys via the party boats that lurked around the railroad towns. (Flagler forbid alcohol and women in the camps) Adolph avoided these dens when he saw other workers struck with syphilis and the clap.

Pigeon Key had become the base of operations for the Middle Keys railroad effort since the moment the tracks were completed from Knights Key. While the larger area at Knights provided for staging supplies and housing for the working crews. A quote from the 1912 Indianapolis *Star described the little city;*

"The railroad construction camps are in the charge of a resident engineer, with the one at Pigeon Key presently the most active. At high tide, Pigeon Key is about two acres in extent and perhaps three acres at low tide. There are four bunkhouses, each designed to hold 64 men; one of them for the foremen, who are housed apart from the laborers. Each has a reading room with good lights. Good mattresses are provided on standard double-decked bunks, with plenty of clean bedclothes; all laundry work being done by the company.

Once a week all beds are washed and thoroughly disinfected to keep any parasites from getting a start. The engineering and office force are housed in a combination office and sleeping quarters. All buildings are erected securely on pilings and well braced to keep them from blowing away. Numerous tents are provided but are not nearly so satisfactory. These tents are set up over a wooden framework and are numbered the same as houses in a city. By far the greater number of laborers are hobos recruited by labor agencies in New York and Philadelphia. Strict discipline as to cleanliness is enforced, and all debris must be thrown into the tide, where it is washed away. A watchman patrols the camp to see that this rule is enforced. Most of the camps have walks laid out, coursed by walls of coral rock and conch shells. Between these, the ground is kept well smoothed and in some instances, flower gardens are in sight."

The railway was completed, the tents were gone now, and the island population had shrunk to a total of about forty men. It was this scenario that Adolph found himself in when he arrived in February of 1912. As the crews thinned, the riffraff also drifted off, and Adolph, as the sole foreman of the line crew found he was in charge of twenty experienced, capable, and trustworthy workers. They quickly developed a routine, with perhaps a half dozen men operating a handcar, leaving in the morning and working their way either up or down the line, performing maintenance and repairs, and responding to any reported problems. The Florida East Coast crews had a tool unique to them; the ability to use a motor launch to inspect the bridges and viaducts by boat. The reliable job routine, decent pay, and job security got in the way of Adolph's plan to work at Pigeon Key for only a few years, and the comfort level increased when no major storms affected the entire keys for years after the 1910 storm. With no harsh winter weather, relatively minor precipitation throughout the year, and a line that saw only two trains a day, the maintenance job was far from grueling. It was an added bonus that Adolph lived in a veritable paradise on his day off. Unlike today's overpopulated and overfished waters, the entire population of the islands from Key Largo to Key West numbered less than ten thousand. Fish abounded, and Adolph could fill a gunny sack full of snapper, grouper, cobia, and hogfish right from the shore of Pigeon Key, or with a short walk up and down the mainline (between trains). Unlike most of the northern transplants, Adolph could swim, but the legends of vicious shark and barracuda attacks kept him out of the salt water.

Wayne Gales

15
Who Says You Can't Go Home?

The Conch Republic Seafood Company is located dockside in Key West Harbor. I was never sure if it was a tourist bar that locals hung around, or vice-versa, but there was always a crowd. A guy with a guitar sat in the corner doing bad Buffett covers while tourists and locals got hammered, all ignoring the impending sunset celebration on Mallory Square a few blocks away. As they say, seen one sunset, seen 'em all, and besides, just like a bus, another one would show up tomorrow. I ordered drinks and Rumpy and I caught up on gossip. Then, something jogged my memory.

"Hey Rump, what do you know about prostitution or white slavery rings operating in this area?"

"That's kind of out of the blue, my friend," Rumpy answered. "Why do you ask?"

I went on to tell him about noticing some strange behavior by a couple of the housekeepers when Karen and I stayed at the La Concha a few weeks ago. Visible bruises and looking very stressed. One of them had a trace of glitter in her hair.

"It just seemed strange," I said. "All of them appeared to be Eastern European."

"Well, that's not uncommon," Rumpy answered. "Most of the hotel labor force down here is from that neck of the woods, Russia, Poland, Czech, or one of the 'Stans. Lots of them are undocumented."

"How do they get away with that?" I asked

"There's a couple of rackets. Companies contract the labor to the hotel, so the hotel doesn't have to do a background check or get proof of citizenship. I hear they will bring in a dozen or so with legitimate papers and work permits, and then sneak in a hundred others without. They just shuffle them around so nobody notices, but I hear that more than one might have the exact same name." He took another sip. "I can understand them doing this to have a cheap labor force, but why do you think it might involve prostitution?"

"I was solicited twice in one week, once by a skinny girl with a Russian accent, and once by a guy over on Whitehead Street by the

Green Parrot. He had a Russian accent too, and he pointed to a girl across the street who looked very much like one of the housekeepers at La Concha. Both girls looked terrified. That's two more times than I was propositioned in the last twenty years in Key West."

"Pal," Rumpy answered, with a thin smile. "I've never paid for it, and at my age, can't even keep up with the free stuff." He briefly smiled. "For that matter, I can hardly keep it up at all anymore, but if I hear anything else, I'll let you know."

We finished dinner and drinks, and I sent Rumpy on his merry way. I walked down Duval and checked into the La Concha where I was treated like a long-lost friend. After balancing their October budget with a week at dog-robber rates in a Duval Street suite with a balcony during Fantasy Fest, I was given VIP treatment and an upgrade this time. I booked the room for the weekend and told them I might stay longer. I didn't have any plans, just needed to climb out from under my rock and get a little dose of Key West Normal in my veins. I picked up the room phone and called Faro Blanco, asking for my suite. It rang a few times and went to voicemail.

"Hi sweetie, it's me. I'm staying back at La Concha, room 425. Pack a bag and join me. I miss you."

Then I wandered outside and took a walk. I didn't want to risk the old haunts, so I opted for the Lazy Gecko. Taking a stool at the end of the bar, I nursed a beer, and engaged in my second favorite pastime, people watching. The Gecko is just a few doors down from Sloppy Joes and draws the same touristy crowd, couples on vacation drinking for effect, boat people, (cruise customers to you flatlanders), and a few local barflies. Wait staff is pretty, the music half decent and it's cozy enough you don't get lost in the mob. From my vantage point, it didn't take long to spot another shady character, working the street very subtly, approaching single guys and talking in a low voice. I looked around the area from my chair, and it only took a moment to spot a scrawny, undernourished girl in a tank top and cutoffs, leaning against a building with her arms clutched around her. It was a different girl than before, but the same look. I did a double-take. It was the maid from the La Concha! It wasn't more than a few minutes before the pimp found a John, and with a crook of his eyebrow, signaled the girl to follow them someplace up the street. They disappeared out of sight from the front of the Gecko. I went back to my beer but filed the scenario in the back of my mind.

Key West has its share of soiled doves, from high-class escorts to back-alley twenty-dollar blowjob girls (or guys, for that matter) and everything in between, but as long as I had lived here, I had never seen such a preponderance of urban-styled action. This smacked of sex trafficking, and I flashed back to my years in the Navy when a pack of hookers would descend on us almost every time we went on dockside leave in a city. Back then they weren't Russian or Eastern European, but American girls, black, white, Hispanic, young, rough and crude, dressed in miniskirts, heels, and garter belted nylons, the perfect depiction of what a prostitute would look like, bringing to mind Jamie Lee Curtis in *Trading Places*. In the seventies, they could give you everything from crabs to herpes to classic Hong Kong drippy dick, but by the early eighties, the crowd started to thin out as a quick fuck could result in a lot more than a trip to the doctor. The standing joke was that sex with a hooker was like bungee jumping; They both cost fifty bucks, they both took ten minutes and if the rubber broke, you died.

Hookers didn't interest me. Violence and abuse of any kind to women does and makes my skin crawl.

After a couple of days, I hadn't heard from Karen and decided to change hangouts. I walked over to one of my favorite old haunts, Casa 325 on Duval Street, and took a unit in the back over the pool. Tree-lined, peaceful, and quiet; you could almost imagine you were living in some sleepy part of New Orleans or Saint Augustine.

From my memory, during most weeknights you usually had the back of the place to yourself and moonlit skinny dips were always a great way to soak the booze out of your skin. And, since most people didn't even know this place existed, it was the perfect hideout for someone who wasn't supposed to exist. The old mansion that most of the Casa 325 resides in is a century-old Victorian-style residence that's been converted into a guest house. It's hidden because there's a row of shops directly in front of it facing Duval. The driveway is a tiny alley that's always blocked by a little kiosk selling dive and snorkel trips. Want to pull a car into the driveway?

141

The salesperson just rolls the entire "office" out of the way and in you go. The driveway was built for the days of horse and buggy, so anything much wider than a Yugo is a squeeze. In the back, there is parking for a half dozen Yugos, along with a couple of Harleys and a bicycle or two. There are also five newer studio units surrounding a nice pool, probably where the old carriage barn used to be. For me, on foot, it was the perfect place. I called our room at Faro Blanco and left a message to let Karen know I had changed locations.

Wayne Gales

16
Schooner Wharf Dogs

As agreed, Saturday afternoon I wandered over to Schooner Wharf. On the way, I passed one of my favorite ships, the schooner *Western Union*. Built in 1939 it was the last tall ship built in the keys and performed as a lookout ship during World War II searching for Nazi U-Boats that were lurking in the Florida Straits. After the war, she laid telegraph cable between Key West and South America along with several islands in the Caribbean including Cuba. She's in bad shape now and needs funding to keep her afloat. It was sad to see the paint peeling from her sides and woodwork in need of attention. I sighed to myself. Things that are truly important don't seem to be important anymore.

I walked in and sat on one of the benches by the bar in the shade with my back to the bandstand. To my surprise, my old friend Mike McLeod was on the stage playing solo. I pulled my floppy hat down to my sunglasses and peeked out of the corner of my eye, and sure enough, he was staring at me wondering if he recognized me. I looked over my shoulder, and Mike had already dismissed the moment and gone back to playing his song about Schooner Wharf Bar Dogs. At least this far away from the music, I would have a better chance to visit with the twins without having to yell. I ordered a beer and a basket of shrimp and fries and waited.

An hour and five beers later, Lex breezed around the corner, followed by Mary Elizabeth ten steps later like an obedient Japanese wife. My fears that Lex would stand out like the reverse visualization of a nun in a whorehouse were eased. She was actually dressed fairly civil, lime green terrycloth shorts that looked nice above her tanned legs, sandals, a floral tank top, beach wrap, and a floppy straw hat to complete the look. Mary had also edged a tiny bit in the other direction, wearing a long sleeveless sundress over her Birkenstocks. I couldn't tell if the baseball cap was meant to look cute or if she just found it at Goodwill, but she almost pulled it off.

Lex did a pirouette. "Do I pass?" she said.

"Yeah, a regular Mother Theresa," I said. "Mary, I'm impressed too. Good changeup. I'm glad you joined the human race." She blushed but smiled. "We're making progress. Sis picked it out for me yesterday. I didn't like it at first, but I think it's okay, and you're right, it's a lot cooler than what I wore before." She smiled again, and I could see there was a very pretty person under that mask. Like her sister but without the big rack. I invited them to sit down and called over the server. Mary sat across from Lex, who sat down by my side. "Corona Light," said Lex. I looked at Mary, and she was borderline in a panic about ordering a drink. Sheesh. "White wine?" I ventured. She was on the verge of saying no, but then barely bobbed her head yes. "And another Miller Lite for me."

The table was big enough for four or five people, but Lex slid right next to me until her shoulder and leg were touching, picked a French fry out of the basket took a sip of my beer, then looked at me and bit into the fry with a little smile. I edged away just a little, and she snuggled right back. I slid away again, threw one leg over the bench, and faced her. "Listen girlie," I said. "This chicken dance needs to stop right now. Your games are distracting. Cool it, please."

Lex didn't answer, but just stared straight ahead without emotion. The server brought our drinks, and she just sat there without speaking, sipping her beer.

Awkward.

I turned to Mary. "So it's been a few days, how are you coming along?"

"I found an apartment in, what's it called? Oh, New Town," Mary started. "Wow! Thirteen hundred for an efficiency AND an extra five hundred deposit for the cats. I feel like I live in San Francisco again. I need to get a job soon."

"Cats?"

"Yes, I have four cats. I had them shipped here Tuesday from home."

"I would have never guessed. Okay, go on."

Mary looked pained. "That's all. I went to the Citizen and filled out an application, but they didn't sound very encouraging. I might have to go back home if something doesn't materialize pretty soon Uncle Bric."

I lowered my voice. "Do me a favor and drop the 'Bric' and for that matter the 'uncle' part too. Just Mister Phillips will do. I'm doing a good job of flying under the radar and want to keep it that way.

"Sorry, Unc... I mean Mister Phillips. I'll remember," she said sheepishly.

"Give them a few days and then check back. I have to do this sort of in a roundabout way, but maybe I can help you with Plan B. I'm staying at Casa 325 in the back, unit four. Just knock anytime you need any more advice." I turned to Lex "That goes for you too kid. I didn't mean to be hard on you. I like you. Heck I like both of you. Pax?" I said. She took another sip of her quickly warming beer and smiled, then stuck out her hand. "Sure," she said. "Got it. Sorry if I got out of line. Sometimes I don't know how to act any other way."

"And how is your career going?" I asked, changing the subject.

"I passed the audition yesterday. The coochie goes public tonight at ten. Come on by for a peek." Mary turned her head away in embarrassment.

"Ah, not likely," I said. "Not into strip joints but too many of my old friends are. Besides, that would be more of you than I plan to experience. Thanks anyway. Where are you staying?"

"I got a loft on Thomas Street in Bahama Village. Like sleeping in a phone booth for twelve hundred bucks a month, *AND*, I have to wear earplugs because the roosters crow all night. Not sure what you see in this town."

"Well, I missed it enough to put myself in danger by coming back," I said. Then I had a thought.

"Lex, while you are at the club, do me a favor and sort of keep your eyes open for something. I've seen and heard about some pretty shady activity going on. Like white slavery stuff. Young, Eastern European girls being abused and such. Where you will be working is the kind of place that sort of thing might be going on in. Just keep your eyes open and let me know if you see anything suspicious."

147

"Sure Unc, but this place seems pretty classy. I'd be surprised if anything like that is going on." Lex said and then had a question. "Not to change the subject, but, like what do people do for real fun around here? Like if I was a tourist and wanted to experience the real keys?"

"Well, there's fun, and there's fun. Key West is as normal as any other little town in the country until it isn't," I said and then came up with an idea.

"Okay, want some fun? Tomorrow morning, seven-thirty sharp, park your car in the public lot on Caroline and meet me on the corner. Bring towels, sunblock, and a swimsuit. Oh, and take some Bonine when you get up."

"What's Bonine?" they both said at the same time. That was the first time the twin thing showed itself.

"Keeps you from getting seasick. We're goin' on a boat ride," I answered. "Now skedaddle out of here so I can enjoy my beer in peace. See you in the morning."

I sat there for the rest of the afternoon, nursing beers and listening to music. Just before dark, a cute-ish but scrawny blonde slid onto a barstool just across from me and ordered a rum runner. I watched the bartender mix her drink. I've tended enough bars in my life to recognize a watered-down drink, and there was a lot more "runner" in this one than there was rum. The girl nodded to the bartender, and the eye contact conveyed some sort of message. She sipped her drink then slowly spun around on the barstool to face my way. I watched her out of the corner of my eye while I pretended to be listening to the music. Mike was singing "Chasin the Wind," a song I had heard a million times. The girl was wearing a cutoff denim skirt, a very *short* cutoff denim skirt, and appeared to be trying to catch my attention. She finally crossed her legs and slid one up the other until, even with a sidelong glance, I could see a little bit of black panty. Then I had an idea. I turned toward her and pulled my glasses down below my nose.

"Sure is nice out," I started. That was all the invitation she needed. She slid off the barstool, letting the skirt ride almost up to her crotch, and sat down on the picnic table across from me. Reaching out as if to toast my beer bottle, she spoke;

"Buy me another rum runner?" she asked.

"You mean another seven-up with grenadine in it?" I answered. "Sure, I'll play the game."

She frowned, but motioned to the bartender with her cup, then turned back to me.

"What's your name?" she asked. Her accent was thick and Eastern European. "You are here on vacation?"

"Sort of," I answered.

"Me too. I'm on vacation and looking for a party."

I've never been much for tact, so I cut to the chase.

"No, you aren't. You're not looking for a party, you're looking for a John. Where's your pimp? Is he watching us?"

"Fuck you," she said and started to get up. I grabbed her hand. "Sit down. What's the price for a blow job?" She tried to pull away and then looked at me for a moment. She sat back down.

"Fifty."

I slid a C-note across the table. I lied to her. "Ok, here's a hundred. I'm parked around the corner behind B.O.'s Fishwagon. Green Ford pickup. Meet me there in five minutes." I walked out of Schooner Wharf turned left toward B.O.'s. and then stopped at the corner under the big Wyland mural where the old Overseas Market used to be. A few minutes later the girl came around the corner. I gave my little tweet whistle, and she saw me. I crooked my finger, and she came over, puzzled.

"Where is your truck?"

"I don't have one. I just wanted to talk to you for a moment. Is anyone following you?"

She turned and started to walk away. "Hey, I paid a hundred bucks for your time!"

She reached into her pocket and threw the money on the street. "Keep it, weirdo."

"I've got four hundred more if you will just stand here for a moment. No tricks. We can even sit at B.O.'s if you want." She stopped, and turned, then picked up the hundred. What do you want to talk about?"

"Getting you out of here and back home."

She looked over her shoulder and walked a little closer. "You can't do that. Nobody can do that."

"Are you being watched?" I asked.

"No. He's sitting at the bar waiting for me to come back. If I don't come back in twenty minutes, he will come looking." She took another step toward me. "If you try to take me away, they will kill you. Other people have tried, and they disappeared." She walked up to me. "Where is the four hundred dollars?" I reached into my pocket, peeled off four more bills, and held my hand out. She reached for the money, and I grabbed her wrist, turning it over. The track marks up her arm were fresh.

"How long have you been using?" I asked.

"Since I get here. They force me every day for weeks. Now I do it twice a day. They know I will come back at night."

I let her go. "Look, you need to go back to Schooner Wharf but believe me when I say I want to help you and the others. If you want help, come to Casa 325, in the back, unit number four." I knew it would not be good if she went back and squealed, but I felt it was worth the risk. She nodded. "Casa 325, number four, ok." She turned and walked away.

Bric old man, I hope you didn't just write your death warrant.

Wayne Gales

Flashback - January 1, 1923, Pigeon Key

Adolph found himself living in the same place on New Year's Day 1923. It hadn't been totally uneventful. World War I had come and gone, and Adolph quickly learned to "Americanize" his German accent and introduced himself as Al whenever possible. The German restaurant in downtown Marathon had wisely changed its name to the "Swiss Garden" and Adolph quickly learned that hailing from Northern Minnesota was much healthier than telling people he was German.

The war had minimal effect on rail operations. Ten years into the completed railroad, the Florida East Coast Railway was operating at a loss. Freight to and from the Panama Canal never materialized in the volume that had been predicted. All the Key West Cigar factories had been lured away to Tampa, and the only reliable cargo was the seasonal pineapple crop that went by boat from Havana to Key West and then by rail to the North, and that was only a few weeks, or perhaps a month a year.

Enjoying the extra day off, he commandeered a hand car, found an agreeable accomplice and they rolled the two miles into the little village at Knights Key. The prohibition act of 1920 meant the sale of alcohol was illegal throughout the US, but the ban hardly reached the Florida Keys. Notice of federal agents boarding the train in Miami alerted communities up and down the islands and by the time they arrived, bawdy bars turned into ice cream parlors, so Adolph and his accomplice had no problem finding cold beer and interesting company. They ran into several coworkers from the Knights Key camp, and Adolph was surprised when his benefactor, Mister Weeks, walked in. They shook hands warmly. It had been eleven years since they had met in Key West. Adolph proudly showed Weeks the Double Eagle from that day.

"I must have been paying you too much if you haven't had to spend that!" Weeks exclaimed.

"It's my good luck charm," replied Wahl. "Keeps the storms away."

"Well," Weeks replied. "It might have brought you more luck today. I came to this bar on business. One of my crew bosses is retiring in two weeks, and I need a replacement. I was supposed to meet a prospective candidate here in an hour, but if you are interested, I can think of no better person for the job." He squared his shoulders and looked at Adolph in the eyes. "One hundred twenty-five dollars a month and a small house. Are you interested?"

The thought of living in his own house and securing a position likely to last for the rest of his working days agreed with him. He hardly hesitated when he answered.

"I'll take it. What location?" He asked, realizing that he probably should have asked that question first, not that it mattered.

"Islamorada."

The Upper and Middle Keys were formed nearly 100,000 years ago by corals building a reef. This formation can be clearly seen today at the Windley Key Quarry Geologic State Park. Native Americans settled in this area over four thousand years ago and the first European to visit the area was Ponce de Leon, who sailed through the keys in 1513. He called them Los Martires. A map of the time indicated an island known as Guarugumbe in this section of the keys. The Indian name was corrupted by the Spanish into Matecumbe, a name that has survived to this day.

In 1733, a hurricane destroyed almost the entire Spanish treasure fleet as it returned to Spain. Some remains of this fleet can be seen on the Islamorada reefs. One ship, the San Pedro, is now an underwater state park.

The first permanent settlers came to the area from the Bahamas in the 1800's. They received land grants and farmed on Upper Matecumbe. The Russells arrived first, followed by Pinders, Parkers, and Sawyers. These families acquired the entire island for about $20, the cost of recording their land grants! Other Bahamian families that had originally moved to Key West as wreckers joined their cousins after the salvage business dried up when a series of lighthouses were constructed up and down the keys, and the number of shipwrecks drastically fell off.

The settlers cleared the jungles, fought mosquitoes, raised pineapples, limes, melons, and vegetables, and fought more mosquitoes. Cephus Pinder opened the first canning factory in the keys to can pineapples. The site was just east of today's Cheeca Lodge. Plantation Key was named for its pineapple plantations.

Islamorada's first post office opened on June 1st, 1908, with John Henry Russell as postmaster, and the Islamorada FEC Depot was constructed next to the Post Office near present-day mile marker eighty-two a few years later.

The railroad that was supposed to bring prosperity to the keys ruined the pineapple business. Cuban produce could be loaded on train cars in Havana, placed on the ferry to Key West, and then travel by rail through the keys to New York, all without being unloaded. The Cuban labor was so cheap the local farmers could not compete.

Adolph Wahl stepped off the northbound train on January tenth, 1923, and introduced himself to the Station Agent, Joseph William Russell. Russell, a native "Conch" had moved to Islamorada with a contingent of other Key West families shortly after the turn of the century. His family farmed, and when the railway came through, he joined the crews, first working construction, assuming the duties of Islamorada Station Manager in 1908. Now in his sixties and in failing health, he was ready to retire and draw his pension. Russell instantly liked the younger Wahl, tall, muscular, and handsome with blonde hair and blue eyes. The elder Russell stepped outside the station house and pointed at a tiny clapboard cottage just a few dozen yards from the depot. Next to the house was a sturdy line shack that housed tools and assorted repair equipment. It was constructed of old railroad ties and hammered together with railroad spikes. The roof consisted of a sheet of boilerplate that had been salvaged from an old dredge. It was probably the strongest building on the island, if not the entire Upper Keys. Beside it was a four-man handcar, a stack of spare railroad ties, and a length of rail. A short walk down a path behind the house was a sturdy twenty-foot motor launch, tightly covered with a tarp, which was infrequently used to inspect bridges. With these meager supplies, Wahl was supposed to keep twenty miles of track intact, repaired, and operating. "That's your home," he said. "It's not fancy, and your predecessor was not much of a housekeeper. I suspect it needs some attention." Russell shook Adolph's hand again and invited him back inside for a cup of coffee, which Adolph accepted humbly. After some idle chatter, he seemed to come to a conclusion.

"Do you go to church, son?"

"Not for many years sir," he answered. "Oh, occasionally I attended services at the camps, but mostly not."

"Why don't you join us for services on Sunday?" Russell went on. "I want you to meet my family. We would welcome a visitor. What's your faith?"

"I was born a Lutheran, but I haven't been too dedicated, I'm afraid."

"We're Methodists. Sing a lot of the same songs I seem to recall. Please tell me you will be there. And we always have a nice picnic after services."

Adolph smiled and gave in. He knew the old man wouldn't take no for an answer. "Sure, I'll see you there."

The German walked to his new home by himself. He realized he didn't have a key to the house, but when he reached the porch and turned the door handle, he found it wasn't locked. In fact, there wasn't a single lock on any door in the keys. No crime and no criminals, although the village residents were starting to voice concern about the nearby World War I veteran's camp. It was well known that an hour after paychecks were handed out, virtually every single laborer in the camp was drunk, and they would beg, borrow, or steal to stay that way until they had to return to work on Monday. There had been no incidents as of yet, but it would probably just be a matter of time.

As Adolph pulled the door open, both hinges fell off the rotting door frame, and he found himself laughing with a door in his hands. He sat the door in the entryway and walked inside to survey his castle. He was greeted by the stench of rat droppings, trash in the corners, and a broken back window. A dove burst from a nest over the dresser and flew out the opening. With his hands on his hips, he wondered where to start. Living in rather spartan accommodations for the past thirty-plus years, he was ready to make this shack into a home. At least, he had plenty of tools and knew how to fix things. He got to work.

Sunday being his day off, Adolph put on his suit and walked the half mile down the tracks to the little Matecumbe United Methodist Church. He found the elder Russell outside and was introduced to sons, daughters, grandchildren, nieces, nephews, and cousins. He laughed. "I think you are related to every person in this town!"

"Other than you and a few colored families south of the tracks, I would say you are probably right." He thought for a moment. "Come to think of it, most the coloreds are named Russell too. Probably former slaves from the Bahamas days before they were freed." Despite being residents in the Florida Keys for multiple generations, most of these former English loyalists had a definite British lilt to their voices.

The pastor called the congregation to service, and everyone strolled inside and sat. Being January, the weather was mild, and the mosquitoes were gone. The church could be stifling in the middle of the summer, especially since the men wore heavy woolen suits and the women were dressed in their Sunday best. Adolph sat when they sat, stood when they stood, and sang along as best he could, using the hymnals in the pews. He had never attended an English-speaking church in his life.

As promised, when church services were over, the congregation gathered under the trees and a picnic was produced. Chicken, fresh vegetables, pineapples, citrus, and tea was served. He couldn't help but notice the occasional flask produced from a hip pocket, but nobody knew him well enough to offer a share. By early afternoon, he was dizzy with all the new names, especially since half of them seemed to be named some variation of John Russell. But one person caught his eye, and he was careful to remember her name. Perhaps fifteen years his junior, she was tall and shapely. A halo of auburn hair jutting from her bonnet framed her attractive face and hazel eyes that seemed to dance with life.

"Mary Jane Sawyer," she announced, shaking Adolph's hand. "Adolph Wahl, but you can call me Al," he replied. He held her hand for an instant longer than necessary which she noted and returned a coy smile. Noticing her wedding ring, he ventured. "And when do I meet Mister Sawyer?"

"Oh, Tom's a seaman," she answered somewhat offhandedly. "He's sailing the ocean blue most of the time." She turned to the elder Russell. "Uncle Joe, can I borrow this strong, handsome man for a few hours? I have a number of items that need fixing and they can't wait until my husband finds his way home again." She smiled, "you can come with him and drink tea so people won't gossip up a scandal."

Joseph Russell scowled. "That scoundrel. It would serve him right if someone took his place. It's fine with me if it's okay with Adolph, but I'm not sure that's how he wants to spend his day off," he said with a wink.

Mary turned her head up. "Joseph Russell, how dare you talk like that! I just need a few hinges tightened and a leaky drain pipe repaired."

Adolph interrupted the conversation with a laugh. "I would be more than happy to come by. Say next Sunday after church and the picnic?"

"That will be fine, Mister Wahl. Bring a few tools if you can." Adolph nodded in agreement and said his goodbyes, which took almost as long as the greetings. Newcomers were rare in this little town, and the locals made him feel more than welcome.

Wayne Gales

17
The Tortugas

The next morning, I met Lex and Mary at the city parking garage on Caroline, and we walked across the street to the ferry terminal, where I bought three tickets for the *Yankee Freedom* to Fort Jefferson and the Dry Tortugas. Mary looked apprehensive but determined and boarded the *Yankee* without a word. The *Yankee Freedom III* is a big catamaran and handles rough seas wonderfully at a fast clip. The water was like glass today, and we virtually flew across the water at thirty knots. In a little more than two hours, the impressive structure of Fort Jefferson loomed into view. For the first-time visitor, seeing this huge red brick fort seemingly rising out of the water is impressive. Lex was up on the deck getting sun, but Mary was fascinated. "How did this fort get built way out here?" She asked. I lapsed into my 'Bric the historian' persona. In my best radio voice, I started;

"Construction started on the fort in 1846 and was never actually completed. By the time the Civil War came around, cannons were shooting rifled shells instead of big cannon balls, and the brick walls of the fort were as much protection as butter. It's only claim to fame was that it was used as a prison for Doctor Samuel Mudd, who was convicted of setting the broken leg of Abraham Lincoln's assassin, John Wilkes Booth, and sentenced to incarceration at the fort. He would have died there, but his work treating the soldiers at the fort for Yellow Fever prompted President Andrew Johnson to give him a full pardon in 1869."

"Wow," she exclaimed. "Why did they build it?" She asked.

"It's a strategic point for shipping going anyplace in the gulf. Ships from New Orleans, South America, Tampa, the Mexican Coast heading towards the East Coast of the US or even England and Europe pass near here. Control of this fort back in those days was critically strategic." I changed the subject. "Ok, enough history. Get your sister and let's talk about snorkeling," I said. Mary went topside and came back in a few minutes with Lex in tow. Mary looked nervous. (When did Mary not look nervous?)

"Ready for a snorkeling lesson?" I asked

"I...I don't know if I can," Mary stammered.

"Can you swim?" I asked her.

"Oh yes, very well. I learned in the pool at mother's house in San Francisco, but I never went into the ocean. It's too cold there."

"Well, it's like a bathtub here," I answered. "Look, I'm a professional diver. This is kind of a busman's holiday for me, but it's some of the best shore snorkeling on planet earth. Do me a favor and let's give it a try, ok?"

"But what about great white sharks and barracudas? Isn't it dangerous?" She asked.

"The car ride to the parking lot this morning was more dangerous than what you might find in the water here," I answered. "The kind of sharks that might be dangerous don't hang around water this shallow. You might see a 'cuda, but I've never had an issue with them while in the water. It's just fine. Just stick with me and I promise a day you will not soon forget."

A short time later the Yankee Freedom III tied up to the dock, and we filed off. A member of the crew was staged at the bottom of the gangplank and passed out dive gear, mask, fins snorkel, and BCD, buoyancy compensation device to everyone.

"I don't need one of those," I growled.

"Oh sir, you must wear one." She started in her tourist training voice. "People don't know how tired they might get in the water. It's mandatory. And it's especially important for our senior citizens."

I let her live.

I counted to ten and with my most gentle voice, answered. I tried as hard as possible not to snarl.

"Listen, sugar. I've spent more time *in* the water than you probably have *on* land, like something on the north side of three thousand dives. This old feeble body can probably struggle around in six feet of bathwater for thirty minutes, thank you. As it is, I feel about as silly as a rodeo cowboy climbing on a plastic horse in front of the grocery store, but I'm entertaining family today, so kindly go enlighten somebody else."

That worked, and she scurried off. I turned to the twins and told them they *did* have to wear BCD's and gave them a ten-minute lesson on snorkeling one point oh.

"First the mask," I started. "The straps are not to stick the mask to your face. Just make them tight enough, so it stays in place." And I adjusted each correctly. "You have the advantage of possessing perfectly smooth faces." I went on. I pointed to my beard. "For me, it's a little tougher." I picked up the snorkels and attached them to the masks. "The snorkel points up when you are in the water face down. If you go under water, just say the number 'TWO!' through the mouthpiece when you surface, and all the water will go out. You might have to do it twice, but the snorkel will clear." Despite her fear, Mary paid close attention and Lex was an eager learner too. Aside from snorkeling lessons, I was half apprehensive about what both would wear. I was afraid Mary would dress like an 1890s photo from the Jersey Shore and was equally afraid that Lex would wear dental floss and two Band-Aids.

We shall see.

The first part of the day trip to the fort was a forty-five-minute tour. I had done it several times but always enjoyed the history. We saw Doctor Mudd's cell, the old armory, the metal tracks that the huge guns used to move smoothly back and forth, endless long halls and lots of blind walls, and "do not enter" signs, all surrounded with millions of blood-red bricks. It was fascinating to think that every single brick was mined, formed, and fired someplace in the Northeast, taken to a harbor like New York, Boston, Baltimore, or Charleston, loaded on a wooden sailing ship and hauled to this place and then assembled, one by one to create this huge fort that was actually obsolete before it was finished. The twins looked someplace between sufficiently interested and totally bored, and when it ended, were more than ready to walk over to the beach. "I need to go to the boat and change. Coming with me sis?" Lex said on the way. Mary, carrying a purse that looked like a cross between a knitting bag and a steamer trunk, nodded and scurried off behind her.

There are a few different places to shore snorkel at Fort Jefferson, but the pristine, white sand beach on the north side by the old coal dock is the best spot. Newbies can get comfortable with snorkeling in four feet of water and there's still lots of tropical wildlife to see. I slipped off my shirt and shorts and waded knee-deep in the water, sitting down to cool off. A few minutes Mary showed up. I had to bite my lower lip to keep from laughing out loud. Underneath a huge floppy hat was this blinding white zinc oxide-covered nose perched below huge sunglasses. For a top, she was wearing a four-sizes too large bulky sweatshirt, with polyester gym trunks that hung below her knees.

"I think this is the first time I saw somebody change into swimwear and come out wearing more clothes than when they started," I said. "What's under the shirt and shorts, chain mail armor?" Mary blushed and didn't answer. She sat down her bag and looked at me, scared.

"C'mon girl, let's get you wet." I saw this was a potential disaster but didn't say anything else. Mary waded into the water next to me with her arms folded like she was freezing in the 90-degree water. "Ah, the hat and glasses need to stay on shore," I pointed out. She obediently waded back to the beach, left the headgear and shades, then came back. I handed her the mask and snorkel. "Let's not worry about the fins for a moment," I said. We walked waist-deep in the crystal clear water, and she pulled the mask over her face. Putting the snorkel in her mouth, she went face-down in the water. "Just breathe normally," I said in a normal tone of voice, and she nodded. After a moment, she came back up with a smile. "I can do this!" She exclaimed. The bulky sweatshirt had already gained about twenty pounds in water weight, and the gym shorts were ballooning full of air. "I figure in about another three minutes you will tip upside down and drown," I said. "Do you have anything under all those clothes?"

She looked pained. "I do, but I don't know if I can wear just that."

"Well, you have two choices. Peel off some layers or drown. What's it gonna be?" Mary hesitated, looked longingly at the water, and came to a decision. She walked out of the water, dragging twenty gallons of ocean with her, struggled out of the sweatshirt, and peeled off the gym shorts. She shuddered like she was naked on an iceberg despite the summer sun. Underneath was an honest-to-goodness Speedo made out of a Brazilian flag. Tight, thin, and

164

French cut. "Much better" I called to her. "Now that's a proper swimsuit. Come on back and try again." She didn't need coaxing and ran back into the water.

I handed her gear back to her. "Now pull your fins on and go ahead and paddle along that wall. It's not deep and lots to see." I turned and looked toward the fort. "It's your sister's turn now." Mary nodded, pulled her fins on, and paddled off. In the meantime, Lex showed up. I chuckled to myself. Lex was more conservatively dressed than her sister for once. Aside from a fairly skimpy bikini bottom, she had on a full-body long-sleeved white Under Armor rash guard, comfortably PG-rated, a good choice on this beach full of kids. "Ready for your turn?" I asked.

"Sure, Unc!" she quipped, looking left and right in an exaggerated way like she was making sure nobody could hear her. She grabbed her gear and waded into the water, leaning backward and dunking her hair in the water. When she stood back up, the seemingly innocent white rash guard was completely transparent when wet. Her brown nipples were pushing on the thin fabric and every curve of her pricey store-bought tits was clearly outlined. And she knew it.

"Gotta love me!" she chirped and then eased back down in the water so only her neck was exposed. I frowned, but, aside from making her put my shirt on, resigned to her victory, and gave her the same snorkeling lesson I had given her sister. Braver than Mary, and a more adventurous swimmer, Lex quickly slipped her fins on and took off down the wall toward Mary. Feeling rather ridiculous, I pulled on the rental gear and in a few kicks, caught up with the twins.

With my beard and mustache, the cheap mask leaked terribly, but I just dealt with it. Catching up with the girls, I floated vertical and pulled the mask up. "How are we doing?" I asked. In twin-speak, they both said, "Great!" I had to laugh. "Ok. Follow me," and, without waiting for them, started slowly swimming away from the wall. I had found an outcrop of coral a short distance from the moat on a previous trip and wanted to see if I could find it again. The girls chugged along behind me obediently and didn't seem to look too worried about getting into deeper water. After a few passes,

I found what I was looking for. A big outcrop of coral, probably encrusting some long-lost piece of ship or part of the fort. Coral doesn't grow on raw sand but if you give it something to hang onto, it flourishes.

The outcropping came into view and surrounding it was a tropical aquarium of yellowtail, gray snapper, parrotfish, angels, Sargent majors, a medium-sized Tarpon, and even a lionfish. Two squid cruised by, and the antennae of at least two lobsters peeked from under the rocks. I could hear the twins hooting into their snorkels in awe. Then I noticed that there was a visitor – just above Mary's back a four-foot Atlantic Barracuda was cruising, using her as a decoy while the unsuspecting fish below swam unaware. I didn't dare let Mary know she was in such close company. The 'cuda had no interest in her and had probably used this system in the past. Suddenly there was a flash of silver, and the predator vanished into the distance with a big gray snapper in his mouth. Neither twin caught more than a flash of motion, and never saw what happened. I floated around and let the twins get their fill of nature for a half hour before I spoke through my snorkel to get their attention and pointed to the shore. They were almost reluctant to leave this natural aquarium, but both nodded, and we headed back. By then the crew was preparing lunch aboard the catamaran, and, after rinsing ourselves off with a fresh water hose, the girls ducked into the restroom to change.

Somebody's grandma came out of the restroom and smiled at me. "I saw how you were teaching your granddaughters how to snorkel. That's real nice."

"Thank you ma'am, but they aren't my granddaughters; they are my nieces." Her smile turned as cold as ice. She turned and walked away and said over her shoulder. "Yeah, right."

Sheesh

About then Mary came out in cute little green shorts and a blouse set with beach sandals and a floppy hat. I whistled approval. Maybe there was hope for this caterpillar after all. I was relieved when Lex emerged in a thin strapped short sundress. At least, the twelve-year-old boys on the boat wouldn't go thru instant puberty today on the way home, as long as Lex didn't get between them and the sunlight as when she walked out of the shade, the dress turned nearly transparent. She tucked her hair under a Salt Life Visor and donned the Gucci glasses.

This girl could make a Richard Nixon Halloween costume look sexy.

Shortly after lunch, the Yankee Freedom crew pulled the gangplank, and we eased off the dock. Aside from a few passing thundershowers, the ride back was uneventful, except when the skipper pointed out a big blue boat anchored off to the south. "That's the *J.M. Magruder*, folks one of Mel Fisher's main treasure boats. She's anchored over the wreck of the *Santa Margarita*, the sister ship to the *Nuestra Señora de Atocha*, the site of one of the richest treasures ever salvaged." The twins glanced towards the Magruder and turned to me. "Wow! Is that where you found the treasure Uncle Brie?" asked Mary.

I put my finger to my lips. "Can you say that a little louder?" I asked. "I don't think that old deaf nun six rows behind us heard you." I sighed. "No, to answer your question. I was several miles that way," pointing to the east and a little north. I stood up. "Let's go topside where we can find a quiet spot, and I'll tell you a story." They followed me up the stairs to the outdoor seating area. There weren't a lot of people topside today, with most everyone opting for an air-conditioned ride instead of a thirty-knot breeze in a blast furnace. Mary held on to her hat and Lex held on to her hem for a moment, and then just gave up and let it swirl in the wind. Thank heaven she decided to wear panties. I sat down and mulled for a moment to decide how to give a Reader's Digest version of this shaggy dog story. Mary broke the silence and asked. "What was it like getting your hands on all that treasure?"

"Honestly?" I answered, "I almost wish I had never found it. It's caused almost as much pain as it has pleasure."

I looked at the clouds for some language.

"Lessee, where to start?" I began. "I was contracted on a salvage boat, following clues of the possible wreck of a Spanish Galleon, over that way." I gestured with my thumb off the starboard bow. "While I was looking for the wreck, I found an old cannon on shore. When we recovered the cannon, I discovered three huge gold bars under it." I held my hands apart to show how big they were. The girls gasped. "It wasn't part of the wreck we were looking for, so I decided to keep them for myself. I went back later and recovered them, only to find out they were just gold-plated lead." The twins groaned. "But...." Mary started. I held my hand up. "That's not the end of the story. Months later, with the help of a good friend, Bo Morgan, we discovered that the lead bars were hollow, and filled with pure gold, a million and a half worth." They both "oohed" and Lex's eyes got wide.

"So you're rich and don't have to work anymore?" Lex asked.

"There's more to tell, a lot more, but I don't want to bore you," I answered.

"Please, please, tell us everything!" they both said at the same time.

I continued. "The wreck turned out to be a salvage vessel that had plundered an earlier wreck off the middle keys in the 1700's. We aren't totally sure what this wreck was, but we knew which ship it had salvaged, based on the markings on the silver bars. The galleon had lots of silver and gold. Not the gold I found, which was strangely from the Confederate side of the Civil War and not Spanish treasure. We recovered a lot of the silver, but not much Spanish gold. We looked everywhere, and only one gold bar was ever turned up.

Then, months later, while looking at some pictures of the treasure, I saw a clue that told me where the gold might be. My boss, Harry Sykas was a genuine slimeball dickwad asshole. I called him up and told him I could recover the gold, but I wanted sixty percent. He bitched and fussed but finally agreed. We were pretty sure the gold was buried in a protected wildlife bird sanctuary, and when Karen and I went to dig it up, we got caught by Fish and Wildlife and had to leave without confirming it was there or having a chance to dig it up. We told Harry we wanted to leave it there until nobody was looking for us, and we went on a long vacation. Harry's Greek mob family decided we were trying to steal the gold, and they kidnapped Karen, tried to murder her, killed other people, and tried several times to kill me." I decided to leave out the rest. The more that story goes untold, the better. Karen actually recovered the gold with some friends and hid it in a museum. We eventually picked it all up, gave Harry his forty percent, and sailed off into the sunset."

"How much gold? What was it worth?" Mary asked.

"A lot," I answered. I didn't see a need to be specific.

Lex looked puzzled. "But all this doesn't explain why you had to make everyone think you died."

I sighed. I was hoping they wouldn't catch that little omission. I chose my words carefully. "I helped the government with a little problem, in exchange for them getting the bad guys off my ass, and it didn't go well. They decided the Witness Protection Program was a solution. It wasn't. Enough said."

The twin diesels on Yankee Freedom changed pitch as we came into Key West Harbor and the speaker came to life. "Folks, we will be docking in a few moments. Please check around you and make sure you gather up your personal items, cameras, dive gear, and kids. Remember that gratuities are always appreciated." Grateful for the interruption, I jumped up, pulled a twenty out of my pocket, grabbed my bag, and started walking toward the stairs. "That," I said, turning back toward them, "is another story."

Flashback - January 18, 1923, Islamorada

The first week on the job seemed to take an eternity. His crew showed up at the line shack shortly after daybreak and introduced themselves to Wahl. Two young men, one from New York and one from Homestead, and a coal-dark black man from Grand Cayman Island. They were capable and hardworking and had the little hand cart on the tracks in a few moments. Adolph pulled his gold pocket watch out and checked the time.

"The train from Key West will be here at nine-thirty" and the crew nodded agreement. "What first?" The muscular Caymanian spoke first. "Washout on the Indian Key Fill, boss. High tide always takes away the grade under dat bridge. I suspect we needs to tend to it first." While Adolph had no particular affection toward "das Schwartz" (African Americans), he respected hard workers and noted approvingly that he was treated as an equal among the crew. They loaded some shovels and picks on the handcart and shortly had the little car moving at a brisk ten miles per hour down the tracks.

When they arrived, the crew lifted the cart off the tracks to make way for the northbound train. Line foreman or not, he picked up a shovel and worked side by side with the crew, stopping only for a few moments when the train roared by with a cloud of steam and a salute of its whistle, and a half-hour break at lunchtime. Adolph had been doing this for years, and the effort took a lot of physical skill but not much mental aptitude, which gave him time to let his mind drift while his arms toiled. All Adolph could think of were those green eyes, auburn hair, and a smile that seemed to have a hint of mischief. At four in the afternoon, the crew returned to Islamorada, stored the handcar, and went their separate ways. That night he worked in his tiny cottage using a kerosene lamp, cleaning and repairing, while he thought about Sunday. "Don't be foolish, man," he thought to himself. "She's married and related to everyone in town. If I laid a hand on her, I would be tarred, feathered, and run out of the keys on one of the rails I put down myself." But it was still nice to imagine.

The week seemed to last forever, but Sunday finally came, and Adolph joined the Russell family again at the little church. It wasn't until just before he sat down that he spotted Mary in the back, wearing a bright green dress, white bonnet, and white gloves. She flashed a brief smile just before the pastor brought all eyes forward in prayer. With services over an hour later, the congregation gathered again for the highlight of the week, the church picnic. Food abounded, but Adolph could hardly eat; This time more than one flask was offered to him. Apparently, he was becoming part of the community. He finally found an excuse to wander near the group of women and he greeted Mary, who was holding the hand of a toddler. She made sure all knew who Adolph was, (not that his name hadn't been on the lips of every woman, married or single for the entire week) and then she announced. "Mister Wahl has agreed to come by the house and repair a broken hinge this afternoon." She leaned down. "Mister Wahl, this is my niece, Amber. Her mother has been kind enough to loan her to me for the afternoon, so I don't get lonely." Adolph could sense the sarcasm in her voice. He motioned to the side of the church building. "I have a bag of tools with me. Hopefully, they will suffice."

"I'm sure they will sir," Mary answered. "Shall we walk?" They said their goodbyes and the three of them headed north up the street. Some looked in suspicion, but most were comfortable that a two-year-old girl would sufficiently run interference and keep the saucy bride from straying.

The tiny Sawyer house was only a few blocks from the church. It was a "Sears house" a three-room building with, a kitchen, living room, and bedroom, plus a small porch and an outhouse in the back. The whole house could be purchased for about six hundred dollars from the Sears and Roebuck catalog and shipped by train or wagon to the buyer. This one looked to be only a few years old, but it had never seen a drop of paint. Building instructions were not complicated, but it appeared that there wasn't a lot of care taken in its assembly. Adolph sat the bag of tools down and took off his coat and tie. "What needs to be done?" he asked.

"No huge rush Mister Wahl. Please sit down. We'll have lemonade. May I call you Al?" She asked.

"Of course," Adolph said and sat down at the small dining table. Amber obviously visited her aunt frequently as she had a small box in the corner with toys. Before Mary could pour the lemonade, Amber brought her own tiny cups and saucers and solemnly sat them in front of Adolph. He hadn't been around little children since his youth, but always loved kids. He played along with the toddler and pretended to drink tea, much to her delight.

They sat across from each other and Mary put her chin on her hand as she leaned over the table. "So tell me about yourself," she started. "Where do you come from?"

Adolph hesitated and decided on a safe answer. "Right here in the keys since 1905," he replied. "I've worked on this railroad almost from its inception. The first time I set foot on this part of the islands, there were no more than a few shacks and some farmland. I guess the railroad made Islamorada."

She scowled at that. "It made it and then it killed it," she retorted. "Cuban pineapples cost a fraction of Islamorada pineapples, and trainloads of them come by here all season. The economy in America is booming everywhere else, and we are struggling. You can keep your damn railroad." She softened. "I'm sorry, that's none of your fault, Mister Wahl. Anyway, back to your story. Before you worked here where did you come from?"

Wahl thought for a moment and chose his words carefully. "Oh, worked here and there, always on the railroads. It's all I have ever done." He changed the subject. "I best get some work done here, Mrs. Sawyer. Point me at your first project." And he stood up.

"The back door," she pointed. "Something appears to be wrong with the door hinges, I think. Go ahead and take a look while I put this little urchin down for a nap."

Adolph walked to the back door and opened it. It only took a moment to see the top hinge had rusted in the salt air and broken. It was not repairable. She walked back into the room from the bedroom. She had changed into a simple shift from her church dress, common apparel for island women especially in the summer, and since this winter day was warm and balmy, perfectly appropriate. That being said, the summer dress, barefoot with no stockings and apparently nothing but a slip underneath, caught Adolph off guard. He couldn't help but stare for a moment, and then turned away, embarrassed. Mary, if she caught the moment, ignored it. Adolph turned back and stammered;

"The hinge is broken. Do you have a Sears and Rocbuck Catalog?"

"We do but it's in the outhouse." She laughed. "I hope the pages you are looking for haven't gone down the hole yet." She walked outside, still barefoot, and came back with the heavy book, sitting it on the dining table. With her standing beside him, brushing his shoulder, Adolph thumbed through the hardware section and found what he was looking for. His hands shook a little.

"*Here.* You need two of these. Two dollars and fifty cents for the pair. Order them by mail and I will put them on for you when they come, hopefully in a few weeks, no more than a month I think." He stood up and put a little distance between them. He caught her smile and wondered if she was playing with him, or maybe playing *for* him? "Show me what else needs fixing," he said. She pointed out a few more minor repairs around the house, which he was able to accomplish in a short time. As the afternoon grew late, Adolph put his coat and tie back on, then held out his hand.

"Thank you for the lemonade," he said. "I'll tell the postmaster to keep his eyes open for a package to you from Sears Roebuck. When it comes in, I'll drop by and fix that door for you. In the meantime, I'll see you at church next Sunday." She took his hand in both of hers and held it for a moment. "Thank you again, Al. It's been a pleasant afternoon. I'll look forward to your next visit, hopefully without that scamp here trying to serve you imaginary tea." And she leaned forward and brushed his cheek with a kiss. Adolph blushed and quickly turned away, mumbling thanks as he fled out of the house. He didn't want her to see how much he was blushing.

Wayne Gales

18
Research

I had almost forgotten my pledge to the Sawyer sisters to help them trace their roots. Mary rather bluntly reminded me one day and after that I committed to an afternoon's research a week, going through historical documents and microfilm at the Key West library with additional day trips to the Florida Keys Historical/Discovery Center in Islamorada. The library also had several books about the railroad and the storm, and Mary and I checked them out and read them one by one. After performing as much casual research as we could lay our hands on, I shared my synopsis with Mary.

"I assume the railroad is what brought great-great granddaddy Wahl to the keys. The problem is, aside from all the top bosses and dignitaries, which I'm sure Adolphus Wahl wasn't one of, there aren't too many names mentioned in these documents." I slid a couple of Xerox copies over to her. "But, I was able to find these. Here are three mentions of great-gramps. The first one documents him running a line crew in 1913 for the Florida East Coast Railway Extension at Pigeon Key." I handed her the second. That name shows up again several years later as the line foreman in Islamorada, and." I handed her the third. "He was listed as missing and assumed drowned in the 1935 Hurricane. Great Grandma Mary Sawyer called the dead guy Al, which is probably short for Adolph, so I'm pretty sure he's the guy we're looking for."

Or so it seemed.

Well, one way to tell. On the way back to Key West, I had Mary pull into a CVS Pharmacy.

"Wait here a moment" and I went inside. I came out a minute later with a Diet Mountain Dew, a bottle of water, and a small package. "Time to solve the mystery." I opened the package, pulling out a cotton swab. "Rinse your mouth out with the water, and then rub this swab inside your mouth, on the cheek."

"What's that for?" she asked.

"DNA Test. It's usually used to determine paternity, but it should easily be able to tell if we shared close ancestors. I have no doubt we share distant ones. All Conchs do, but they will be able to tell the difference I think." I demonstrated by rinsing and then doing my cheek. That resulted in me having to go back inside the store as Mary refused to drink from the same bottle as me. Sheesh. Eventually, we got the task done, and I packaged everything up.

"What's your address?" I asked, "I don't have one." She gave me her address; I wrote it on the envelope and then dropped it in the mailbox at the Key West post office when we got back to town. "Let me know when the results come back. The three of us can open it together," I told her.

A few days later I was already in bed when I heard a soft knock at the door. I slipped on a pair of shorts and looked through the peephole. In the dim light, I made out an older blonde woman in dark clothes. She looked nervous.

"Sorry, I didn't order any pizza," I said through the door.

"You said you wanted to help," the voice said quietly. "May I speak to you?"

Trick? Trap? I peered through the window curtains and scanned the pool deck below. It appeared she was alone. "Just a second," I answered and went back to the bedroom and slipped on a tee shirt. I opened the door, and she quietly stepped into the room.

"Have a seat," I motioned toward the chair. She nodded thanks and sat down. I would guess she was in her mid-fifties a little worn out but was probably a looker in her younger days. She wore a dark tank top, sunglasses even though it was the middle of the night, and a pair of shorts. Her left arm was decorated from wrist to shoulder in a vivid color tattoo of a nude woman apparently making love to a snake.

Weird.

"Can I get you something to drink? Diet Coke? Water?"

"Water, thank you." Her voice was also thick with an Eastern European accent. I got a bottle of Zephyrhills out of the fridge and gave it to her, then took a dining chair, flipped it around, and sat down on it backward. I decided to let her start talking. She took a sip and looked at me.

"You spoke to a girl the other night and told her you wanted to help her get to a safe place," she started. "In just doing that, you put her very much in danger." She stopped. "I'm sorry, I have not introduced myself. My name is Ludmilla," and she reached out her hand. I shook hands with her. "You can call me Mister Phillips," I said. "Pleased to meet you."

Ludmilla went on. "I work for some people, some very bad people," she continued. "I guess that makes me a bad person too, but I want to help now." She stopped and took another drink, and hesitated.

"Let me make this a little easier for you," I said. "I think I know what's going on. I saw pimps and prostitutes working the street on several occasions, and at least once, I know the hooker was also working as a housekeeper in a hotel. I'm guessing you guys are luring girls out of Eastern Europe, offering them jobs as hotel maids, and then turning them out as prostitutes. White slavery."

"You have part of it right, but there is more. Much more," Ludmilla answered. She hesitated again and seemed to come to a decision. "I don't know why I should trust you, but I have no one else to bring this too. If I go to the police, I will likely go to prison or be deported, and if they don't believe me and send me away, I will be quickly dead." She looked into my eyes. "Why do you say you want to help?"

"Multiple reasons," I answered. "Most of these girls are young enough to be my daughter and I'm disgusted with what's going on. I'm sure they are being hooked on drugs, and who knows what happens when they are used up. I guess I just can't ignore what I'm seeing." Then I had a question.

"If you are a big part of this gang, why are you coming to me now instead of ratting me out to your goons?" She looked down in shame.

"Years ago, I was one of their top working girls in New York. It was different then; at least, that's what I made myself believe. No drugs, none of this luring young girls to come to America under one promise and then forcing them into prostitution. They took care of us; we paid for that protection. It was okay. I got older, and they put me in charge of the crib. I helped the girls with abortions and took them to doctors when they got a venereal disease. Then a year ago, they moved the operation to Key West, and started this new way of importing talent." She turned her arm over and showed me the tracks on her wrist. "Now they make all of us shoot up. They beat and rape the girls until they submit to working the streets. Those that don't work, die." She squeezed her eyes shut and almost whispered, "It has to stop." She opened her eyes and looked up at me. "If I help you and give you information, what will you do? Will you go to the police?" She asked.

That resulted in a thin smile. "I'm not a bad guy like your bad guys," I answered. "But let's say I don't want to get the police involved. Look, this town isn't that big. What can this be? A half dozen girls. I'll chase away the baddies and get the girls to a safe place off the island. That will be it. No biggie."

"Oh, it's so much more than that," Ludmilla answered. "What you see is, how do you say, the tip of the iceberg. What if I tell you that they have brought in over four hundred girls in the past year?"

"What would I say?" I answered. "I would call bullshit on you. Hookers and housekeepers total, there's hardly that much demand for either on this rock and they ain't the only people supplying talent."

"That is true," she answered. "Key West is just the drop-off point. It's where they start, but they leave here pretty soon. It's just that this is the perfect location for this business."

"Really? One road in, a tiny airport, immigration agents up the ass because of the Cubans. I would think this is the worst place to organize a white slavery ring."

I could tell she had more to say but was struggling with opening up with the whole story. I needed to bump the needle off-center. I stood up.

"Lady, I appreciate your coming to me. I will not tell anyone you came, but unless you give me some real details and not just pieces, I'm just as well off figuring this out on my own." And I started to walk to the door.

"Wait! Sit down. I will tell you everything I know." I went back to the chair and sat. "Ok, spill it," I said.

She took a deep breath. "There is an organization operating in Eastern Europe, the Middle East, and Russia," she started. "They advertise for young girls to come to America and become housekeepers, hotel maids, things like that. When people respond, they screen them and decide if they are pretty enough and young enough to fit their needs, and then take them to Istanbul whey they are put on a ship to Southeast Asia. From there I don't exactly know how they get here other than by a big ship. When I talk to the girls, they say they are put on a ship, locked in a small cabin with just some mattresses and a bucket for a toilet, and brought food. They are there for weeks. Then they are taken off that boat and put on a smaller boat, made to strip and put other clothes on. A little later, they see the lights of Key West. They are told to act like they are having a party. They dock, get off the boat, and are taken to an apartment where they figure out very quickly what they are actually here for. They usually ship a dozen or so at a time." She looked relieved to be able to tell the story.

"Do you know of a party boat called *Moonlight Madness*?" Ludmilla asked.

"Vaguely" I answered. "Some drink and drown boat that goes out all night long into the gulf stream so people can get hammered and look at stars? I hear it's not too popular."

"It does not have to be. Someday next week, I will let you know when to watch. It will leave with only fifteen people, but if you try to book it, they will say it's sold out. But when it comes back, there will be twice that many people on it."

"So they go out and rendezvous with a ship and transfer the girls to the party boat?" I said, almost to myself. "How slick is that?"

Ludmilla stood up. "I will leave a note under your door to let you know when the next group of girls will be arriving so you can see for yourself. I don't know when I will risk coming here again. It is very dangerous for both of us."

"Thank you for taking that risk," I said. "I'm glad you want to help. I don't know what I'm going to do or how to do it just yet, but these kids need to escape. I'll think of something." And with that, she left.

Her question was valid. What was I going to do, and for that matter, why?

I can't fix the world.

But maybe I can make a little difference.

Wayne Gales

19
Happy Surprise

A few days later I rented a cruiser bike from a shop on Truman and peddled my ass down Duval Street.   With a decent beard and full mustache, wearing a Ricky Ricardo shirt, black shorts, and a Celebrity Cruises baseball cap, I could have probably walked into my mother's house, and she wouldn't have recognized me. I was growing weary of playing rich recluse, and it felt good to be out among 'em in daylight. I had the advantage of being able to grow facial hair. It would be tougher for Karen if she were here. She would have to dye and cut her hair and maybe wear big movie star sunglasses and a floppy hat, but the chance someone would recognize her was much greater. I'm not sure how to deal with that in the long run, but, for now, it was just me in Key West, and nobody knew her in Marathon.

First things first. Breakfast. Pepes? Blue Heaven? Two Friends? Let's not push the envelope today, buddy boy. Ah. I know just where to go where nobody knows my name. I peddled the bike down Duval, with a longing glance at Buzzards as I cruised by. I wonder if my Gibson Ripper Bass was still residing in the closet. I was sure it was long gone. It's far too valuable a collector's item to be sitting there gathering dust. Probably long-ago somebody pinched it and sold it to the highest eBay bidder from Norway. I turned my head away and pedaled on. No sense crying over spilled milk.

I went left at the end of Duval and right on Simonton and leaned the bike against the fence at the Southernmost Café. I sat at the bar and had eggs benedict and a cup of decaf, peering over my shades to see if the world had indeed forgotten Bric Wahl. So far, so good. Where next? I had all day and was already running out of things to do. Well, a swim will clear my head, so I got back on the bike and headed for my old hobo bathing spot on Smathers Beach. It seemed like an eternity since I went for a dip, met Rio Rio, and left for my European adventure a few days later, but it had been less than a year. Rio was likely long gone. According to her, when we

183

were staying on her derelict boat, she had terminal stage four cancer with no intention of getting treatment. My vision blurred for a moment as I thought of her and all the other people in my life who had been taken far too soon by cancer. We never really clicked. She was a tough, cynical bitch sometimes, but underneath that shell was a big heart and a vulnerable little girl. I thought of Rio often.

Like any other Tuesday in Key West, Smathers Beach was more or less empty this early in the day, just a gay couple walking their Pomeranian, an old black man with a fishing rod and no apparent desire to fish, and a few Canadian tourists, shirtless and snow white on beach towels, slowly turning lobster red. I had swim trunks on under my shorts. I hung my clothes on the bike, and started walking toward the water when I saw one other person, sitting solo in the sand, smoking. The hair stood up on the back of my neck. Short stubble for hair, tall and slender, sitting cross-legged, wearing short tattered cutoffs and a camouflage wife beater tank top. It couldn't be her. I walked closer and caught the whiff of cannabis. I was close enough to know for sure.

It was Rio.

"Last I heard those things were illegal in Florida," I ventured.

She didn't even look up. "Helps with the chemo nausea. On the other hand, go fuck yourself."

"Ah, that's my Sabine," I replied.

Her head snapped around, and she squinted into the sun for a moment. I flashed a smile through my beard and just stood there.

"Bric." It was so soft it was almost a whisper. She gracefully unfolded herself from the sand, stood up, put her arms around me, and quietly sobbed on my shoulder. After a minute she finally said, "I thought you were dead."

"Baby, you took the words right out of my mouth," I answered. "You are the last person I expected ever to see on Smathers Beach. You said chemo. Change of heart?"

We sat back down on the sand, and she offered me the joint, which I declined and then spoke, staring not at me but at the ocean. "Because of you. Remember your parting words that I was living my life in denial? Well, after you left I got drunk and stoned for three weeks, woke up one morning, and decided to end the pity party. Left the SS Titless, caught a bus to Miami and checked into U.M. Sylvester. Come to find out I wasn't as bad off as I had been led to believe. Eight months of treatment, a little radiation here and there, no more cigarettes, at least the kind with labels on them, and a lot less alcohol, and I'm in remission." She took a breath and looked at me. "Not out of the woods for sure, but they think I've bought a few years." She flashed that heart-melting smile. "And here I am. Now your turn Bric. I went to your fucking funeral. I saw your friends and your kids cry. Hell, *I* cried. You've got some explaining to do."

I didn't know where to start, or what to leave in or take out. Bric Wahl was two names ago, and it was probably foolish to have even opened this chapter back up, but, as they say, the cat was out of the bag. I gave her the short version, left out a lot, but not everything. Her eyes got bigger and bigger and then narrowed some when I told her that Karen was alive, kicking and holed up on Islamorada. Rio and I were never an item, but we both know we could have been, under the right circumstances.

"So you told me back then that your treasure had been lost. I take it you found it again?" She asked.

"Yes, I found it. More than I knew I had," I answered. Then a light came on. "Hey, do you need anything? You helped me out when I didn't have a pot to piss in or a window to throw it out of."

She stiffened up. "I don't need charity. I make my own way."

"I got that," I answered. "Not charity. Consider it as payback for your kindness. What can I do for you?"

She stood up and brushed the sand off her cutoffs. "No need. I'm good for now." I stood up, and she gave me another hug. "Great to see you *mon ami*. How do I find you?"

"You don't, at least not right now. I'm not even supposed to be alive, much less in Key West. Tell me where you are staying and I'll keep in touch," I answered.

"I'm renting a loft in an old Conch home at the corner of Eaton and Elizabeth. A retired dentist owns it and comes down to the Rock like twice a year, so I have the place more or less to myself. Big backyard and a pool. I amuse myself by looking lustfully at Julio the pool boy twice a week." And she smiled again. "Come by and see me sometime." And she turned and walked up the beach. Suddenly I had a thought.

"Wait!" I called. She turned around.

"What?"

"I'm working on something, sort of a rescue mission to help out some people. I'm starting to come up with a plan. Would you be interested in helping me? It might be interesting, and it could be a little dangerous." I smiled thinly. " Actually, it could be a lot dangerous." She walked back toward me.

"Maybe," she said. "How dangerous? Tell me about it."

"Not just yet" I answered. "I'm not sure I even want to get you involved. I'll come by in a few days and fill you in."

"What's the worst that could happen?" She said. "Last time I chatted with the docs my 'use by' date wasn't that far off anyway. I think that's how you and I are alike. We both need a little adrenalin rush to get us up in the morning."

"Do you have a driver's license?" I asked, changing the subject.

"International," she answered. "My Florida license was revoked after my fifth speeding ticket, but my International license is still valid. Why?"

"Just a thought," I said. "I'll talk to you later." She nodded and walked away.

I headed back to Casa 325. My message light was blinking. I retrieved the message and heard Karen's voice.

"Hi, it's me. Thanks for the invite, but I think I'll stay up here for a while. Maybe I need a little space and time, and maybe you need to get away and breathe for a while. Enjoy Key West. I'll talk to you soon. Hugs."

And she hung up.

I wasn't sure how to take that. It sounded like somewhere between "here's a hall pass" and "go fuck yourself." I guess I'll never figure out women. I mentally shrugged and crawled into bed for some TV and eventually dozed off. Like about every other night in my life, the dreams came; vivid, manic, and in Technicolor. Sometimes I would wake up after a full night's sleep needing a rest. In my dream tonight, I was running from the law after committing some sort of terrible crime. I had buried a body in the basement and thought I'd gotten away with it, but they kept coming to my house asking questions like they knew the truth. Suddenly I was hiding in a room where I thought nobody could find me and then there was a soft knock at the door. I ignored it. They knocked again, and again, this time, harder. Suddenly I realized the knocking was real and not in my dream. I lay there for another moment, and there was another knock. I got up and pulled on a pair of shorts and went to the peephole. The blonde pixie haircut of either Lex or Mary was visible through the little glass. I opened the door a crack and was suddenly enveloped in a five-foot, nine-inch tall sobbing girl, wearing a pair of fuck-me heels, a short silk wrap, and apparently nothing else.

"I'm so scared!" Lex sobbed, holding on to me with both arms. "They tried to drug me; they were going to try and take me away!"

I held her for a moment and then slowly untangled her. "Here, sit down. Let me get you a bottle of water." I said.

"Do you have something stronger?" she asked.

"I don't keep liquor in the place," I lied. "It's a little too much temptation for my old bad habits." She nodded and sat down, and I got water out of the fridge. I sat down on the other chair facing her.

"Ok, tell me what happened."

Lex shuddered. "So I did my first dance at about eleven. Lots of tips. I'm good." She gave a half smile. "Afterward in the dressing room, two managers came back. It's like any other place I've worked. The owners just barge into the back room unannounced whether you are dressed or not. You just deal with it." She took another sip of water. "They had European accents, and they told me how good I was, and that they had big plans for me. They asked if I was busy after we closed at two, and that they had a 'private party' I could 'dance' at and make some real money. I told them I had something to do tomorrow and needed to go home." She shuddered again. "One of them left the room and the other one kind of lowered his voice and told me that extra work was part of what was required to have a job there. Then the other one came back in with a drink and gave it to me. I said I don't drink on the job, and he said that drinking with the customers was also a requirement. I sat it down, untouched, and he said 'Drink it!' I threw the glass on the floor."

She started to cry.

"And then?" I asked.

They both said they would deal with me shortly and to not plan on going back on stage, and then walked out of the room. As soon as they did, I climbed out through a back window, slid down the roof jumped into the alley, and came here."

"Dressed like that on Duval?" I asked.

"I didn't have a choice. Hell, I saw people wearing less than this on the way here."

"You have a point," I answered. "So, your career as a stripper has just ended," I said. Monday you can start looking for a position as a server. Might not pay as much but at least, you will live through the night."

She nodded. "I'm afraid. I don't want to go back to my place. Can I just stay here tonight?"

"Sure," I answered and got up and walked toward the bedroom. She got up and started to follow, but I met her at the door with a pillow and a blanket.

"Couch is all yours, kid. Sweet dreams." And I closed the door.

Wayne Gales

20
Moonlight Madness

Things were starting to come together for the twins. A few days later I helped Lex get a job behind the bar at A&B Lobster. Good tips and a somewhat more civilized clientele. She struggled with the conservative outfit the managers required but succeeded in wearing shorts that were a little tight and a blouse that gapped enough between the buttons to reveal some well-tanned cleavage. The goon squad either hadn't figured out where she went or had turned to more cooperative or at least less resistant victims. *Of course, it might have had a little to do with me paying a visit to the club late one night to convince them that she wasn't worth the potential pain.*

With a little help from Rumpy, Mary had landed with the new Florida Key's tabloid, the *Conch Crier* as the City Editor. For me, I was worried that Karen hadn't called again or come down, but not overly concerned. If she needed space, so be it. I was sleeping a lot during the day and hanging out in the shadows at night, trying to get my arms around this white slavery thing. It was pretty obvious there was a lot more street action in town than when I lived here before. The cops either weren't catching on, had better things to do, or were in on the action. I hadn't heard back from Ludmilla yet on when the next "shipment" was scheduled to arrive.

Why care? Maybe because I was bored, maybe because I had watched a nine-year-old child in Bangkok turning tricks before she had gone through puberty, giving five-dollar blowjobs in back alleys covered with bruises and scars from abuse by her pimp, slowing dying from drug addiction, knowing if she survived the abuse, she would die from Aids. That vision has stuck in my mind ever since, and seeing these young girls in a similar situation with nobody to save them, nowhere to run, and no place to hide, called me to take action. Right now I'm watching, but eventually, I'll need to do something.

Then things started to develop. I came in late one night and found a note slipped under the door.

One sentence.

Tuesday night, Moonlight Madness, fourteen newcomers.

That was tomorrow. I slept all day, got up late in the afternoon, dressed in my best tourist outfit, and headed to Schooner Wharf. Learning my lesson, I sat on the other side of the bar, far from the bandstand, and nursed an order of peel-and-eat shrimp and a few beers, watching the *Moonlight Madness* docked across the harbor. At about five p.m. in the gathering dusk, the crew boarded the boat, followed by a half dozen people, all men. I paid my tab and walked over to the catamaran. With a little bit of a drunk swagger, I approached the gangplank. Rough-looking crew. In my best cockney accent, I called; "Ev'nen gents, is it boarding time?" The whole crew and passengers all froze and turned to face me.

"Private charter." One of the crew said in a thick accent.

I reached into my pocket and pulled out a piece of paper, which happened to be my Schooner Wharf tab, waving it in the air. "No, mates, I've a ticket for a sunset cruise," and started to board. A bulky guy in a dirty shirt blocked the entrance. "Not on this boat," he said. "Private."

"Aww, c'mon mate" I slurred my voice a little. "Tripadvisor says this is the best booze cruise in Key West. I can't leave without a trip on the *Danger*."

"This not *Danger Charters*. *Danger* is at Westin Marina." He pointed toward Mallory Square. "That way."

I looked at the receipt, pretending it was a boarding pass. "Ah, there you go matey. Looks like I got the wrong boat. Sorry about that gents! I'm off! Cheers!" and I wobbled off down the street, then turned right and doubled back to the White Tarpon for another beer and a dozen fresh oysters. I realized that if I sat there and nursed beers until that boat showed back up, I would be shit-faced drunk, so I headed back to the Casa for a little TV and a catnap. About eleven, I changed into darker clothes and wandered back down to the marina, took a seat at the Conch Republic, and ordered iced tea. Eleven thirty. Twelve. Twelve thirty. The crowd was starting to thin out, and my bladder had absorbed about as much tea as possible when I saw the dark shape of a sailboat emerge around the breakwater. The *Moonlight Madness* pulled into the slip, obviously with more people than they left with, just as Ludmilla promised. A dozen or so girls, all dressed in flowery tourist colors were sitting, subdued and quiet. It looked like a strange way to end a booze cruise, but by that time of night, the customers at the Conch Republic were all too hammered to notice.

One of the crew said something to them, and they all rose and walked off the boat. None of them were wearing shoes, and all looked pretty scared and confused. Two vans pulled up in the circular driveway at the Conch Republic. The girls got in one van and the crew and "passengers" in the other, and they drove off. I noticed Ludmilla was driving one van.

By chance, I saw Ludmilla walking down Duval by Aqua a few days later. I was hanging out across the street, watching one of the girls work the crowd out in front without much luck, as the regulars were mostly gay, and the tourists were couples. Ludmilla happened to glance in my direction, and I tipped my hat toward her. She recognized me and, without drawing attention, motioned for me to follow. I ambled down the street, staying on the other side of Duval and several yards behind. She ducked into the Walgreens located in the old Strand Theater. I crossed over and stepped inside, wandering the aisles until I saw her by the feminine products. She was adding various items to her basket; I walked up and turned my back to get a few medical items. Never know when you might need a Band-Aid. I just hoped I didn't need one to plug a sucking chest wound soon. Ludmilla spoke in a quiet stage whisper behind me.

"I told some of the girls there is a person that wants to help," she started. "How are you going to do this?"

I didn't have a plan yet. I just planned to make one up as developments, well, develop, but I didn't let her know that.

"I'll take one at a time. Tell them to look for a man with a reddish beard. I will use the code word 'Marathon'. They will answer with your name. I'll give them instructions as to what to do next." I looked over my shoulder. "I'm not going to tell you how I'm getting them off the island, or where they are going." (*Hell, I didn't know myself just yet*) "That will protect you, them, and me in case something goes wrong. Got it?"

"Understand," she said. "Marathon. My Name. Okay." She

finished her shopping and started to walk to the cashier, then stopped as if to look at a hat. "No more meetings. People are watching us all of the time now. Good luck." And she walked away.

That was the last time I would ever see her.

Flashback - February 12, 1923, Islamorada

Adolph skipped church the following week, and when Mary noticed Adolph she motioned him to come over. "Mister Wahl, I would like to introduce you to my husband, Thomas Sawyer. Tom, Mister Wahl is the new line foreman and has been kind enough to do a few handyman projects around the house."

They shook hands and sized each other up. The muscular German was nearly a foot taller and ten years older than Sawyer, who was slender, with a thin mustache and greased back hair. Wahl seemed amazed that this poor specimen had managed to land a wife as stunning as Mary.

"Mary told me you had come over and helped with some maintenance. I'll be happy to pay you for your time, Mister Wahl," Sawyer said.

"No, please, it's not a problem," Adolph replied. "Joseph Russell asked me to lend a hand, and I'm more than happy to. After all, Joseph has been very helpful in getting me situated here in Islamorada. It's the least I could do for his niece."

"I would feel better if payment was sent to your home," Sawyer said, stiffly. Will three dollars suffice?" Wahl nodded, sensing the tension between the two.

Sawyer left the following day on the morning train to Miami. Two weeks later the hinges arrived by U.S. Mail, along with another package from Sears. As promised, after his days' work, Adolph grabbed a few tools and walked down the tracks to the Sawyer house. He knocked on the door, but no answer. He shrugged and walked around to the back of the house. Doors in the middle Florida Keys were never locked, and he let himself in, sat the other parcel on the table, and started making repairs. Fifteen minutes later he heard the front door open.

"Mrs. Sawyer, it's Al! I'm fixing your door!" he shouted.

"Just let yourself in, did you?" she asked.

"I, I, I'm sorry. I just thought….."

Mary laughed. "Of course, it's alright. I was just poking fun at you. I'm glad you're here. I just spent a boring afternoon quilting with the Ladies Church Auxiliary. I swear that pack of hens can talk your head off. I need some more pleasant conversation. Are you finished?"

"Almost. Just hanging the door back on now," he replied.

"Wonderful. Perhaps you will join me for a beverage after," she said. He grunted in agreement as he lifted the door and tapped in both hinge pins.

"There," he said. "Good as new!" He walked toward the kitchen but Mary was not there, and the package was gone.

"Just a moment!" she called from behind the bedroom door. "The day is far too nice to be underneath all of these petticoats." A moment later the door opened, and Mary walked out. Adolph was stunned. Mary was wearing a salmon-colored dress, short, just below the knee, bare-shouldered and sequined, with a deep plunging neckline and nearly nothing underneath. She twirled around in the middle of the room. "Like it?" she asked. "I saw it in the Roebuck catalog when I was ordering the hinges. It's the latest fashion from Chicago. It's called the Flapper dress!"

"It's beautiful," Adolph answered. "But I don't know how it will be received at the Sunday Church picnic."

"Oh heavens, I would never wear it there," she quipped. "I doubt anyone beyond Key West would dare walk outdoors in it, but I just had to have it. It cost nine dollars and came with a hat." She twirled around again in her bare feet and danced to the icebox. "Let me make you that drink. Please sit down. I'll make us some Planters Punch." Adolph sat down at the little dining table. Mary got a pitcher from the cupboard and juice from the ice box. She added some clear syrup, grenadine, and a few squirts of seltzer, then reached into the back of the pantry and brought out an earthenware jug. "Dark Rum," she said. "We get it from our Bahamian relatives when they visit." She poured a generous portion of the rum into the pitcher, hesitated, and poured a little more with a giggle. "I just can't stand drinking alone, and I don't dare drink with Tom. He can't hold a drop of liquor." Mary chipped some ice off the block into two glasses and poured them full. "Cheers!" she said. Adolph took a sip. It was like nothing he had drank before, sweet and fruity, and very strong. He preferred beer, but this was tasty, and so was the company. They chatted for a while, and he finished his drink. He began to stand. Mary said, "Please don't go! We have lots of punch left and the evening to pass. You have to wait until it's dark now so you don't cause a scandal walking out of my house at dusk in plain view." Adolph shrugged and held out his glass. "I'm an honorable gentleman, Mrs. Sawyer, but I'm not a fool. Pour away!"

· She stood, already a little wobbly, and reached for the pitcher. Adolph jumped up to help her and she turned toward him. The first kiss was schoolboy awkward, but the second had better aim. His hand slid down her back and confirmed she was indeed nude under the dress. He finished the kiss, scooped her up in his muscular arms, and strode toward the bedroom.

It wasn't the dusk he was worried about now; it was the following dawn he would need to avoid.

Wayne Gales

21
Hatching a Plan

After a few days at the library pouring over the internet, I came up with a possible plan. The next morning I packed a small bag, had breakfast at Two Friends then walked over to Rio's place. I knocked on the front door, no answer, and walked around back and looked over the fence. Her scooter was sitting there, so I went through the gate into the yard and banged on the back door. Still no response. Nothing I could do but sit on the steps and wait. Two hours later I heard a door open and out she walked, naked with a towel over her shoulder. She jumped when she saw me and then recognized who it was.

"Come here often?" She asked, and walked past me, towel still over her shoulder.

"Just for the floor show," I answered. I then saw her destination, an outdoor shower underneath the stairs. She turned the water on, got wet, lathered up, and rinsed while I watched. The huge tattoo of the Tree of Life on her flat chest glimmered in the morning sunshine as if it were a real oak. Rio was beautiful in her own way, graceful, and comfortable in her skin. I waited for her to dry off, and she wrapped the towel around her waist, sat on the bench next to the stairs, topless, and lit a joint. After a few minutes, I broke the silence.

"I told you I was working on a little rescue project." I started and filled her in on the details. "Do you want to help me?"

"*Oui, monsieur*, most certainly. How do we do this?"

"We start with a little trip," I answered. Care to take a bus ride with me? Probably be gone three or four days."

"When?" She asked.

"Bus leaves at noon. We need to get moving."

"Give me five minutes," she said and went inside. Fifteen minutes later she emerged, wearing shorts, a gray tank top, sandals, sunglasses, and swinging a knit purse.

"You travel light," I observed.

"Toothbrush, my pills, and associated supportive medication. Enough to last for a few days. Who needs more?"

The Greyhound bus leaves from the Key West airport. We strolled over to Simonton Street and hailed a cab. An hour later we were riding up the keys on the bus and four hours after that we were in Homestead. We jumped in a cab at the bus station and told the driver to take us to the nearest used car dealer. By dark, we were motoring north in a late-model windowless Dodge cargo van. I paid for it with my Amex and had it registered to Rio, or more accurately, to Ms. Sabine Annette Ponsette of Key West.

I never knew her last name, or for that matter, her middle name until then.

We made one more stop along the way to buy a couple of throw-away cell phones and a couple of bean bag chairs at Wal-Mart. I was getting tired of zero communication. It was time to get back to the present. The first call was to Faro Blanco, and I asked for my room. I left a message for Karen, gave her my number, and told her I was off the island on business for a few days. When we stopped for gas, I got back in the passenger seat. "You need to get used to this barge," I said.

"Where to?"

"Drive north on 95 for three hours. Melbourne."

I was positive that Rio couldn't be as much of a juggernaut in a four thousand pound van as she was on a fifty c.c. scooter. I quickly realized I was wrong - she was twice as crazy. She buried her foot into the floorboard and shot up on the turnpike, hitting almost ninety and using all three lanes and occasionally the shoulder, to pass traffic, all of which seemed to be virtually parked. A life of combat, commando, Navy SEAL, deep water tech dives, shootouts, and hurricanes, and this was the first time in my life I was genuinely scared. It occurred to me that we would either be in Melbourne in an hour and a half, in jail, or lying on a stone slab at the county coroner with a toe tag attached.

"Ah, care to take it down to a little below light speed? I want to live through the night, and we don't need to be stopped right now." Rio didn't answer but eased off the pedal a micron, backing

202

off to a leisurely eighty-five. My fear level also backed off to just slightly below stark raving terrified for the next hour or so. When we stopped in Fort Pierce for gas, I dove for the steering wheel.

Enough of that for sure.

We got off U.S. 95 at Highway 192. It was a little after two a.m. I pulled into the Holiday Inn and got a room. "Two beds, two keys," I told the front desk agent. Taking a key, Rio turned toward the entrance. "I'm going outside for a smoke. See you up there,"

I went to the room, stripped, and was asleep before I hit the sheets. I never heard Rio come in, but when I woke up a few hours later; she was in bed with me, arm around my waist, nude, spooned up, and sound asleep. I thought of Karen and considered moving to the other bed, but she was asleep. I didn't want to disturb her and, well, it felt good.

What the Hell.

The next morning we checked out and went to breakfast at the Blueberry Muffin on A1A. She looked up over a mouthful of pancakes with her coffee cup in hand.

"What now?" She asked. "And why this little town?"

"I saw a story on the news about a guy that runs a mission here. Pastor Dave Jordan. He helps the homeless but has a particular focus on helping prostitutes get off the streets. He gets them back together with their families, helps them with drug problems, like getting them methadone maintenance, and in at least one case, helped get a girl repatriated back to her home in Eastern Europe. I thought he might be a possible pipeline for these girls in Key West."

I got a copy of the local paper and checked the classifieds. I didn't see anything that looked like what I was looking for. Also nothing in the phone book. How was I going to find this guy? Ah. The best way to find someone who helps the homeless? Find a homeless person. We crossed back over the Intracoastal on Highway 192 and into downtown Melbourne. Like almost every other city in Florida, the term "downtown" was a loose description of what made up Melbourne a hundred years ago. Now it's a sprawling community of strip malls and trailerhoods, choked in traffic and blue-haired grandmas in minivans, all hell-bent for the nearest Walmart. The old main street, East New Haven Avenue, had been resurrected from a tired avenue of consignment shops and dingy cafes to a trendy block of upscale shopping zones and fun nightspots. I ignored New Haven and turned down the alley behind the street. It didn't take a minute to find a bag lady pushing a shopping cart down the alley. I stopped and rolled down the window, holding out a twenty. She looked at me suspiciously.

"I'm looking for Pastor Dave," I said, holding out the money. She hesitated and then snatched the bill out of my hand. She pointed south and mumbled through toothless gums.

"East Melbourne Avenue. Two blocks and turn right. White church." She scurried away, pushing her cart, anxious to get out of sight before I asked for the twenty back.

We found Dave at his office. I expected a kindly old man in a black frock and white collar and was surprised to find a thirtyish, very good-looking guy with a wedding ring on his finger, wearing a Ron-Jon surfer shirt, blue jeans, and Sperry topsiders. We made introductions, and I briefed him on my plans.

"How many girls?" he asked.

"Probably, at least, a dozen, and maybe twice that many. I don't know how many I'll be able to get out of Key West before they figure out who and how."

"A dozen all at once will tax my resources, but yes, I'll take every girl you drop at my door. We'll figure out a way to take care of them."

I pulled out my wallet and counted bills. "All I have in cash is a thousand." I handed the money over. "I'll have Rio bring more when she comes up." Then I thought of something. "Wait. I have one more item you might be able to use." I reached into my jacket pocket and brought out a purple Crowne Royal bag,

"I was supposed to throw these off a bridge a long time ago and never did. I don't know if they have brought me good luck or bad luck. I guess it depends on how you look at it, but it will probably do you more good than it's doing me," and I handed him the bag. The pastor opened the bag and looked inside, then whistled. He poured out the emeralds onto his desk. Raw, uncut, some poor quality, but several perfect. "Find a jeweler in town. Give him a story that it was an anonymous donation to the church. I'm not sure how much you can get for them, but I suspect it will be substantial." Dave hesitated.

"Are they stolen?" he asked. "I can't touch them if they are stolen goods."

"They were recovered from a three-hundred-year-old shipwreck," I answered. "I split part of the treasure with the company I was working for. Sort of a finder's fee. These were part of the treasure." I decided that was as much of the story as I wanted to share. It was the truth, but not exactly all the truth. He accepted my story without comment and pocketed the bag of emeralds, nodding thanks.

"Wait," I said. Looking at the stones on the table, I selected the largest and clearest emerald. Putting it in my shirt pocket, I explained. "I lost the other one in the wreck. I need this in case a certain person says yes someday." Rio scowled and turned away for a moment.

We parted with one final instruction. "Don't tell anyone these kids are from Key West. If anyone asks, just say they walked in the door. That's to protect them, you and us." Pastor Dave agreed, and twenty minutes later we were back on 95 headed south.

Rio sat in silence for nearly an hour before she spoke. "Bric, when you were talking to the pastor, you said 'until they find out who and how.' What happens to you when they do?" I drove on for a while before I answered. I think she was starting to believe I was just ignoring her. I finally answered.

"I don't plan on them finding out 'who.' It's a small advantage of being a dead guy. I'm hard to track down, and I will have no remorse in making some of these guys go away. After all, dead men tell no tales."

Rio looked at me, maybe in a different way than she ever had. "You have killed people?"

"I was in an elite combat group in the Navy," I answered, somewhat evasively. "Sometimes you have to kill bad people to save good ones." She chewed on that for a while and then answered.

"I don't think you are telling me the whole story." I thought about how to answer that for a while longer and then decided not to. We drove in silence all the way back to Key West. I parked the van

205

on Simonton Street by Rio's place.

"Keep the van here," I said. "That is if you are still in." I turned toward her.

"I need to know you are okay with this. Look, this isn't your fight. If it's outside your comfort level. I understand. I can get someone else to make those trips or I can do it myself." She answered quietly.

"Yes, I'm still in. Just sometimes I'm not sure you are telling me what the real story is."

I pulled the keys out and handed them to her. "Baby, sometimes I feel the same way. If I'm holding anything back, it's to protect you, not to keep you in the dark." I gave her a hug. "Keep the phone handy. I'll call you in a few days."

I opened the door, got out, and walked back down Truman Avenue.

I chose the following Saturday night to attempt my first rescue. I called Rio and told her to stage the van in the public parking lot on Peritonea at Duval by the Bourbon Street Pub at about eleven p.m. I figured I would start at the 801 Club and work my way up the street. Dressed in a loud floral print shirt, cargo pants, beret, and cheap sunglasses, I barhopped my way up Duval Street for an hour or so. A little after midnight, I made it as far as La Te Da and was about ready to call it a night, when I saw a prospect sitting on a barstool. Toothpick legs, sticking out of oversized shorts, tank top, and lots of makeup. I took the stool next to her and nodded hello. She responded in a European accent and it only took a minute to get a proposition out of her. "Want to party?" That's the classic "I fuck for money" code. "Yeah, maybe, where's the party at?" I said.

"Right around the corner," she answered. "Just you and me."

I gave her a silly grin and decided to try what Ludmilla and I had worked out.

"Sure, nothing like this ever happens in Marathon." She froze in her tracks and stared at me. "You're the guy Ludmilla told us about. You just want to take me out of here so you can put me to work someplace else."

"No, I want to get you out of here so you can go home."

"Mister, this is Hell, but home is a worse Hell. I'm from

206

Kosovo." She slid off the seat. "I will pass on your offer, but I'll tell the girls you sound legit. She started to walk away and then turned around. "You know they will kill you if they find you doing this."

"You gonna turn me in?" I asked.

"They are monsters. I don't fucking care if you kill them all." And with that, she turned down Duval Street into the dark.

I was puzzled. I just thought these women would jump at the chance to be rescued, but here's one that didn't. Am I wasting my time?

I walked up to Petronia and found Rio napping in the van. I slapped the side of the door with an open palm, and she woke with a start. "Let me in. No joy tonight." She started the motor, and we drove down Duval toward Front Street. Even though it was well past midnight, the party crowd was at full song, and every bar you drove past poured out the sounds of live music and over-served customers. I was a little bummed. It was starting to look like nobody wanted to hide behind Superman's cape.

Then, luck took a turn for the better. We were at the light at Greene and Duval in front of Sloppy Joes, and a girl walked up to the passenger side of the van. "Looking for a good time?" she asked.

"Sure!" I said and then thought 'Oh what the hell, nothing to lose.'

"Can you party as good as the girls in Marathon?" Her head jerked toward me, and then she said one word.

"Ludmilla."

I reached back and opened the side door. "Get in," and she jumped in back, pulling the door behind her. We had a few beanbag chairs on the floor of the van, and she plopped down on one. "What now?" she asked. I pointed to my driver.

"This is Sabine. She's going to take you someplace where you will be safe. It's a long drive. Nobody will know where you are." I turned to Rio. "All set?"

"Yep," she said. "I have the cash you gave me, and I know where I'm going."

"Do me a favor," I said. Don't try to set the land speed record. Stay inside the speed limit and be cool. See you in a couple of days."

207

I leaned over to give her a peck on the cheek, and she turned toward me, grabbed the back of my neck, and gave me a long, hard kiss, with just a hint of tongue.

"For luck!" she said and hardly waited till I was out in the street before she barreled off down Duval, making a right on Front Street, nearly on two wheels, and out of sight.

One down.

Wayne Gales

Flashback - April 1, 1923, Islamorada

The affair went on for nearly two months. Adolph waited till late in the evening and then walked quietly down the tracks, loitering when he saw other people out for a stroll. He lingered till shortly before dawn and made it back to his shack before the town was up and about, taking one of the winding paths that crisscrossed the island. The sneaking around was necessary to keep the affair discreet, but it didn't fool a single soul in town. Adolph had stopped going to Sunday services and wasn't there when Mary announced to all that when her husband had last visited two months ago, he had left her with child. Nobody in Islamorada cared for Thomas Sawyer. His Key West family was wealthy, and they felt he flaunted his stature to the public while forcing his wife to live in a rundown shack. Although the community felt it was more than likely the baby wasn't Sawyers, they kept the gossip to themselves. Mary told Adolph the next time he visited and confirmed he had to be the father. "How do you know?" He asked. "Because that worthless husband of mine stayed drunk every night he was here," she said. "He possessed neither the ability to perform nor the memory that he didn't." She held him close. "Oh Al, I should so like to tell the world the baby is yours and kick that worthless souse to the street, but his high and mighty Key West family would surely cause such a fuss. Nothing good could come of it, so the secret must remain ours alone."

Seven months later Mary gave birth to a blonde-haired, hazel-eyed boy who she rather brazenly named John Albert Sawyer. The father was away on a ship, and the boy was five months old before he saw him for the first time. Adolph and Mary continued their liaison, but less frequently, and a supply of condoms purchased in Key West ensured there would be no more surprises. The town kept their collective heads turned the other way, and as little Johnny Sawyer grew old enough to know, Adolph stopped visiting altogether. Just as the affair grew to a quiet end and the economy began to slow, Thomas Sawyer lost his maritime job and came home to stay. Adolph returned to attending Sunday Services and picnics.

Ten more years slipped away.

The Florida Keys prospered during the roaring twenties, even though the Florida East Coast Railroad didn't. In fact, the railroad never saw a truly profitable year from the day it opened. When the stock market crashed in 1929, the economy collapsed and by 1931, the population of Key West had dwindled to less than half. In 1934, Key West and Monroe County, once one of the largest and richest cities in Florida, went bankrupt and made itself first a ward of the state of Florida, and eventually of the United States Government.

Adolph's bank account at the First National Bank, which had grown to nearly four thousand dollars over the years, vanished in a single day when the bank declared itself insolvent and closed its doors. Adolph shrugged with indifference. It was gone, but he still had a job, a roof over his head, and food on the table. That was better than most could say. The railroad chugged along, so to speak, albeit a little inconsistently. America was in love with the automobile and in an act of Congress, President Franklin D Roosevelt and the Federal Government had funded the construction of a highway between Miami and Key West, intending to employ World War I veterans. Camps were set up in two locations down the islands, one at Windley Key and the other on the beach at the foot of Lower Matecumbe Key next to the ferry dock. More camps were built, nothing more than tent cities, until over a thousand veterans were housed to work on the highway project. While a plan was created in theory, to quickly evacuate them should a storm approach, there was little or no true organization to implement it. It was a catastrophe waiting to happen,

In 1935, Key West had a population of over twelve thousand, but fewer than one thousand people were scattered between Key West and the mainland. Across those islands, there were only two communities with electricity; one in Tavernier and one in Marathon. The rest of the keys were without power and nighttime found the residents of the tiny community of Islamorada using their kerosene lanterns. The railroad was looked upon by residents on the mainland as the economic savior for the keys, but island people had a different opinion. Despite better transportation and a source for shipping produce, the locals eyed all the causeways that had been built for the railroad to save money. Unlike bridges, which allowed tidal water to flow freely from Florida Bay to the Atlantic Ocean, the solid causeways, some as much as thirteen feet high, were nothing more than giant dikes. Their fear that the inevitable hurricane would cause water to pile up on the causeways until it would "drown us like rats." Little did they know this concern was about to become a prophecy fulfilled.

Old Ice House near Schooner Wharf –

Jimmy Buffet's Studio

22
Almost Busted

A week later, we were back on the streets, this time at Schooner Wharf. Rio parked the van on Greene Street by the Conch Republic Seafood Company, and I walked around the wharf, past the old ice house that currently houses Jimmy Buffet's occasional recording studio, and took a seat near the water with my back to the boats so I could scan the crowd. Two beers and a basket of shrimp later and the girl I had made first contact with wandered in. Ten feet behind her was a dude who made a good body double for Mister Clean.

Bald, an earring in one ear, and a lot of muscles bulging under a white tee shirt. A body builder no doubt. She took a seat at one end of the bar, and Mister Clean sat down on the other side. The same bartender that served her before made her a drink without asking and did the same for the guy. She lit a cigarette and was trying to strike up conversations with the bar crowd, flipping her hair and showing lots of leg. The local regulars were ignoring her – they knew the act, and so far, I didn't see any tourists rise to the bait. I was concerned that she had an escort. I didn't want to create a ruckus and definitely didn't want someone who could go back to the crib with my description. I was ready to bail when she saw me. Like before, she slid off the barstool letting the skirt ride up past her thighs, and made her way to my table, stumbling while trying to walk on gravel in four-inch platform heels. She stopped in front of me and held out a cigarette.

"Got a light?" She asked.

"Don't smoke," I answered. I might have a book of matches in my car." And I hooked a thumb over my shoulder.

"Let's go get them, handsome." And she walked past me down the wharf. I was paid up, and I dropped a few bucks on the table for a tip and caught up with her in a few steps.

"Want out?" I asked.

"One girl is missing," she answered without turning toward me while we walked. "They don't know where she went, but all of us

215

have escorts now, at least part of the time. Dennis will be following us." I reached into my pocket and accidentally dropped my wallet on the sidewalk. When I bent over to pick it up I glanced behind me, and he was back there, standing with his hands in his pockets looking at a boat.

"Does he have a gun?" I asked.

"No, just his bare hands. He is very strong and very mean." She took my hand. "I want to get away, but I don't think you can do it right now. He will kill you if you try."

"Let me worry about that," I answered. We walked past the Sebago, and Rio saw us from her seat at the Conch Republic. She started to jump up, and I motioned her to sit back down with a low wave. She looked puzzled, then shrugged her shoulders and sat down. I turned toward the van, and she held up her hand waving the keys. I nodded and winked, hopefully without the goon behind us noticing, and turned away from the restaurant. The pay parking lot on Greene is small, tree-lined, and pretty dark. The van was parked in the corner of the lot, and I walked the girl around to the right side.

"Let's wait here for a moment. We can pretend we're getting intimate." I thought for a second. "You know, I never asked for your name."

"Yuri. My name is Yuri."

I turned to my right and Mister Clean was standing there, two feet away. I turned to face him. "Hey buddy, I didn't know this was your girlfriend. She didn't tell me she was with anyone."

"Not girlfriend. You pay her. I wait outside of van to make sure she is safe."

I looked stunned. "She's a prostitute? My heavens I didn't know that. Look, this is all a mistake. This isn't even my car." I turned my pockets inside out, and both were empty, except the key that fell back out on the street. I bent down again to pick it up, figuring I had one shot to land the first punch. As expected, he took a step towards me and as I stood up, I launched a stiff finger punch right into his windpipe. He grabbed his throat with both hands, and I reached up, caught the side of his head, and slammed it into the side of the van. He went down on one knee, and I gave him a quick kick in the face and then slammed his head on the back bumper of the Dodge. That pretty well took the fight out of him. Yuri backed up and instinctively screamed, and suddenly the whole side of the van was bathed in blinding light. "Stay right there," a voice said over a speaker. Oh shit. Talk about bad luck. I take a guy out right while a cop car is cruising by. I put my hands out to my side and called over my shoulder. "You better call an ambulance. This guy just slipped on a pile of dog shit and bumped his head."

By now we had a crowd gathering, two more cops showed up, and an ambulance. I was shitting donuts figuring my cousin, Officer John Russell would show up, and there would be a whole lot of explaining to do, being he attended my funeral a year earlier, but, fortunately, it was a couple of young kids that didn't know me. The guy wasn't dead, which was a good thing and a bad thing. They took my statement, decided I just defended myself from an assault, and were a little impressed that this bearded senior citizen managed to bitch slap the hoodlum.

"Do you have any guns, Mr. Phillips?"

"No sir. I don't believe in guns. They should take everyone's gun away like they do in England."

"Any knives?"

"Knives? Heaven's no, officer. Heck, I get faint trying to stab the little plastic straw into a juice box."

They finally let all of us go, and the crowd went back to drinking. I signaled to Rio that the party was over, and she came to the van. I put Yuri in the back and gave Rio some extra cash.

"Before you come back, make sure this is a blue van. When Baldy wakes up, he's gonna be pissed, and he's gonna be looking for a dude in a white van." I reached into my other pocket and smiled at Yuri, handing her a roll of bills wrapped in a rubber band. "I figure you can use this more than your buddy did. I pulled it out of his pocket when he went down."

I walked back down Greene, stopping at Sloppy Joes for a beer and watched Pete and Wayne sing "Looking to Breed in Boca," then headed down the block and back to Casa 325. I needed a shower but just headed toward the bedroom for sleep. I didn't even notice the person sitting in the easy chair in the dark corner of the room.

I was unarmed, and if this person had a gun, I was also dead.

Then she spoke.

"I believe this is where I came in."

Karen

"Looks like you have been busy tonight. I assume all the flashing lights and sirens over on Greene Street have something to do with you?"

"Yeah," I answered. "I sort of got jumped by a bad guy."

Karen stood up. "I think it's a little more than that," she said. "I've been reading the papers for the past few days and figured out you were back at it again. Bric, I'm done. Why can't you just live your life? Every time I turn around, people are chasing us, people dying, running for our lives, hiding. I'm through with this game. You want to be Batman, Superman, Robin Hood, Dick Tracy, and all four Beatles. I let you run off to Key West for a few weeks to see if you could get this silliness out of your system with that little trollop Lex, and I find you with someone completely different, and God knows how many corpses in your wake." Karen walked toward the door. "Whoever your new girlfriend is, good luck with this one. He's a runaway train. For me, I'm done being an extra in a Tom Clancy novel. I'm going back to Oklahoma. Keep the money, it's been nothing but pain and sorrow since the day we found it."

And she walked out.

I stared blankly at the door for a moment. What I said was too late for her to hear.

"I love you, Karen."

As convenient as Casa 325 was to me, every day I was there the more I put myself and people around me in danger. I told Rio about Karen confronting me and the visits from Ludmilla. "I think it's too easy for people to find you," she said. "Next time you walk in, and someone's already in the room it might not be a friend. It's time to move." I agreed.

"Yes, but where?" I said. It's so easy to come and go from here in the dark, and nobody notices my apparel changes. It won't be so easy at a regular hotel."

"Then don't go to a hotel. Why don't you move in with me?" She suggested. "I can stand outside the gate and let you know when it's clear. Nobody will ever know where you are. It's perfect. And besides," she added. "I'm lonely." I looked up at that. With Karen out of the picture, was Rio claiming turf that quickly? She was staring directly at me in her matter-of-fact way. Regardless, once I thought it over, I knew it was a good idea. It was either that or moving back into a van, an alternative that I didn't relish.

"Okay, Rio. We're roomies again. At least this boat doesn't leak."

She smiled.

It wasn't bad. Rio's place would make a phone booth look spacious, and the corners and crannies were a constant danger to clip your head when you walked from room to room, but it was definitively safe and well hidden. The old man that owned the place showed up maybe three times a year, and since he didn't have a phone, dropped a postcard to give a few weeks warning he would be down. Rio was the perfect house sitter, never venturing beyond her little flat, aside from using that precious outdoor shower and sunning on the old wooden chaise lounges in the backyard. We avoided splinters by spreading a big beach towel on the wood, and, never wore a stitch.

I guess Rio and I more or less entered into a physical relationship without a formal commitment. She had a double bed in the tiny apartment. I was a guy; she was a girl. Stuff happened. You never know how such things develop. I didn't know if it was going to be mechanical, missionary, and self-gratifying, or if it would be off-the-leash monkey sex, swinging from the rafters, screaming orgasms, and weird positions. As it turned out, let's just say it was someplace between the two.

How does the song go? It's not love but it's not bad.

Flashback - Islamorada, August 31, 1935

Other than a storm that brushed by Key West in 1919, the chain of islands had been virtually tropical storm-free since the devastating hurricanes of 1906, 1909 and 1910. The majority of the young population in Islamorada had never experienced a storm. The Civilian Conservation Corp, mostly comprised of World War I veterans who were in the keys to work on the overseas highway, didn't even have a hint of the devastation a storm could create.

Adolph and the town's people first heard of a storm that had formed in the Bahamas by the FEC Stationmaster in Islamorada. The newly formed Weather Office in Miami issued a storm warning from Palm Beach to the Keys. People began to board up their houses, and families up and down the keys started to prepare, pulling boats into sheltered inlets, cooking and canning food, and collecting candles for what could be weeks or even months without resources. By late afternoon, the next weather report advised the small "Tropical Disturbance" had attained "considerable intensity" and was about sixty miles east of the Bahamas.

In the wee hours of Sunday, September 1, the Miami weather station compared barometric readings at his station to that of the office in Key West and was alarmed to see that the Key West readings were considerably lower. This meant the storm was closer to the keys. Along with the barometric readings, the locals were interpreting other signs that a storm was approaching. A hurricane's wind creates huge swells that overrun normal wave patterns. Residents in Islamorada noted that breakers, which normally come as frequently as twelve to fifteen per minute, had slowed to only three to five per minute. While not large, they were already larger than normal waves. Also, the skies were showing curved bands of wispy white cirrus clouds, and the sunset was spectacular.

The bathtub-warm waters of the Gulfstream between the Bahamas and the southern tip of Florida created the perfect scenario for the storm to strengthen. By late afternoon, fishing boats, enjoying a holiday weekend offshore from Miami started to run from the intensifying storm. Winds at the center of the storm had increased to eighty-five miles per hour, and the storm track had turned slightly to the north, a move that, without satellites and numerous weather stations, was totally unexpected.

It was two hundred miles from Islamorada. By seven p.m. the storm had slowed and turned even farther north and continued to gain strength. Sometime during this period, between the night of Sunday, September 1, and the afternoon of September 2, the storm underwent what is known today as Rapid Intensification. A combination of circumstances combined at the same time and place – exceptionally warm water, no wind shear, high pressure aloft, and no land with mountainous terrain – so that the hurricane turned from a minimal to a moderate storm to become one of the most powerful hurricanes ever to strike the United States, before or since.

The scene was set for disaster

When Sunday services at the Matecumbe Methodist church were completed, the worshippers gathered out in front, not for the Sunday picnic, but to discuss the bad weather that might be coming. They knew there was a lot of work to do, and families immediately went their separate ways to begin preparations. Adolph, the only member of the line crew that attended the church, walked back to his cottage and began putting loose items away. The sturdy storage shed next to the house, built with railroad ties and spikes was elevated nearly three feet off the ground was one of the strongest buildings on the island, and would be a good shelter if a blow came. The only weak spot on the shed was the door, an old door from some Conch house that had been demolished. He would need to look at ways to make that spot stronger. Adolph hauled a lot of loose items out of the shed to make space and brought them into the house, and returned with some blankets, rain gear, waders, his duffel bag with most of his clothes, and a large Thermos of hot coffee and what little canned food he had in the pantry. Realizing he may get wet, as a last thought, he took his gold watch and the twenty-dollar double eagle stuffing them deep inside the duffel bag. He suspected that gold coin had run out of luck anyway, Lastly, he made his way down the path toward the bay, where he checked the motor launch, making sure the tarpaulin was secure, and the heavy line was tied firmly to a palm tree.

After that, there wasn't much else to do but wait.

Monday morning, September second, 1935, dawned gray and windy. Adolph heard that a train would be sent south from Homestead to evacuate the veterans and citizens, but no train was available in Homestead and a train would have to be sent down from Miami later in the day. His house was just across the tracks but a good six feet lower in elevation, and less sturdy than the train depot. If the train didn't arrive to pick up the workers and citizens, he would resolve to ride out the storm there.

By one o'clock the winds began picking up, and Adolph noted the paper on the roof at the Islamorada train depot started peeling away. Branches and loose items began to fly around and he heard a window break in the distance.

Time to hunker down.

Wind is a deadly weapon during a hurricane. At seventy-four miles per hour, a man can lean into the wind and walk, but flying debris makes it dangerous to be outside. At a hundred and twenty, the wind can lift a man off the ground. This storm was destined to become much stronger. Adolph checked around his tiny house one more time to see if there was anything else he might need, then closed the door behind him and fought the wind and rain for the fifty feet between his house and the shed. Inside, he braced the door to the shed with a two-by-four and sat down on the little bench under a kerosene lantern hanging from a hook on the wall. The door had a small, four-pane window in it. Despite it giving some outside light, and also providing Adolph with a view of the storm outside, he would have been happier had the door been solid.

By four p.m., the winds were well over one hundred miles per hour, and the wind moaned against the shed while occasional thunder drowned out the pelting rain on the metal roof. Adolph was close enough to the tracks that he would easily be able to hear the rescue train, and he planned to abandon the shed the instant it arrived, provided the train was able to make it through the storm. As a line foreman, he was very aware that much of the right of way was only a few feet above sea level, and this much wind would probably flood and eventually undermine the tracks. He smiled grimly to himself. There would be a lot of work for his line crew after this.

Despite it being late summer, by six o'clock it was almost dark outside. He looked out the window toward the tracks and could see the little train depot was slowly coming apart. He couldn't see his house, but he was certain it was suffering a similar fate. The winds were getting stronger by the minute.

Still no rescue train.

Then he heard someone calling his name. Wondering who might be out in this weather, he opened the door to the shed and was surprised to see Mary at his nearly destroyed house next door. She was soaked to the skin. "Over here!" he called, and she ran through the downpour and up the steps.

"What in heaven's name are you doing out in this?" he asked.

"Adolph, it's terrible. Tom and Johnny went to Key West four days ago to visit family. Most of the roof on our house is gone and the windows have blown out. I didn't know where else to go, so I came here."

"You're soaked. Get out of those wet clothes." And he reached for one of the blankets he had brought over from the house. Mary pulled her dress over her head, hesitated for a moment, and peeled the wet slip off too. Wearing only a camisole, lace panties, and shoes, Adolph wrapped the blanket around her and cleared a spot on the bench where she could sit. He hung the clothes on a nail by the door. In the damp humidity, it was not likely they would dry soon.

"Any word on a train to get us out of here?" she asked.

"It's supposed to be on the way from Miami, but I don't know if it will get through. It depends on where the storm will hit."

"From what I can tell, it's hitting here," she answered, shivering.

"Would you like some coffee?" Adolph asked. "I made a pot and filled my Thermos before the storm." She nodded and Adolph poured a tin cup for her and filled the lid for himself. "Sorry, it's black. I didn't think to bring cream and sugar. I didn't know I would have company," he smiled.

"It's just fine like this. I don't even know how it stays hot. What did you call that?"

"A Thermos. I bought it in Miami a few months ago when I was off-island. Very handy when you're gone on the line all day." She

224

nodded again and sipped the hot coffee.

"Enjoy that hot coffee, Adolph noted. "It could be a while before you get another." He turned the wick on the lantern up a little and they sat on the bench in the flickering light as darkness approached outside. The wind was getting stronger, and the weak door rattled. Mary drew close to the German.

"Come closer, Al, she said quietly. I'm cold, I'm wet and I'm scared. He slid over to her side, and she turned and kissed him softly on the lips. "I've missed you," she said. Adolph brushed his face in her damp hair and drew in her familiar scent. They sat in silence and listened to the storm rage outside. Adolph got up and opened the downwind door, peering outside. In the flickering light of frequent lightning, his fears were validated. "Water is rising!" he said. He closed and blocked the door again. "If that train doesn't come soon, we'll be swimming. Can you swim?"

"Like a fish," Mary said.

"I'm not sure that will do you much good in this wind, and I hope we don't have to leave this shed. We're safe here as long as the water doesn't rise much more."

She put both arms around his neck. "Oh Al, I so wish we could be together forever. She hesitated a moment and then looked at him, smiling. "When this storm is over, I'm going to divorce Thomas. Everyone in town knows who I really love, and most know who Johnny's father is. I will be yours if you want me."

Adolph did not answer. He pulled Mary closer to him and just silently held her.

He thought for a moment and came to a decision.

"There's something I need to tell you. Call it a confession, but I need to tell this to someone. Who knows, we may not live through the night." He clenched his eyes shut. "I am not who I have told you I am." My real name is Joseph Mueller. I was born in Munich, Germany. I have been in and out of prison since I was a teenager. I escaped and took a train to Hamburg and signed on with a ship as a seaman, and saw the world for three years. In 1903, we came to America, to New York. I got a job on the subway, repairing tracks and doing other maintenance. One night I got into a fight in a bar. A man pulled a knife on me, and I hit him with a fireplace poker.

225

Two of his friends came for me and I struck both of them. I ran from that place, hid in an alley, and sneaked out of town the next day. I made it to Baltimore and went to work for the B&O Railroad for a few years, then heard about the Florida East Coast Railway extension that was being built to Key West. I rode a boxcar to St Louis and caught a paddle-wheeler down the Mississippi. I met another German, and we traveled together to Saint Augustine, Florida." He put his head in his hands and began to sob. "I was so afraid that people would be looking for me. An escaped convict and murderer. I killed him in his sleep, took his name, his clothes, and his watch. I started a new life here in the keys, and I haven't broken the law a single time since." Mueller took the pocket watch out of the duffel and showed it to her. He opened the back and showed her the inscription.

Presented to Herman Adolphus Wahl for 25 years of loyal service. The Union Pacific Railroad Company. January 25, 1889.

"I have lived with this terrible crime every waking day of my life since." He buried his face in his hands and sat silently.

Mary sat in the flickering candlelight, not sure how to respond. She finally straightened up and took both of his hands in hers. "My love, my one true love," she began. "People make mistakes, especially young people. I must confess, I have been within an inch of killing that worthless bastard of a husband in his sleep more than once. I know that's different. I hate that man for his abuse, his drunken rages, his leaving me alone in that shack for months at a time." She looked into his eyes. "I'm sure you felt at the time there was no other way to start a new life. I can see in your eyes you regret what you did. What you did is not mine to forgive."

They held each other in silence for a long time.

The storm grew in intensity every minute.

Wayne Gales

23
Tropical Breezes

SPECIAL WEATHER STATEMENT

NATIONAL WEATHER SERVICE MIAMI FL
1251 AM CDT THU JUL 14
OKZ015-140600-
1251 AM EDT

...TROPICAL STORM WATCH...

AT 1251 AM CDT...A TROPICAL STORM WATCH EXISTS
FROM 20 MI NE OF MIAMI FL TO NAPLES FL INCLUDING
THE FLORIDA KEYS. AT 060Z TROPICAL DEPRESSION 91L
WAS LOCATED 130 MI SE OF GUANTANAMO CUBA.
WINDS ESTIMATED AT 30KTS...
MOVING EAST AT 15 MPH. SOME STRENGTHENING IS
EXPECTED OVER THE NEXT 24 HOURS. RESIDENTS OF
SOUTHERN FLORIDA, INCLUDING THE FLORIDA KEYS,
SHOULD MONITOR LOCAL WEATHER BULLETINS.
SHOULD THE DEPRESSION REACH 35KTS OR 39MPH, THE
TROPICAL STORM WILL BE NAMED BEN.

SEVERE WEATHER IS NOT EXPECTED, AND NO
WARNINGS ARE ANTICIPATED FOR THE NEXT 24 HOURS.

It was time to plan another raid on the Islamorada Historical
Society and library to see if we could glean any more information
on our phantom ancestor. Mary was in Miami for a few days
attending some sort of bookworm/spinster/hopeless virgin/cat
hoarding seminar and agreed to meet us there on her way home. Rio
was up north delivering my latest rescue, and I suggested while she
was there she get a room at the Hilton on Melbourne Beach and chill
for a couple of days. I told Lex to meet me at Two Friends for
breakfast, and we would motor up the keys in the Porsche. This
morning she chose to wear a pair of very short, loose silk shorts with
a matching nearly sheer blouse and wicker platform wedge sandals.

Like most days with her, it caused about a hundred eyeballs to audibly click when she strolled in. (*Ok, ninety-nine as one-eyed Walter was nursing a Bloody Mary at the bar.*) She dove into a three-egg omelet like it was the first meal in a week. Talking around a bite, she spoke.

"You sure we should make this trip? There's some sort of tropical storm thingy out there according to the news." I interrupted shoveling down my eggs benedict long enough to answer. "It's too early for anything significant to develop in the tropics and anyway, the 'thingy' is far away and moving slowly. We can get everything done we need to do up there by three and be home by five, far ahead of any bad weather. Besides, this high pressure over us should make it stay well south, probably under Cuba. No biggie."

"Well, you're the expert, Unc. Let's burn some road up." The Porsche was parked at a meter around the corner on Simonton, top-down and pretty. Lex slid behind the wheel and, showing a lot of leg, spun the little Porsche around and up Simonton, to Truman, past Searstown, and off the island. It was steamy hot, but the sun felt good, and I relaxed while she drove, sneaking an occasional peek to the left as her blouse gaped in the breeze revealing a pair of well-tanned, nicely shaped albeit artificial breasts. My desire to counsel her on appropriate attire for visiting a library and historical society was tempered by the free show. The voyeur in me has got me in trouble more than once, and, if I include that incident in Paris, almost killed. Well, as Popeye, says, "I yam what I yam."

We got to Islamorada about ten, well ahead of Mary's ETA, and looked up Benjamin Thomas, at the local library. Benjamin was an amateur Conch family historian and expert on Keys history. Thomas was in his seventies and was born only about ten years after the 1935 Hurricane that killed most of the residents on the island. Like Key West, the library had digitalized all the microfilm and, although the images were sometimes faint and hard to read, it was a heck of a lot easier than mounting spools of film on a projector and peering through a viewfinder for hours. Records before the Hurricane were fairly sparse; most of them had been destroyed that Labor Day weekend. We also went through scanned copies of the Miami and Fort Lauderdale newspapers. Hurricane coverage was so sensationalized it was hard to glean the truth. Accounts of thousands of dead people were exaggerated, and hard news was sparse at best. Lex, who normally has the attention span of a two-year-old, was genuinely engaged this day, and the morning passed pleasantly. At about noon, the librarian stuck her head into the research room. "That depression is now a storm," she announced, "and it's speeding up. We're under a tropical storm warning now and a hurricane watch." You might want to put the top up on that little car out there. It's starting to rain." We ran outside and put up the convertible on the Porsche. I looked at the sky. High cirrus clouds overhead with a dark band far out to the southeast. The breeze had picked up, but I guessed it couldn't be more than ten miles per hour. "It doesn't look that bad yet. Call Mary and see what the hold-up is." Lex punched in Mary's number and spoke quietly for a few minutes, then hung up. "She's not coming," Lex announced. "The news stations in Miami say that they expect a mandatory tourist evacuation order will be issued for the middle and upper keys sometime later today. She's gonna chicken out and stay up there for another night." I shrugged and shook my head. "That girl is afraid of her own shadow." I turned to Lex. "While we're here let's make the most of it. I've got to believe there other more traces of this elusive ancestor." She nodded, and we went back into the library. The old man stuck with us and found a file with a lot of 1935 Hurricane aftermath photos. The destruction from Long Key to Tavernier was near total devastation. Only a handful of buildings were standing after the storm and almost every tree, other than palm trees was gone. Miles of railroad track had been washed out, and, aside from the locomotive, the entire train had been washed off the right of way, with some cars ending up over a hundred and fifty feet from the tracks. Thomas stopped when he came across a photo of an attractive woman and a pre-teen boy, standing in front of a strange building. "That's your great-grandmother," he said, nodding to Lex. She was one of a handful of survivors. Her husband, Thomas Sawyer, and their son John Albert were in Key West and were spared." He handed over a printout of an old microfilm. "Here's Sawyer's name in the 1910 Key West census. It shows he lived on Fleming Street." I looked at the address, it was familiar, and then it came to me.

"Well, I'll be damned. That's the house my late wife Wendy was born in. I've been there hundreds of times. Wendy's mom still lives there, but she's getting old." I turned to Lex. "It couldn't hurt if you and Mary dropped by and paid Granny a visit. She loves company and will share journals, stories, and fossilized Oreo cookies with you all day." Lex nodded absently but was engrossed in the 1935 Hurricane. She turned to the old man.

"How did she survive this mess?" Lex asked. Benjamin answered. "I seem to recall she hid in a boat. That's all I know about that."

"What kind of house is that?" Lex asked. "It looks like a log cabin or something."

"It's an old storage shed for the railroad," he answered. Made of railroad ties soaked in creosote. It's built like a fort and survived the storm. It's still standing a little ways south of here, just a few yards bayside from the highway but it's covered by bushes. It's on private land, so nobody ever touches it." The librarian came back into the room. "We're closing at three," she announced. "I need to get home and get some things secured. Best you find some shelter. It's getting pretty nasty outside."

"Just a little longer," Lex said. "We're finally getting somewhere." The librarian threw up her hands in exasperation. "Thirty minutes and we're closing. You have to leave then."

We turned back to the photos. "Any pics of Adolph Wahl?" I asked. "Not by name, but here's a picture of a line gang near Islamorada in 1932 in a handcar. He's likely in the photo, but no way to tell who." I peered at the poor resolution. She pointed at one of the crew, a muscular black man. "Well, we can rule him out at least." Mary chuckled.

Then I remembered. "Wow! You won't believe this but I may have met his great-grandson in the Cayman Islands a few months ago. What a coincidence."

The rest looked the same, mustache, cap, white shirt with suspenders. We stared at the photo for a few more minutes when the librarian came in the room again.

"We're out of here! I'm locking the doors. I suggest you find a place to hunker down. It's getting nastier out there by the minute!" We thanked the old man, and I offered to pay for a cab. "No need," he answered. "Beth," he said, pointing at the librarian, "is my niece. She will give me a ride home."

We walked out the front door to a completely different scenario. It was raining sideways, and the wind was blowing at least thirty knots, with some higher gusts. We stood on the step and watched a plastic trash can fly by, heading west and gaining speed. I turned to Lex. "Think you better let me drive. We might be dodging a few obstacles down the road." She nodded nervously and handed me the keys. I folded myself behind the steering wheel, and we motored off down A1A. With the wind at our back, I almost didn't need to use the gas pedal to get up to speed. We approached the bridge at Tea Table Key and found the highway completely overrun by waves. No way this little low-profile German machine could navigate that. I flipped a U-turn and headed back north. "We need to find a place to hole up, this weather is too nasty to try and make it home." She nodded, scared now. I hadn't gone more than a few blocks when I had to slam on the breaks. A power pole was lying completely across the road, and the blue flame of arcing electricity was dancing along the downed power lines.

I pulled the Porsche to the left and down on the frontage road. It was almost dark now, and the only visibility was from a combination of the car's headlights which were a little more than a foot above the highway, and frequent flashes of lightning. I didn't see the road was under a foot of water until the little sports car splashed to a halt, and the motor died. Lex let out a gasp. "We walk from here!" I said. "Get out!" I grabbed the key and opened the door. Just as I stepped out I noticed a little LED flashlight in the door pocket. Smart girl. I grabbed it and stepped out into the dark water. Lex was still sitting inside. "Come on!" I yelled, and walked around to her side, yanking the door open. I took her by the hand and dragged her out into the street. "It's only a foot deep," I said. "We can walk up the road and find some shelter." She nodded, and I started leading her up the street.

We were both soaked to the skin and in better circumstances, I would have been enjoying the impromptu wet tee shirt show. For now, I just wanted to get out of this weather. The water was almost to our knees by now. It wasn't really a storm surge, just bay water being pushed inland by the wind, but I didn't want to wade around in it any more than necessary. Then, a flash of lightning illuminated a small building to the left. In the brief moment of the light, I recognized it. "This way!" I yelled over the wind, taking her hand. She stumbled along behind me, blinded by the rain, and suddenly stopped. "I lost my shoe!" she said. "For chrissake, I'll buy you another pair!" I answered, turning and scooping her into my arms. I approached the doorless shed and walked up the steps, putting Lex on her feet. At least we were out of the water.

I turned the flashlight on and scanned inside for wild creatures. There was nothing in the room but a bare wooden floor, covered with dirt and leaves, a small bench on one side, and nothing else. Well, at least it was dry. "Sit" I pointed toward the bench, and she did. I sat down next to her and turned off the light. "This flashlight will burn through the battery like popcorn. Need to save it for later." She didn't answer. A few moments later she said. "I'm cold." I slid next to her and put my arm around her. She buried her head in my shoulder and began crying. "I'm afraid," she said. I put my other arm around her. "Nothing to worry about. This shed has been here for a hundred years. This little storm isn't much of a threat. We just hang out here, ride out the storm, and find help in the morning." She nodded and turned her head toward me. Instinctively I kissed her forehead, and she turned her face up until her lips touched mine. I kissed her gently. She returned the kiss with a little more passion.

No, Bric, I said to myself.

Oh, what the Hell.

She was shivering from the wet clothes, and I reached around her with my right hand. I was sure she would be grateful if my hand cupped her round, firm, albeit artificially enhanced breast with the rock-hard nipple, to help keep at least that body part warm.

Yes, she did appear to appreciate that selfless gesture.

No, Bric.

Oh, what the Hell.

Oh, what the hell.

234

Wayne Gales

Flashback –
Islamorada, the afternoon of September 2, 1935

By mid-evening, it became evident that the rescue train wasn't coming. The residents and Army veterans had no idea that the train, which had been delayed for hours, would be washed off the tracks by powerful waves just a short distance from the Islamorada station. As the eye of the powerful storm approached, the water level continued to rise, not from the inevitable storm surge, which would rise to over eighteen feet at its peak, but from wind-pushed waves coming ashore as the railroad causeways to the south blocked the water from flowing back into the Atlantic. In the lantern light, Adolph noticed muddy water seeping through the floorboards of the shack. He reached down and dipped his finger in the water and put it to his tongue and noted that it was salty. The shack was built nearly three feet off the ground, and that part of the island was, at least, a few feet above sea level.

They were trapped. The wind outside was howling at over one hundred thirty miles per hour. Adolph and Mary had no idea how much worse the storm might get, but Adolph was certain if they stayed here much longer they could drown. They needed to escape.

Options were considered. How high would the water rise? It was already higher than either had ever seen and appeared to be rising higher. The only viable solution was the boat. It had a tight tarpaulin cover over it and had a motor. He came to a decision.

"I have a boat about a hundred yards away bayside," Adolph said. "I think we need to get to that boat before the wind and water gets any worse." Mary nodded, wide-eyed, and stood up. "I need to get dressed," she said. "No," answered Adolph. "That big dress will only get waterlogged and drag you down. This is not a time for modesty if you want to live to see tomorrow." She swallowed hard and nodded again. Adolph stood, and looked around the room. He took the lantern down and reached for a length of rope. In the gloom, Mary noticed several initials carved on the shed wall.

"What are those?" she asked.

"I guess everyone that has worked here or lived next door left their mark," Adolph answered.

"Where are your initials?" she asked.

Adolph pointed. "Right there. I carved the initials of my real name. J.M. Mary stood, the blanket falling on the bench. "Give me your knife." He reached into his pocket and opened the pocket knife, handing it to her. Under his initials she first carved a plus sign, then the letters M.S. "There!" She said, handing the knife back. It's official. He smiled a thin smile. The wind outside seemed to be increasing by the minute. He looked at Mary. "Well, it's now or never." She shook her head.

"Maybe we should wait for a few……" Her voice was cut off as the door to the shed was suddenly ripped off its hinges, vanishing in an instant into the storm. In a second, the shed was a maelstrom of vertical rain, screaming wind, and flying debris. The kerosene lantern blew off the wall and crashed to the floor, extinguishing the flame. Now the room was illuminated only by the constant flashes of lightning.

"Let's go!" Adolph yelled over the wind. He took Mary's hand and led her outside. They were both instantly blinded by the sand-filled wind. Turning their backs to the wind, Adolph led Mary down the steps into the rising water. He knew the direction to go, but the wind, blowing sand, debris, and sea water confused him. Holding Mary's hand, he started walking in the direction he thought the boat was stored. Water was over his waist, and nearly chest-high to the shorter woman. Suddenly she tripped over something and went completely out of sight. Adolph held her hand firmly and pulled her to her feet. She came up coughing and gasping. "My underwear!" She exclaimed. "Come on!" Adolph said, literally dragging her down what he hoped was the right path. In five minutes, the trees opened up, and the boat came into view in a lightning flash. You couldn't tell where the land stopped and the ocean started, it was all water. The ocean was now up to Adolph's armpits. The boat, normally sitting in a wooden cradle, now bobbed in the wild sea, straining at the rope that secured it to the palm tree.

The German went to the back of the boat and loosened the canvas tarpaulin. He reached for Mary and hoisted her into the boat. "I'll be right back!" he shouted above the screaming wind. "I need to re-tie the boat higher up the tree!" Mary nodded and ducked under the canvas and out of the rain. Adolph pulled himself along the side of the boat and found the line, which was now under two feet of water. He tried to untie the knots, but the boat's straining against the wind and water had made them impossible to loosen. He pulled his pocket knife out and began sawing on the one-inch line. After a minute, he managed to cut through the line, but to his dismay, he couldn't hold the boat against the wind. The line slipped out of his hands, and the boat vanished into the darkness in seconds.

Several hours later Mary woke to the dawn and the sound of an airplane. She was lying in a pool of dirty water at the bottom of the boat, nude from the waist down. She crawled to the back of the vessel and peered out from the corner of the loose canvas. A float plane was circling the boat. Ignoring her nudity, she stood and waved with both hands. The plane circled a few more times, waggled its wings, and flew off. Mary knew they had seen her and would send someone. She slipped the knot that held down the tarp and opened the boat up to the morning sun. Florida Bay was choppy and full of debris. Trees, part of buildings, and several bodies were floating around her.

The skies were still overcast, but at least it wasn't raining. She surveyed the contents of the boat. In front of the motor was a wooden box where she saw a small box of tools along with a canteen half-full of water, which she happily opened and drank her fill. In the tool box was an old rusty pocketknife. She pried the knife open and began cutting the stiff canvas. Eventually, she had a square of canvas, and, using the rope, fashioned a makeshift skirt, setting it aside until a rescue boat arrived. Mary was appalled at the number of bodies floating in the bay. She wondered if anyone else had survived. She lay there, floating all day Tuesday and through the night, regretting she had not been more conservative with the water. She took her last sip from the canteen about noon on Wednesday, and it wasn't until Thursday morning that she heard the noise of a boat in the distance. Wrapping her canvas skirt around her, she stood and waved her arms. The large motorboat came alongside and pulled her aboard. In the back of the boat, a dozen bloated bodies were stacked like so much cordwood. At the front sat one other person, wrapped in a blanket. She rushed to his side, but sadly it wasn't Adolph, but a teenage boy with a bloody bandage around his head. She looked south toward Islamorada and wondered what had happened to the man she loved.

One of the most powerful hurricanes in history, the 1935 storm was so intense, it literally tore Islamorada in two. As a category five storm; with winds over 180 miles per hour, many of the smaller islands had completely disappeared, and hundreds of people were reported as missing. The survivors, what was left of them, crawled out of their shelters and took part in the search for those missing. In the end, the middle keys were all but destroyed; the houses were now rubble and debris and when the gruesome search for the dead was over, the death count was simply unbelievable.

24
Alone Again, Naturally
Flashback - September 3, 1935, Islamorada

As daylight approached, Adolph could see from his perch high in the palm tree the unbelievable devastation that had come during the night. The lush tropical vegetation, almost every tree and the entire village of Islamorada were completely obliterated. He was battered and bruised, and the side of his face along with much of his back all the way down to his ankles was bruised and sandblasted from the wind-blown debris. The wind had torn all of his clothes off save his shoes. He tried to recall the night but it all seemed like a nightmarish blur. When he cut the rope to free the motor launch, the wind immediately jerked the rope out of his hands and the boat quickly vanished into the darkness with Mary inside. It was the precise moment the storm surge arrived and he quickly found himself armpit deep in windblown churning seas. Not knowing what else to do, he took the remaining rope and began climbing up the palm tree. Climbing above the water line, he wrapped the rope around the tree and tied himself to the palm. In moments, the water had risen two more feet and he worked his way up the trunk, staying ahead of the surge. Within ten minutes he was nearly at the top of the twenty-five-foot tall tree. Palm trees, unlike sturdy oaks and brittle fichus trees, bend with a storm. Palms may lose a few fronds but they are built to survive storms. When it appeared the water would rise no higher, he tied himself extra tight and hung on. He stayed that way all night.

As daylight began to color the horizon, Adolph began untying the knots with shaking fingers. The wind and lashing water had stripped every fragment of clothing from his body. The knife was long gone and he began to wonder if he would ever be able to untie them at all, but eventually, the knots came free, and he painfully climbed down from the palm, skin scraping against the rough bark. Looking toward Florida Bay, he could see no sign of the launch or Mary. The launch was well made and with the tarpaulin secured across the top, he felt it was, at least, possible she survived the storm. He turned and walked away from the beach toward the village and the tracks. With most of the foliage gone, he saw, with some surprise, that the maintenance shed was still standing. In fact, it was one of the strictest in sight that had survived the storm. His house had been completely washed away, and the depot had been reduced to a pile of splintered timber. The post office and other houses up and down the road were all either gone or nearly destroyed.

Climbing the steps to the shed, he peered inside. The ocean waters had scoured everything out of the little shed, but after a second glance, he noticed that his duffel, although waterlogged, had remained jammed under the bench where he had left it. He pulled it out and set it on the bench and began going through the contents. He chose a shirt, trousers, and a small-billed cap and laid them out on the steps to dry. After a few hours, they were sufficiently dry to put on. He dressed and then retrieved his pocket watch, frozen at 10:15 pm, the time the cabin flooded, along with his twenty-dollar gold piece, and thirty dollars in cash. He threw the still-dripping duffel bag over his shoulder and began walking, shoeless, up the island.

The devastation was incredible. Dead bodies were littered like so many dolls, some jammed among piles of debris, some hanging from trees, naked like him with their clothes torn off by the wind. A twelve-foot hammerhead shark lay across the railroad tracks, and numerous other fish and birds could be counted among the dead. Even though it was only a few hours after sunrise, the bodies were already starting to bloat, and flies, who somehow managed to survive, were already starting to hover over the carcasses. He walked for two miles and as of yet, had not encountered a single living soul. Ahead was the veteran's camp. Built mostly of canvas tents, it was in worse shape than the village. Virtually nothing was left standing, and human bodies floated in shallow pools staring lifelessly upward. He came across one individual who had drowned and noted he was about his age and build. He thought for a moment, about his past, about his confession, about Mary's telling him she would be leaving her husband for him. He looked again toward Florida Bay, thought for a moment, and reached into his pocket for the watch and gold coin. Checking the body to make sure it had no wallet or other identification, he slipped the watch and coin into his pocket, standing up only after removing the corpse's shoes, which thankfully fit his blistered feet. and, without a backward glance, turned toward the railroad tracks and started walking north toward Tavernier, and Miami.

25
Change is Good

Three weeks later, I was reminded just how lazy I was getting. I've become way too much of a creature of habit when someone knows how to find me on any given Saturday morning. If a set of identical twins can effortlessly track me down, so could a pack of bad guys with guns. I need to start changing my routine.

I was sitting outdoors at Pepe's a little after eight. My ham, cheese, and mushroom omelet was finished, and the plate was pushed aside. I was cruising through the Conch Crier and enjoying my second cup of decaf when Mary and Lex bounced into the restaurant. I was mildly amused at the slow transformation of the two. It seemed like every time I saw them, Lex was trying to become a little more conservative, and Mary came a little farther out of her cocoon. Today Lex had on a bright lime green floral sundress, likely, from my recognition, out of the window of the Lilly Pulitzer store on Front Street. It wasn't low cut, see-through, or, for that matter, very short. I suspected she was growing weary of low-life tourists whistling at her every move. Mary was wearing a pair of white Terrycloth boy-shorts and a tank top under a white long-sleeve blouse, tied at the waist and looking darn near sexy. Another month and she would be giving her sister a run for her money.

I put my paper down. "Good morning ladies. What's up?" Both girls dutifully kissed me on the cheek. (Lex slipped a tiny bit of tongue in my ear) and took chairs at my table. Silently, Mary pulled a large white envelope out of her purse and handed it to me. The envelope was addressed to Mary in my handwriting and the return address said "Home DNA.com." It was unopened.

"Ah, the mystery will be solved today!" I said. I cleaned the butter knife off with my napkin and slit the end of the envelope. There was a two-page letter enclosed, with the second page being some kind of graph. I set that on the table and began reading the results, then picked up the graph. I knew the answer but wanted to give it some dramatic effect.

"Let's see here. Lots of little codes that I don't understand, some sort of probability index. Well, no surprises here. It says we are both ninety-eight percent European, with about half of our heritage German and the other half English with a little trace of Nordic. Must have been that time in the tenth century when some Vikings snuck across the English Channel and nailed our distant ancestor. That makes sense. Ah, here it is. It says you're related to Chewbacca. I guess that makes me a monkey's uncle." I grinned. Lex stood up and put her hands around my throat, mock-strangling me.

"I'll 'uncle' you in a minute!" Lex said. "What's the verdict?" I tossed the paper on the table. "We're less than four percent related, girls. We're cousins, but at least a half-dozen generations apart. I know what that guy said his name was but he wasn't my great great grandfather. I don't have a clue how he ended up with Grampa's watch. Unless," I mused, "The only other possibility was that he was great grandpa and *didn't* father little Johnny and, your great-great grannie," I nodded to Mary, "was a real slut." Mary blushed, but not as much as she used to. She spoke. "Reading that diary, she seemed pretty sure who the father was. I guess our quest has hit a dead end." I remembered something else.

"Hey, did you guys ever go over and visit Grandma Sawyer?" Mary looked sad.

"We missed her by a month. We knocked on the door and there was no answer, then a neighbor came out on the porch next door and told us she passed away. I would have loved to hear anything she knew. She was actually alive in 1935. Now we'll never know."

ANNE'S BEACH

TO COMMEMORATE OUR RECOGNITION OF

ANNE EATON

WHO LIVED ON THIS ISLAND FOR MANY YEARS
AND DEDICATED HERSELF TO MAINTAINING THE
BEAUTY AND SERENITY OF THESE KEYS
ANN HELPED BRING THIS PARK TO LIFE.

SHIRLEY FREEMAN
MAYOR OF MONROE COUNTY

JACK LONDON
MAYOR PRO-TEM

KEITH L. DOUGLASS
COMMISSIONER

WILHELMINA G. HARVEY
MAYOR EMERITUS

MARY KAY REICH
COMMISSIONER

1995

26
Anne's Beach

For people that frequent US1, driving from the mainland to Key West hell-bent on hell-raising and spending the weekend in a blurry stupor, the sign for Anne's Beach at Mile seventy-three is little more than a mental note that you have about two hour's drive left. Or maybe signifying the unofficial point where you cross from the Upper Keys to the Middle Keys, launching the true "overseas highway" feel that driving with the multicolored ocean on both sides of the highway offers.

For James and Sheila Tucker, along with their four-year-old daughter Tequisha, Anne's Beach was the destination for today. Just a few hours south of downtown Miami, Anne's Beach offered a tranquil setting with warm shallow waters for the little girl to play in, and few enough parking places to ensure the area was never overcrowded. James, at six foot six, was able to make the second string on the University of Miami basketball team but never had a chance of getting a shot at the NBA. He parlayed his partial athletic scholarship into a Bachelor's Degree in internet marketing and landed a white-collar job in an industry that was poker chip white in almost every aspect. Life was good.

James and Sheila sat their beach chairs down, opened two Colt 45s, and watched their baby play in the shallows. They always sat in the same place, and it was Tequisha who noticed something was different. A dozen yards offshore, two seagulls were perched on something floating. The tide was coming in and the flotsam finally grounded in the shallow water ten feet from the couple. Tequisha waded out, and the sea birds flew off. She stopped a few feet away, and yelled, "Mommy, come look!" Humoring her daughter, Sheila waded out into the warm water. A few feet from the object, her eyes widened, and she let out a scream, and then became violently ill. Her husband ran out and saw the horror. The headless upper torso of a nude woman was already attracting small crabs and fish. He couldn't help but notice one arm was a completely tattooed sleeve of a woman intertwined with a serpent.

Wayne Gales

27
Never Bring a Gun to a Street Fight

I heard the news on the radio and picked up both Key West newspapers on the way to breakfast. The stories were about the same. An unidentified, partially decomposed headless torso of an adult Caucasian female was found at Anne's Beach. The part that caught my attention was the description of a full-sleeve tattoo on her arm. A snake intertwined with a nude human female.

It had to be Ludmilla.

I gleaned all I could from the papers, but there wasn't much more. Figuring currents and the Gulfstream, they probably brought her out on the *Moonlight Madness* to pick up another group of girls and dispatched her there, decapitating her and throwing the body in the ocean. It wasn't a ritual killing or designed to get someone's attention. I'm sure they thought anything dumped that far out would be subject to predation long before it came to shore. She told me that what I was doing would put everyone in danger. It's just that I figured I would be the target before she was. Probably one of the girls ratted on her in exchange for a favor or more drugs. I looked at the sky for a moment and wondered how much they got out of her before they whacked her. It was time to be a little more careful, at least for a while.

I still had a mission. It was no time to chicken out.

I went back to the house, and Rio was just waking up. I usually got up a lot earlier than she did and she usually just opted for a bowl of granola and a big joint for breakfast when she woke. When I came through the gate, she was sitting in the backyard on the bench, nude, smoking her morning doobie. "Shower?" I suggested. She squeaked out a "Sure." Before exhaling and stubbed the end out in a flowerpot. I stripped and turned the shower on, letting it get warm before I stepped under it, motioning to Rio to join me. We lathered each other up, rinsed off, threw a couple of towels on one of the big wooden lounges, and spooned up to enjoy the coolish morning before it got steamy hot. I lay there with my arm around her, idly tracing the scars on her chest. I was still quiet, thinking about Ludmilla.

"What's wrong?" she asked.

"The woman that helped me get this rescue thing going was murdered I think," and I went on to tell her what was in the newspaper. "I'm surprised she didn't get consumed by the pelagics before the body got to shore," I said. "It's quite a ways from where they meet the container ship and Anne's Beach."

"No way," Rio countered. "I can guarantee you she didn't float that far. Somebody cut her head off and threw the body in the water close to shore. They wanted someone to find the body and make the news." She sat up and turned toward me. "Bric that was a warning to *you*. They wanted you to know that you are next."

I hadn't thought of it that way. I sat up on the other side of the lounge and then stood. "Well, they aren't going to scare me off," I said. We need to try a rescue tonight and also get on the scoreboard." I pulled my shorts on.

"What do you mean?" She asked.

I took a moment to answer. "Look, Rio, you can stay home tonight. I'll take the van and meet you back here with the girl if I'm successful. You can leave for Melbourne from here."

"No fucking way," she answered. "We do this as a team. You can't have all the fun by yourself."

"I'm not sure I want you to become an accessory to murder, Rio" I answered.

"It's not murder when you're killing pigs," she answered. "I'm in. What are you planning?" I thought for a moment. "A little change in tactic. Instead of acting like a tourist, I think tonight I walk the streets as 'me.' See if I can flush out a crook or two."

"Do we need guns or something?" She asked.

I smiled grimly. "I never bring guns to a street fight."

I almost forgot what the "real me" looked like. I dug out my Columbia fishing shirt, khaki shorts, Alabama Jack faded orange fishing cap, Reef flip-flops, and mirror Costa sunglasses. It was night, but I opted for the glasses to make sure that, even with the beard, somebody local didn't accidentally recognize "Bric." I got up to leave and gave Rio a hug and a kiss. "Leave in an hour or so and cruise around until you find a parking meter on Caroline behind the Bull. Between, the Bull, the Whistle, the Garden of Eden, and

Fogartys, I'm sure I'll be able to scare up something."   I walked over to Caroline and headed toward Duval Street. It was a typical Friday night in Key West; dim lights, thick smoke, and loud music filled the air. The locals were either working one of their three jobs or safely away from Duval. The tourists, who mostly were just arriving from the mainland by this time of day, were already working on their third beer and first drunk of the weekend.   I decided to start from the top and work my way down. I climbed the fifty or so steps from street level to what the locals call the Top of the Bull but is really named the Garden of Eden. It's the last clothing-optional bar in Key West. There used to be Atlantic Shores that was located on the water between Simonton and Duval Street. It was a clothing-optional bar with a swimming pool a sunbathing area and a short pier with steps into the water that was affectionately called by the locals "dick-dock." Also, just around the corner from the Bull and Whistle was a bar that is currently occupied by Smokin Tuna called Naked Lunch. It was hard to find and failed after a year or so, but I did play there one Fantasy Fest, and it was a crazy scene. But anyway, if you wanted to get legally and publicly naked on any of the fifty-one weeks besides Fantasy Fest, you went to the Garden of Eden.   I rarely went there, even when I was "alive", mostly because ninety-nine percent of the time, the only people you would find there were, shall we say, "eccentric" men, who got their jollies by taking their clothes off around other men. Oh, occasionally a few tourists would go up there and talk their ladies into stripping. More often than not, the women who took their clothes off looked a lot better with them on. Tonight, it wasn't much different. One guy, a regular named Dennis dancing in just his Birkenstocks, two guys at the bar trying to impress the waitress, and one couple sitting on the wooden bench. He had stripped and thus far coaxed his woman into unbuttoning her blouse. That wasn't going anywhere.

I didn't expect to find any hookers up here, but it was worth the try. I strolled down the steps to the middle bar, the Whistle. Nothing there either. I walked down the back steps from the Whistle and saw Rio in the van cruise by, still looking for an open meter on Caroline. She threw up her hands in exasperation. I gave her a thumbs-up and made a circling motion with my finger. "Keep looking," I mouthed to her as she drove by. She smiled back and flipped me the bird. I stepped into the Bull, took a seat at the bar, and ordered a beer, acting just a little too loud and sloppy. I pulled a wad of bills out and dropped several on the floor. The crowd couldn't help but notice that they were hundreds. I stooped down and picked them up and almost fell over. I sat back down, drained my beer, and yelled for another. "Whassa guy gadda do to get some service around here? I thought this town was full of action!" The bartender frowned but poured another beer. He put it in front of me and quietly said, "Cool it buddy or I'll have you eighty-sixed." I gave him a drunken nod and started nursing my beer quietly. I hung around for another hour listening to the mediocre band when a short guy with a big black mustache sat down on the stool next to me. I expected another bad accent but was surprised to hear this guy was a Brit. He ordered a drink and then turned toward me.

"Fancy a little company?" he started.

"What kinda company?" I slurred.

"Whatever you want. Tell me what you want and I'll deliver it."

"Two girls. No, make it three. Young. Younger the better long as they're legal age."

He smiled. "I can make that happen, but it will cost you a thousand for an hour."

"Fuck you," I answered. "I wouldn't pay a thousand for a whole weekend. I'll give you three hundred bucks, or you can shove it up your ass." With his accent, I was wondering if I was dealing with the right people, but it was not likely there were two such organizations in the same little town.

He checked his phone for a moment and typed something, then looked back at me.

"Five hundred. Three young white girls. Delivered to your room. Now."

"I wanna see the talent before they get delivered. Bring them down the block on Caroline in fifteen minutes." I jerked my thumb toward where Rio was parked, and then reached in my pocket and flashed the dead presidents. "If you bring what I asked for, I'll give you six of these, and you can bring them to my room on Sunset Key.

256

I'll be standing out in front of The Lost Weekend liquor store. Just parade them by and I'll let you know if I approve."

"Highly irregular way to do business," he replied. He pulled his phone out and did some more texting. Okay. Fifteen minutes. Sergi will bring the girls over. I have other things to do."

"No," I answered. I want you there too. Do other things later. Deal or no deal?"

He sighed, tapped on his phone again, and put it in his pocket. "Very well, Sergi and I will be there. You better be there too."

"No problem, amigo. I'm heading out there right now." And I stumbled off the barstool and staggered out the front door, turning to the right on Duval, and right again on Caroline. Rio saw me walking that way and reached to start the van. I made a motion for her to roll the window down.

"Pull out and turn around. Park the van in the same spot pointing the wrong way. Cops won't care. We will be out of here one way or the other in fifteen minutes. Oh. Make sure the cargo doors are unlocked and the passenger door too. It might get lively in a few minutes." She didn't ask any questions, just nodded and pulled the van out, doing a donut in the middle of Duval Street and right back into the same space.

I stood in front of the liquor store in the dim light with my arms folded, letting my eyes get accustomed to the darkness. I slipped off my flip-flops and stood in bare feet. A quarter of an hour later, I saw a thug wearing a jacket standing across the street from the Bull with three girls in tow. That must be Sergi. They were dressed casually, probably because he already had a sale and didn't want to draw too much attention. He stood on the corner and surveyed the surroundings. I scanned the area too. I was comfortable taking on two, or maybe three but didn't want to confront an army. In a moment, the Brit showed up on the corner at the Bull and nodded to Sergi. They crossed and headed toward me, Sergi in front and the Brit taking up the back of the troupe. I nodded to the thug as he approached. He stopped and turned toward the girls. The Brit spoke. "Meet your approval, my friend?" He asked. I leaned against the post and acted as casually as possible.

"Depends on what they are here for," I answered. They both

looked puzzled.

"What do you mean?" Sergi asked.

"Well, if they are here for fucking, then no. But if they are here because Ludmilla sent them to be rescued, then I'm all for it." It was almost comical. All five froze when they heard Ludmilla's name. I didn't move, but just smiled, but I was watching their eyes, and more importantly, their hands. I was at a little bit of a disadvantage as there were two targets, separated by three innocent girls. I was beginning to wonder if we were all just going to stand there all night. Time to break the impasse.

"Who will answer for Ludmilla?" I said.

"You will!" the Russian said and reached behind his jacket. He never got to his weapon as Rio slammed the passenger door of the van open, and the rearview mirror caught him square in the nose. The Brit crouched in a defensive posture, which meant he didn't have a gun. I took two steps toward him, pushed one of the girls gently aside, and launched a spin kick into his right temple. He fell and clipped his head on the bumper of a Jeep that was parked behind the van and went out cold. I turned my right to see Sergi holding his nose with one hand and a nine-millimeter stainless Beretta with a silencer in the other. Rio slammed the door open again but this time, it missed him, and he started to bring the gun up to the window of the van. I was there in two steps and locked his arm under mine. I swung it away from the van, pointing it at the Brit, where I helped Sergi pour three rounds in his direction. Two hit. I slammed his hand into the side of the van, and he let go of the gun, then kicked him hard in the balls. That took him to his knees. From there it was one swift twist of the neck and, no more Sergi. Total elapsed time, about eight seconds from start to finish. We hadn't even drawn any attention yet. Rio got out of the van and stepped over the body. The three girls were standing on the sidewalk, frozen in horror. I turned to them.

"The code word is Marathon," I said. One of them answered, stammering in fear.

"L..L.Ludmilla." I reached for the cargo door. "Get in!" The girl who spoke didn't hesitate and climbed through the door. I turned to the other two. "Now's your chance. I won't stop you if you run away, but please don't tell them how it happened or more people will die." They looked at each other and nodded.

I got a three-fer.

I climbed in the passenger seat and had Rio drop me off a few blocks away. I gave her a goodbye kiss and off she went to Melbourne. "Bring back a green van!" I shouted before I closed the door. As she motored up Front Street, I heard the wail of sirens to my right. I turned and walked toward A&B Lobster, whistling Paul McCartney's "Live and Let Die" to myself. It wasn't until then that I remembered I had slipped off my shoes before the fight. Oh well, I'll find some new ones in the morning.

It had been a good night.

Wayne Gales

28
Hello Again, Goodbye

It was a quiet week between rescue attempts and I needed to touch base with an old friend. Bo Morgan had been clear that I stay away from the compound when all the crazy stuff was going on, but I was pretty sure the trail was cold enough that nobody was watching his houseboat or tapping his phones for that matter. Regardless, I thought it best to just quietly drop in one night for a visit. I asked Rio to drop me off in front of the gate well after dark. I could see over the fence that lights were on at his place. My houseboat next door was eerily dark.

"I'll find my way back," I told Rio and gave her a kiss goodbye. I waited outside for a minute after she drove off to get my eyes accustomed to the dark, and listened for any activity in the area.

Old habits are hard to break. It's why I have lived this long.

Strange, I had lived here off and on for years, but just realized I was standing right on top of the right of way for Henry Flagler's Florida East Coast Railroad. This hundred-foot-wide strip of land was man-made by Flagler's railroad company, dredged out of the ocean, and piled up to make dry land. The tracks came off the main island right where the driveway for Banana Bay is now, and then came down this piece of land to the terminal. I guess I always knew that fact, it just never crossed my mind. Standing in the darkness, I wondered if I could hear the ghosts of railway workers past. Relative or not, did my so-called ancestor pass by here?

I looked at the bell cord hanging outside the gate and considered announcing my presence, then decided against it. The rots would alert Bo and a half dozen houses on both sides that someone was there. I quietly clicked open the compound door and stepped inside. Scooter and Devvi were trained surprise attack dogs. If they were outside, which was likely since they stunk like the city dump, they would be well aware I was there, and they were sizing me up from a dark place to see which appendage to rip off first, provided I didn't let them know who I was. I didn't need to. While I was standing just inside the gate, Scooter stuck his muzzle into the back of my hand and gave a quiet, recognizing "woof" to let Devvi know it was a friend. They were both rewarded with a couple of Beggin Strips which they accepted happily. The porch light came on and Bo stuck his head out of the front door.

"Who is out there that my dogs know?" He asked. I stepped into the light.

"An old friend," I answered. Bo stuck his hand out and welcomed me into the houseboat. "Have a seat," he motioned toward the couch. Without asking, pulled a couple of glasses out of the cupboard and poured each half full of Appleton's. Handing me one, we clinked glasses and silently toasted a lot of water under the bow. After a moment he spoke.

"Your friend Tim let me know that you survived that storm." he began. "But that's all I know. How long have you been back in town?" I took another sip, mulling over how much or how little to share.

"Couple of months," I answered. Karen and I have been hanging out at a place up the keys, but I ran into some distant relatives and decided to come down this way for a while. Got a new name and changed my look. I think all that craziness is finally behind me." I filled him in on the Wyoming trip, the near miss in Mobile, Belize, Panama, Cabo, the Russians, Grand Cayman, and how we got back to Key West. Bo just sat there, holding his rum in both hands, and listened silently with his eyes nearly closed. I thought the story was a pretty good yarn but my friend showed no emotion at all. I guessed I could have added that I was abducted by aliens and spent the weekend with Jimmy Hoffa and Amelia Earhart and he wouldn't have shown emotion. I shrugged and changed the subject.

"Seems like a waste to have my place next door stay vacant. Would you be interested in leasing out the units and splitting the rent? Houses are happier when they are occupied."

"Sure," answered Bo. I can turn it back into a four-plex without too much expense. I'll deduct whatever I spend out of your half until it's covered. I'm sure I can rent it pretty fast." I nodded ok. We sat in awkward silence. Bo seemed to be in thought. He carefully examined his glass for a few minutes and finally spoke. "So it calmed down enough that you decided to light some new fires?" He asked and then looked straight into my eyes. I looked away.

"It's not like that Bo," I answered. "I'm trying to help some people who can't help themselves. People that have no right to be on this earth are interfering with my efforts. That's all."

Bo mulled over what I said. "I suspected it was something like that," he said. "Bric, it's none of my business, and I'm sure you feel justified in what you've been doing." He stood up and walked to the door. "You don't have to answer to me or anyone else, except maybe the law and your maker, but the list may be long come Judgment Day." I stood up and he gave me a man hug. "Bric, I hope you make peace with the world before the world finds peace without you."

I found myself standing alone in the middle of the compound with both Rot's sitting expectantly in front of me in case I had more treats. I absently reached in my pockets and found a few more Beggin Strips and distributed them. I looked back towards the houseboat and watched the porch light go out. I shrugged again, walked out the gate, put my hands in my pockets, and made my way up Hilton Haven Drive into the darkness.

Wayne Gales

29
Night Vision

After creating an honor guard for Ludmilla, I backed off on the violence. It was dangerous to keep killing people and besides it was starting to make more than local headlines. I was rather amused that I had been described by CNN as a "large gang of vigilantes" that had taken the law into their own hands to attack and kill or injure illegal aliens with criminal backgrounds. Thus far nobody had connected the dots to sex trafficking, organized prostitution, or the Russian Mafia, but I needed to concentrate on the task at hand and save as many girls as possible before I had to fold the tent.

Bo's words were heavy on my mind and I decided to take a week off from my *Save The World* mode and relax a bit. How can you get a taste of Key West Normal when you hardly ever see the sun? Rio was growing weary of the seven hundred mile round trip commute too. I put on my best disguise, and we decided dinner at the Conch Republic Seafood Company wouldn't be too risky. I hadn't seen any girls work there, perhaps because the *Moonlight Madness* was docked almost right in front of the place. I ordered a rumrunner on the rocks and Rio opted for a cosmopolitan. She was dressed in her normal disregard for fashion, a camouflage-colored tank top, tattered cutoffs, a Salt Life visor, and K-Mart plastic flip-flops. As of yet, I had no concern that any of the bad people had seen who drives the van, and for that matter, I wasn't positive they had connected the van to my activity. Either way, it was fun to be out among 'em, relaxing, listening to music, and consuming adult beverages.

"How much longer are you going to do this?" Rio asked. "Until someone manages to kill you?"

"Actually, I'm starting to think about wrapping up the party," I answered. "Think I might borrow Rumpy's boat some evening, follow these guys out to the container ship, so I can get the name of the vessel and leak the info to the proper channels. I know my CIA spook sort of friend Tim is offline nowadays, but I think if I get him some info he can call the right people. Maybe we can at least shut part of the pipeline down for a while."

"How about tonight?" Rio asked.

"Hunh?"

"Turn around," she pointed. I craned my neck around to see the marina. Sure enough, there were four guys on the *Moonlight Madness*, obviously prepping it for a run. Keeping my eyes on them, I pulled my phone out of my pocket and dialed a number from memory. It rang three times then picked up. I started to talk when a recorded voice came on.

"Hi, you have reached Rumpy. You know the drill." And then it beeped. This was his home number and he was the only person I know that; A. Didn't have caller I.D. and B. Had one of those old answer phones with a little cassette and a speaker. Come to think of it, he also had an eight-track in his Toyota. I spoke into the cell phone. "Rump! Pick up! It's me." There were a few moments of silence and then I heard a click.

"Hello, me. What's up?" I had him. Now I had to figure out how to talk him into a night boat ride.

"Let's go swordfishing. I hear they are killing them out past the color change." The phone was quiet for a moment. Rump was either lighting a cigarette, taking a pull from his rum drink, or both. He finally answered.

"Sure, pal. I could be talked into going out for some swordfish. How about next Tuesday?"

"How about tonight?" I answered. "Say, in about forty-five minutes."

"The *Wave Whacker's* out of gas, I don't have bait, and I'm about half a boat drink away from driving the '*Whacker* into a reef."

"It's a special kind of swordfishing," I answered. "We don't need bait. You get the '*Whacker* to the Marina by the Conch Republic ASAP, and I'll buy the gas, and I'll drive the boat from there. When we get back, we go to Fancy Seafoods and pick up a dozen swordfish steaks."

"Ah, it's the super sleuth at it again. I got it," he answered. "Tell you what. You can come get the '*Whacker* and bring her back full of gas. I think your version of Swordfishing is too dangerous for me. Oh, and I will take those steaks, though."

"Okay, I answered. I'll be there in fifteen minutes. Get her warmed up." And I clicked off the phone. I threw some money on the table, and we bolted out the side entrance. It was a ten-minute brisk walk to where we had the van parked, and this time, I was happy to let Rio play Mario Andretti out of town up to Big Coppitt Key. She pulled the van around the side of the house on the grass, and we jumped out. Rumpy was in the *'Whacker* making sure everything was up to speed. He stepped out as I jumped in, helping Rio over the side.

"Cast off!" I said to Rumpy. He untied the bowline, threw it in the boat, and slipped the loop off the cleat at the back. "I'll be back in three or four hours," I yelled over the engine noise as I gently spun the boat around in the narrow canal.

"Aren't you gonna introduce me to your friend?" He asked.

"Rio, Rumpy. Rumpy, Rio." I said. "That will have to do for the moment. See you later!"

We idled out of the canal. The route out of there is tricky on a good day, but Rump's Garmin has it well marked and I dialed in Conch Marina as my first stop. I pushed the throttles down, and the twin-hulled boat came up on plane. We shot the little pass, turned left, and crossed under A1A, then back around to Conch Marina to fill up. The attendant at the Marina recognized the boat and looked at me suspiciously. "Where are you heading?" He asked. "And where's the owner?"

"We're just going out for a little moonlit boat ride," I answered. I realized I should have put a few rods on the boat before we left to make it look like a legitimate fishing trip. "We invited Rumpy, but he was one rum drink over the line and declined." I reached into my pocket for the phone. "You can give him a call to verify it's cool if you want." He shook his head. "That's okay. You know his name. That's good enough for me." I paid for the gas and then motored out of the marina and due south, pushing the boat up to speed once we cleared the markers. Rio had been quiet in the rush and now slipped her arm around me. "How are we going to find a little dark boat, on a dark night in the middle of the ocean?" She asked.

"We look for a big boat that's stopped," I answered. "The

Moonlight Madness can sneak around without lights, but that cargo ship has to be well-lit. There can't be more than a couple out here tonight, and I'm guessing it will be pretty easy to figure out which one we are looking for. Remember it will be coming from the Panama Canal so it will be heading east." I powered out to about eighteen miles from the island and shut down.

"Now we wait," I said. We sat in silence with a quarter moon hovering above us. There wasn't a cloud in the sky, and the Milky Way was shining in all its splendor. I picked out my favorite constellations and enjoyed the peace and quiet. Rio doesn't chatter for chatter's sake, and she was enjoying the moment too. I threw a couple of towels down on the bow, and we both laid down to enjoy the moment, looking up occasionally to make sure some big cargo ship didn't run over us out here in the shipping lanes. At about eleven, I saw lights to the west. Now, along with some fishing poles, I regretted not grabbing Rumpy's binoculars. Wait, they might be someplace on board. He liked to keep them around when the ladies at Marvin Key started skinny-dipping. I checked under the seat and in the storage compartment. No joy. Ah. The little compartment on the dash where he put his phone and cigarettes. There. A vinyl case containing a beat-up pair of Ricoh low-light 10-A marine binoculars. Perfect. I cleaned the lenses and put them up to my eyes. The ship, which was more than two miles away jumped into view. Big container ship, going very slow. There was a floodlight over the starboard side. I could just make out the black hull of a black trimaran alongside.

"That's our boy," I said to Rio. "All we need to do is hang here till it passes by, read the name, and go home." She nodded a quiet agreement. It was nearly one a.m. before the big ship got back underway and up to speed. As it loomed closer, Rio put her hand on my shoulder. "Looks like it's going to run right over us," she said. "Nah, it will miss us by a thousand feet to the south, or more," I answered. "We need to be close enough to read the name." The big boat lumbered past, close enough to hear the motors rumbling and even a few voices from the deck. Even in the low moonlight, the words MAERSK were easily visible on the side. As it passed, I fired up the '*Whacker* and eased closer to the stern. As I had hoped, the stern was lighted with the name clearly visible. *"Maersk Dasha"* and under that the country of registry, Monrovia. Lots of ships were registered in the tiny country. It was called a "Flag of Convenience" and Monrovia, like Liberia and Panama, offer low licensing fees and few regulations. I found a piece of paper and wrote the name down, and then we headed back to Rumpy's. He was sound asleep when we motored in so I parked the boat, slipped a couple of twenties under the ashtray on the back porch, and we headed back to town, getting to Rio's place just as the morning sun started to light the eastern horizon.

30
Cheaper by the Dozen

The next rescue was only two nights later and almost too easy. I was minding my own business eating a dozen raw oysters at the White Tarpon when a couple came in. The guy was a young tourist in his mid-twenties and from what I could pick up on his accent, probably Brazilian. The girl was Asian, I would guess Chinese and looked like a working girl from head to toe. I would guess he had paid for an escort for the whole night, and since this dude could in no way be "me" her pimp/bodyguard had taken the night off. I was technically "off the clock" too, and Rio was home asleep. Still, just for shits and grins, I wondered if this gal wanted a ticket home. The guy was about half-drunk and after a few beers wobbled to his feet and headed for the men's room. When he was out of sight, I turned to her, raised my beer bottle, and spoke.

"Nín hǎo."

She looked at me quizzically and answered.

"Nín hǎo." (Hello)

"Nǐ hǎo ma?" (How are you?")

"Hǎo." (Sort of means OK) I had her attention. She was wondering how the white boy knew Mandarin. Actually, I was approaching the limit of my Chinese skills, so I switched to my mother tongue.

"Come here often?" I asked. "I usually hang out in Marathon." That got her attention. She cut right to the chase.

"You can get me home?" She asked, hopefully.

"Sure." I looked toward the men's room. Studley was still in there, probably trying to keep balanced enough to stand and not pee all over himself. I turned back toward her.

"Get up, right now and walk that way." I pointed toward Front Street. Go to the Rum Barrel and sit at the bar. Watch for a dark green van. It will take you to safety. Go!" She looked anxiously toward the men's room door. "He paid for the whole night," she said.

"How much of that grand do you get?" I asked.

"Maybe twenty," she said, hanging her head. I reached into my pocket and waived a hundred. "Here, take this and run. He will come out in a second. I'll create a diversion. No problem." She hesitated for a second, made up her mind, and got up, snatching the bill out of my hand when she walked by. About ten seconds later, the kid came out of the men's room and saw the empty table. "Hey, where is she?" He asked. I pointed toward the east entrance to the open-air bar. She ran out that way," I said, "toward Schooner Wharf. She was running. You better hurry." And with that, he half ran, half stumbled out the door. The waiter started to run after him as the beers hadn't been paid for but I stopped him and handed him a twenty, then punched up Rio on my cell phone. By the sleepy voice, I could tell I woke her up "Got a customer. She's in the Rum Barrel on Front Street. Asian chick." Rio mumbled ok and hung up. I paid my tab, wandered down Front Street, and parked myself across from the Rum Runner. I could see the girl inside at the bar. She was nursing a drink and watching the street. About twenty minutes later, I saw Rio come down Front from Duval. She saw me to her left and pulled up. I walked around to the passenger side and got in. "She will see you in a moment. I want to talk to her for a moment before you guys head up the keys." Rio nodded in sleepy acknowledgment. "I need coffee," she said. "Drive through the McDonalds on your way out of town. Get a room on the way if you need." I put my hand on her shoulder. "Sorry to do this to you on short notice but it kind of happened by accident." There was a tap at my window, and I turned to see the girl standing in the street.

"Back door's unlocked. Get in." I said. She got in the back and sat down on the beanbag chair. I motioned to Rio to drive off, and I crawled in back and sat in one of the other bean bags. I held out my hand. "Russell," I said. "Rosie," she answered. "That's not my real name, but it's the one they gave me." She looked at me for a moment. "Where are we going? There are a lot of girls missing over the past several weeks. Are you taking me to the same place they went?"

"Sabine will take you to the same place, but some may already be gone, either home or to other places. A friend will help you when you arrive." She pondered this for a moment and then responded. "Anything is better than this. I'm glad to be leaving. Many of us were going to be taken away tomorrow anyway." I leaned toward her, suddenly interested. "Where?"

"I don't know. Maybe Los Angeles or San Francisco, even Denver. Cities that have large conventions. It happens all the time."

"How many girls?" I asked. I was thinking of a plan.

"About a dozen," Rosie said. "A big, fifteen-passenger van with dark windows."

"How many men?"

"One guy usually from Key West and he picks up another guy in Miami. They always drive straight through. A really bad dude named Sergi used to drive us, but," her eyes got big. "You killed him! Oh, Mister Russell, I could give you a big kiss right here. He used to beat us and make us do things." I smiled grimly. Behind the wheel, Rio turned partially around and snarled toward the back of the van.

"You plant one on him and when I'm done with you, those eyes gonna slant the other way."

"RIO!" I raised my voice. "Let's be a little civil up there."

"Sorry, little Chinese lady," Rio said, a little calmer. "I didn't get enough sleep, and I don't feel that good." I looked at her, concerned now. Might be time to get her back to U.M. Sylvester in Miami for a checkup. I turned back to Rosie.

"So who will take you now? Well, not you, but the rest of the girls."

"I don't know, but I know we were told to be ready by six a.m. tomorrow." I mulled this information over for a moment and then came to a decision. "Rosie, want to be a hero?"

"Where I come from, all the heroes are dead. What do you want and what's in it for me?"

I thought for a second and came to the right answer.

"The satisfaction of saving eleven girls besides yourself, a ride back to China if you want it, and five thousand bucks cash."

"OK, you have my attention. What do you want?" She asked.

"I want you to go back to the crib tonight and ride that van tomorrow." She was quick to answer. "Dead people can't ride in airplanes and spend money. If they know I have been in this van, I won't live to get in that one."

273

"You have the hundred I gave you. Walk back home, give them the bucks, and tell them the Brazilian dude got weird so you walked. They won't even question you about it when you hand over the bucks." She seemed to think for a moment.

"Okay, so I do this, and we all get in the van tomorrow. How do I become a hero?"

I smiled. "It will be easy. About ten minutes after you leave Key West, tell the driver you gotta pee really bad. Do it just before you get to the Circle K on Big Coppit Key. The driver stops, and I convince him to trade places with me. I drive the van out of the keys and everyone gets away."

"How you gonna convince him to…." She stopped and glared at me. "Wait a minute. You're gonna kill the driver. Look, Mister Russell. If it's Andreus, don't kill him. He's the only guy that's ever been nice to any of us. Promise me you won't shoot Andreus."

I smiled again. "Well, for one thing, Rosie, I don't shoot people."

"Yes you do," she argued. "The papers said that Freddie was shot twice."

"I didn't shoot him," I replied "Sergi did. Well, now that you mention it, I helped Sergi shoot the Brit but technically, it was Sergi. His hand, his gun." I thought of something. "Hey, how will I know its Andreus?" Her answer was matter of fact.

"Just ask him. Okay, Mister Russell, five grand, a plane ride home, and a ride to freedom for me and the girls. I might make a few substitutions tonight. There may be a few girls who get sick by morning." She looked out the front window and yelled up to Rio. "Hey nice bitch, where are we anyway?" I could see Rio rise to the bait, and I interrupted. "Looks like we're at about Simonton and Truman. Rio, turn right on Truman and then right again to the west end of the cemetery. Rosie can walk from there." Rosie looked surprised. "You know where the house is?"

"Sweetie, I know more than you will ever believe." When she got out of the van, I gave her one last instruction. "Oh yeah, tell your bosses that you think you saw the guy that they have been looking for, and that he offered you money to join his crib in Miami. Tell them that he was about six feet tall, kind of fat with long hair and no beard." Rosie smiled. "Got it." She closed the door and walked away toward William Street.

I roused Rio up at five the next morning. "You can go back to sleep in the van," I said. She nodded, pulled on some clothes, and staggered down to the van. She plopped herself on a beanbag chair and lit a joint. I started the van and headed up the keys to the Big Coppit Circle K. At five in the morning there weren't many people there, just some fishermen on their way to work. I backed the van to the left of the ramp that led up to the store and waited. Six a.m. came and went, then six thirty. Maybe this plan was a bust or they twigged that Rosie was lying. I was about to turn the key when a Dodge fifteen-passenger van pulled into the lot, throwing gravel as it skidded to a stop. The door opened, and Rosie jumped out, heading up the ramp. She threw a glance in my direction and gave a little nod. I turned toward the back of the van and called Rio's name a few times until she woke. "Showtime girl. When I get out, you get behind the wheel and be ready to drive back to town if I'm successful in hijacking this van."

"How will you get back?" She asked. "You won't dare drive that van back to Key West."

Not Key West, but maybe Miami, or even Orlando, and then I'll fly home. I'll let you know." She came up and gave me a kiss before I opened the door. I started walking toward the store as I eyed the van. Like Rosie said, only one guy was sitting behind the wheel. I sized him up. Hard to say in the early dawn, but I was pretty comfortable with one-on-one odds. Okay, here goes. I stopped and bent over like I was looking under the van. Then I pointed toward the back.

"Hey buddy, you got something leaking big time there at the back of the van. You better take a look." He looked at his rear-view mirror and then opened the door. "Where?" he asked. "At the back." And I pointed again. "There." He followed me around to the back of the van and bent down. "I don't see anything," he said. It sounded like a French accent. "Hey," I said. "Is your name Andreus?" He stopped and looked at me. "How do you know my name?"

"A mutual friend," I answered and clipped him in the jaw. He went down like a sack of potatoes, and I quickly caught the body, dragged him to the front of the van, and gently lay him down. "There you go, buddy. Pleasant dreams." About then Rosie came down the steps and saw the body. I answered before she could ask. "No, he's not dead, just taking a nap. He will wake up in a little while with a sore jaw, but he will be okay." I took her hand. "Let's meet your friends. I opened the side door to the van and spoke to eleven very scared girls. "Good morning. My name is Russell. I'm Ludmilla's friend that you have probably heard of. Do all of you speak English?" About half nodded their heads. "Okay, those that can, please translate for those that can't. I'm here to offer you a way out of here. I will take you to a safe place, and if you want, eventually get you back home. There are other options. You don't have to go, but I'm afraid that if you don't, I will have to drop you off in Homestead so I can get a head start before you talk to your bosses." I waited for a moment so the girls could translate. I closed the side doors and jumped into the driver's seat. "Are we all in? Any questions?" Slowly, one by one all the girls nodded their heads. Then one spoke. She turned her wrist face up, showing tracks, and said in halting English. "We need medicine." I nodded to her. "I know most of you are strung out on heroin. Pastor Dave will get you on a methadone program as soon as you get there, and get you off the hard stuff. It's part of the deal." Again more murmuring among them and then smiles. "Yes, Yes! We go!" I waved at Rio, and she nodded, and then I started the van and pulled it up onto US1.

Next stop, Melbourne.

31
If It Wasn't For Bad Luck….

Despite Rosie giving her bosses a false description of me, Andreus got a very good look at my face. I needed to change my description as much as possible. I wish I could have shaved the beard off, but too many of my old Key West chums knew this mug. I decided to make another visit to Goodwill. This time, I opted to look a little chubbier than normal and picked up baggy pants that were about four sizes too big, and a couple of flannel shirts that I could wear over two tee shirts. A little Grecian Formula in my beard to make it darker and a cheap pair of wire frame sunglasses under a floppy hat and, at least, I thought it was enough of a change not to draw immediate suspicion at first sight. I opened the gate, and Rio was already sitting in the van, smoking a joint. I frowned in disapproval when I got in the passenger side.

"Think that's a good idea?" I asked. "I need your senses sharp in case something goes wrong."

Rio took another long drag and flipped the blunt out of the window. "This does make my senses sharp," she answered. "Besides, this is our fifth or sixth rescue, and so far it's gone without a hitch."

"Yeah, if you call two dead guys and two in the hospital without a hitch," I answered. "I ain't no spring chicken, and eventually, one of these young studs is gonna get the drop on me. I'm sure Andreus made me, and they are probably beefing up their security a lot after I stole their van and a dozen girls at once." Rio shrugged, started the van, and we drove off, heading slowly up Truman. "Where to?" she asked.

"Hog's Breath," I answered. "Haven't been near there for a while." I turned to Rio. "Listen, I don't think we're going to be able to safely do this much longer. I want to plan a raid on the crib soon, grab as many as we can, and then leak what we know to the law so they get shut down."

"Why don't you just go to the authorities right now, or give me enough info that I can go?" Rio asked.

I thought for a moment. "If they raid the place with twenty girls inside, they will probably get caught in the crossfire. Some might get hurt or killed, and worse yet, thrown in jail for prostitution. Better to clean them out and then bust them before the next shipment comes in."

Rio pulled up behind the Hog's Breath on Front Street, shut the ignition off, and turned toward me. "You know you can't stop this," she said. "They will just start up in a different place. It's too lucrative. You might as well try to stop the ocean from coming ashore. You can't win."

I opened the door and stepped out of the van. "I can't win the war, but I can win a battle. If we save a dozen, then we have won a little. Hell, if we saved one, that's a victory." I started to close the door smiled at Rio and pointed. "Park down the street. You know the drill. Do you have all you need to get to Melbourne?"

"All good" Rio answered. "Plenty cash, plenty stash. Good for a round trip."

I frowned my disapproval again, turned, and walked up the street to the Hog's Breath. I sat down at a small table outdoors, ordered a beer, and started people-watching. Hog's Breath is always a mix of locals and tourists, with the odds leaning towards tourists if there was a cruise ship tied up at Mallory Square. I didn't have to look toward the water to know there weren't any cruise ships in port. Not a single senior citizen in white tennies, calf-high athletic socks, aloha shirt, Bermuda shorts, and skin either snow white or beet read. No ships tonight and not much of a crowd either. Two beers and an hour later and I was beginning to wonder if the evening was going to be a bust. So far the success ratio has been about one for every four sorties, about equal to a cheetah in Africa. Since one of the baddies got a look at me before he got away the other day, I was starting to feel they might have become a little more cautious. I needed to change my modus operandi, but I wasn't sure how.

By midnight, it was beginning to look like another no-go when I saw a girl walk into the bar from the Duval parking lot. I ordered one more beer and watched her out of the corner of my eye. Thin, almost gaunt, small frame, lots of makeup, leggings, heels, and a tank top. They all seemed to dress alike. She sat down at the bar, and I watched the bartender make her a drink without her asking. I could also tell it was just club soda with a slice of lime. She sipped her drink from a straw and started working on eye contact with the half dozen single men sitting around the bar. A couple of smiles, a wink and she caught the attention of a biker dude sitting across from her. She slid off her chair and walked around to his side, sitting down beside him. They shook hands and started chatting. Ten minutes later he was running his hands over her ass and kissing her neck. She whispered something in his ear. He nodded, and they walked out on Front Street, likely heading for a dark alley. It was getting late, and I was considering calling it a night but thought I might hang for a bit longer. Sure enough, fifteen minutes later the girl came back to the bar, and the bartender made her another drink. In the parking lot, I heard the rumble of a Harley as the biker rode off in apparent satisfaction.

Well, now or never.

I picked up my beer and moved over to the bar, just across from the girl. She didn't wait long and caught my eye with a wink. I smiled over my beer glass, and with a hand, invited her to join me on my side. She looked good at fifteen feet. Next to me, she looked like she was made up to look good at fifteen feet. Lots of makeup, but beneath that, dark circles under her eyes, teeth going bad and thin, skin and bones thin. She forced a smile on me and introduced herself.

"My name is Jane," she announced in a bad accent. She was no more a Jane than I was Mickey Mouse.

"Pleased ta meet cha," I slurred back, not offering my name. "Buy you another drink?" She motioned to the bartender, and he nodded, moving around to the other side of the counter so I couldn't see he was making another club soda.

"Where do you come from?" she asked.

I figured it was best to cut right to the chase. "Marathon," I answered. "They ain't many purty girls like you up in Marathon." And I looked her in the eyes.

She looked surprised. Then a little scared. She answered with one word, and it was a whisper. "Ludmilla"

"I know she's gone," I said. "She was trying to help."

"You are in danger," she whispered. "They are looking for a

man with a reddish-gray beard. They are watching all of us."

I thought for a second. Risk one more rescue, or try to get them all? I came to a decision.

"I'm sure you know what girls you can trust. Listen. I'm going to try and get everyone out I can. Let them know I'm working on a plan. Can you do that?"

"Yes," she answered and I slid a hundred toward her. "Ok, if your boss asks, just tell him I was too drunk to get it up, and that I wasn't the guy they are looking for. I'll use the same code word 'Marathon' next time I run into one of your friends. Got it?" She nodded. I stood up and staggered out of the back of the Hog's Breath toward the van where Rio was parked. Nobody was behind the wheel. She was probably taking a nap in the back.

I just barely caught motion to my left in time to react.

Wayne Gales

<h1 style="text-align:center">32
Double Trouble</h1>

Key West Conch Crier – Tuesday, October 15

ANOTHER DOUBLE HOMICIDE IN OLD TOWN

Two unidentified men were found murdered in an alley on Front Street Monday night. One person was apparently dead from a blunt-trauma head injury and the other had suffered a fatal knife wound to the chest. The two-hundred block of Front Street has been cordoned off while the police investigation continues. No suspects have been arrested, and neighbors reported no unusual noises during the evening. This makes the second double homicide in Key West in three weeks. Authorities suspect some sort of fundamentalist vigilante gang from the Midwest is targeting Eastern Europeans. Key West police have asked for help from the FBI.

It was four a.m. Rio parked the van around the corner from her house, and we sat there for ten minutes to see if anyone suspicious was around. "I think we're clear," she said. "Can you get out on your own?"

"Not sure" I answered. "This cut on my leg is bleeding pretty bad. I think you might need to help me." I turned around to check on the girl. She was huddled on a beanbag chair, arms clasped around her body, shivering from fright. "You just stay right here," I told her. "Sabine will be back down shortly and drive you to safety. Understand?" She nodded, and Rio opened the side door. I gingerly eased out to the street. Rio hooked my arm around her neck and closed the door. It was just a few dozen feet to the back gate, but every step was agony. I had the cut pretty well bandaged, but it wouldn't be long before I would be trailing blood. We saw another couple walking down the street, coming toward us. I did my best to just look like another drunk staggering home. Thankfully we ducked into the backyard without any other attention.

"The steps are gonna be a bitch," I said. "One at a time."

"You need to see a doctor," Rio said, keeping the weight off my left leg as we made it up the steps.

"Those two bodies are gonna be splashed all over the papers in the morning," I answered. "If I go to the hospital, I would instantly be suspect number one. It's not a bad cut, just messy. All I need is some antiseptic and a few stitches, and I'll be good as new. Two years ago and he would have never got to me. Guess I'm slowing down."

We made it to the loft, and I laid back on the couch. "Let me get a towel," she said. "Take your pants off so I can see what needs to be done, and then I'll go to CVS and get what we need."

"Everything I need is in a bag on the floor in the bedroom," I answered, pulling my pants down. "Anti-B, peroxide, alcohol, butterfly Band-Aids. I even have a needle and some dental floss if we need to stitch it up."

I leaned back on the couch and winced from the knife wound, then looked up at her. "Please bring me those medical supplies before you head out. I need to get this cleaned and bandaged." Rio went to the bedroom and carried out the bag with the bandages, then knelt in front of me. "Let me help," she said and opened the bag.

"Really, I'm ok. Thank you for offering, but I can clean and bandage this. It's messy but not too bad. You get on the road and get this girl to Melbourne.

"Bric, no, I....."

"Git!" I said. "Thank you, but I need to be alone for a while." She reluctantly rose, then leaned down and kissed me on the forehead.

"I'll be back in two days." She said and walked toward the door, opened it, and turned back toward me. "It's not that you treat women poorly, it's that you don't know when you need them near you." And she left, closing the door behind her.

I sat there for a few minutes feeling sorry for myself, and then it was time to tend to my wounds. Yes, wounds. I carefully peeled off my flannel shirt. The red of the shirt hid the growing red stain on my left shoulder. I took the scissors out of the bag and cut the tee shirt away, then wet a gauze with peroxide and started wiping away the caked blood. I took the little mirror out of the medical bag and examined the hole. Small puncture wound just under the collarbone. My left arm wasn't going to be much good for a few days. Like the leg, it was a flesh wound and it didn't appear to have nicked any critical parts. For the moment, I put some anti-b on a four-by-four and taped it up. The leg needed a little more attention. I cleaned all around it, took out the curved sewing needle and a length of dental floss.

I don't care how macho Rambo was. Five stitches hurt like fuck, but ten minutes later, the wound was closed and bandaged. Using the chair as a crutch, I stood up and nearly fainted. Pain, loss of blood, and the adrenaline wearing off all combined for a knockout punch. I needed to get all the standing done all at once. I peed and then went to the cupboard. Behind the Cheerios was a bottle of Jack. I lied to other people (and myself) about no booze in the place. I grabbed a glass, filled it with ice, and hobbled back to the couch, then poured myself three fingers of painkiller, then reached into the bag, and opened a bottle of Percocet. I tossed three down my throat and followed them with the Jack. Then I laid back on the couch, closed my eyes, and drifted off.

Ah, the dinosaur dream. I had been reliving this dream since I was a little kid, obsessed with dinosaurs. Running through city streets, hiding behind cars, under beds, in dark alleys, being chased for what seemed like days, always being chased by a T-Rex. The only difference was after I grew up, I would know it was a dream, but that didn't make it any less scary. I was running, running, pouring sweat, lying quietly under a car, listening to see if the Rex knew where I was. I could hear my own breathing... and then another sound, a distant sound, growing closer. Something was standing over me.

"whuf.. whuf..Bric.. Bric.. BRIC!"

I woke with a start. My eyes were swollen, almost closed, and stinging with sweat.. the couch was soaked. I tried to sit up and couldn't. I squinted at all the people standing over me.

"Who?" I croaked.

Rio leaned down and put a cold, wet cloth across my eyes. "Friends," somebody said. I heard another voice. "You're burning up, buddy. Need to get you to the hospital."

"Tim?"

287

"Yeah pal," another voice said. "Your friend here came and found me, and I rounded up Bo Morgan and Tack. These other two just showed up outta nowhere. Looks like your homemade doctoring sucks."

"Rumpy?"

"You gone and done fucked yourself up good, honey!"

"Scarlet! Where did you come from?"

Another voice came from across the room. I lifted the washcloth and saw a burly figure with a mustache in the shadows. It took me a moment to recognize him. "Hey there, Bric. Don't worry about those pussies down the street." He pulled a medium-sized cannon out of a side holster. "The posse's here and I got your six."

Caretaker? What the hell was he doing here from Vegas?

Tim spoke again. "We've got an ambulance coming over right now. Don't worry. I told the hospital I have a subject in the witness program so they won't ask questions about whom or why, but we either need to get you some attention or go to Home Depot and buy six brass handles.

"How long?" I asked.

"Five days from what Rio says," Tim answered. "She needs to learn that when you say 'leave me alone' she shouldn't leave you alone."

"Karen?" I asked.

"Flew the coop," Tim answered. I spoke to her yesterday when I was looking for you. She left Marathon and headed back to Okie. Not to worry. I've got her back, and some locals up there will keep an eye on her. I think you have managed to make that trail cold at least, but you sure got one helluva hornet's nest stirred up here."

I heard the whoop of an ambulance outside. Then I remembered and tried to sit up.

"Girls," I said. "We need......"

"No rush," Rio said. "Gone. Everyone. The cops raided the house this morning, and it was empty. The baddies and all their girls are long gone from Key West. Guess they figured flight was better than fight the Phantom Menace – namely you. Likely setting up shop on Saint Somewhere as we speak."

The crowded room got more crowded when three paramedics

came in. Two minutes later I was hooked up to all kinds of machinery, and they were talking in code.

"BP seventy over thirty, pulse one sixty and thready. Temp one oh four. He's borderline v-tach." They turned to Rio. "We need to transport him now." They were talking like I wasn't there, or like I wasn't going to be there long. As it was, I was almost feeling like I was outside looking at everyone from above. They were trying to talk to me.

"Mister Phillips, we're gonna take you to the hospital. Do you understand?"

I understood but didn't want to talk to them. I just wanted to sleep.

Sleep.

I was dozing, but I could hear people talking.

"BP down to fifty! We're losing him!"

What were they losing? I don't care. They were losing something and I'm going to sleep through it.

The scream of the ambulance siren woke me back up. I opened my eyes and Rio was sitting next to me holding my hand. I could feel the hard plastic of an oxygen mask on my face and my arm was being squeezed with a blood pressure cuff. I looked up at Rio.

"Are all those guys coming to the hospital?" I asked.

"What guys?" She answered.

"Tim, Bo, Scarlet, The Caretaker, Rumpy, everyone," I answered.

"I don't know what you're talking about," she answered. It was just me in the house. You kept talking like you were talking to other people, but it was just me."

"Am I dying?" I asked.

She squeezed my hand and answered softly, almost to herself.

"You can't die. Superman never dies."

Wayne Gales

Epilogue – One Year Later

"Rumpy! Refresh mine too!" and I handed up my empty red Solo cup. The crystal clear waters of Boca Grande never felt better. It was a Tuesday afternoon and I could only see two other boats in sight. Two decent Cobia and a twenty-pound Blackfin Tuna were chilling in the ice chest. We could have caught more, but that was enough meat to last both of us for a while, and would nicely supplement the freezer full of lobster tails. We were anchored up in four feet of water, and the Wave Whacker lazily bobbed on a slack anchor line, just a few hundred yards from the spot where I tripped over that Spanish cannon, what seemed like ages ago. Rumpy handed both refills down to me, then pitched a float in the water and gave me a plastic tub full of jumbo Key West pink shrimp and a Tupperware bowl of horseradish-laced chilled cocktail sauce. He came back down the steps, recovered his drink, and dove into the shrimp, peeling the crustaceans clean and throwing the shells over his shoulder. The ocean is an unacceptable trash can, but shrimp shells are organic, and in a few minutes we had an audience of various species eagerly making off with our tossed shells and tails. Hanging around the outskirts were a few needlefish and, at least, one juvenile barracuda enjoying the target-rich environment.

The food chain was healthy.

Drink in hand, Rumpy was satisfied to relax, dip chilled shrimp into the sauce, and listen to Bill Hoebee tell bad jokes on WAIL Radio.

"You know, next time we come out this way, we should load the boat with some extra cargo of the female species. People gonna start thinking we've gone Brokeback Mountain."

"Ah, I don't go that way, but if I decide to jump the fence, I'll be sure to call you first," I replied.

"Well, then, I'll round us up some female talent for the next excursion," he said. "You prefer blonde, brunette, or redhead?"

I closed my eyes for a moment and looked at the clouds for guidance.

"Not just yet, my friend, not just yet."

He turned and eyed the storm cloud to the west.

"Think it'll get to us, mister weatherman?" He asked, changing the subject.

I eyed the cloud, felt the wind direction on my face, and wet a finger. "It'll miss us to the west," I announced, sounding as convincing as possible.

Rumpy stared at the phone for a few more minutes. "I think we'll get wet, but then we are already wet. I can live with it."

I chuckled at Rump's eternal optimism, ate a shrimp, and sipped my rum drink. The cloud might be coming, but the sun felt good on my shoulders right now, especially the left one which was permanently a little stiff. I smiled to myself and took a moment to think back.

It had been an eventful year.

I was in the hospital for nearly two months. It took the docs a few hours to find the real problem. My bandage job on my thigh was just fine, even if it was a little sloppy, but that little hole up in my shoulder was a different matter. X-rays showed a foreign object and the surgeon removed a nine-millimeter slug, along with a patch of flannel shirt later that day. I didn't know I had even been shot, or shot at for that matter. Docs said it was already deformed when it hit me and was apparently a ricochet. Had it been a direct shot it would have probably blown through me, nicked a lung, and put me six feet under the lawn. As it was, my putting a patch on the hole with a gauze bandage almost did the trick. I guess it was nip and tuck for a few weeks, but I don't remember any of it. I have no clue why the doc's didn't report the bullet wound to the cops, which would have made me the prime suspect in four murders. Tim wasn't even in the state that night. I guess it's a mystery best left unsolved.

About the time I got out in late February, Rio started getting sick. The cancer had come back with a vengeance, and there was little we could do but make her as comfortable as possible. She passed quietly in a Boca Raton hospice with me holding her hand. Rumpy and I spread her ashes over the beach at Boca Grande, a place we often visited near the end.

I shall miss her.

Bo Morgan sold his compound, the two houseboats and the

Captain Morgan and moved to Fort Lauderdale to be with his family. Ironically, his houseboat caught fire due to a propane leak a few months after and burned to the waterline.

Tim retired from the agency, moved to Ensenada, and now manages a brothel called the Hookery. Based on my recent activity, Tim assured me that his staff is voluntary, professional, happy, well-paid, and tested monthly. He doesn't work much, just pours drinks and chats with the patrons. We keep in touch via Facebook now. He says they are closed on Sundays. The sign on the door says "Closed today. Beat it." He also joked that he tried to set up Driver's Ed and Sex Ed classes at the house, but the donkey got too tired.

It could be worse.

I called Karen a few weeks ago. The conversation was cordial but cool. I filled her in with my current endeavors in the hope she might come back, but I think that chapter has closed.

As they say, you don't know what you've got till it's gone.

Mary Elizabeth blossomed like a caterpillar turning into a butterfly. The last time I saw her, she was as pretty as her sister, maybe prettier, dressed tastefully and walking like she didn't have a care in the world. She recently moved back to California and had become quite worldly. She works for the San Francisco Examiner and last I heard she was engaged.

Lex met some sheik or Sultan, gave the Targa to a home for pregnant nuns, and moved to Dubai. She probably won't hit the ground till she's in her forties. I don't know if she's chasing or running, and if she will ever be really happy. Hopefully, I can keep track of her through Mary.

No, Lex and I never did it, but we just about nearly almost did in that shack during the tropical storm.

Rumpy, bless his heart, announced last month that he was retiring and would start drawing Social Security. This stunned me. Retire from what? I never saw him work a day in his life, aside from promoting the occasional fishing tournament or bikini-clad beauty pageant. The rest of the time he fishes, takes people fishing, gets other people to catch his lobsters for him, and sits in the bathtub-warm water on Marvin Key, eating chilled Key West pinks and sucking down boat drinks.

I should have copied *his* lifestyle.

Me? Well, to start with, I bought Grandma Sawyer's mansion on Fleming Street from the family, with a little money laundering assistance from Rumpy. I couldn't prove who I was and I didn't dare let Wendy's relatives find out who I *really* was. The old place was over a hundred fifty years old and close to falling down. Now it's undergoing a ground-up renovation, complete with a modern kitchen, central air, and a little pool with a Jacuzzi in the back. Hopefully, it will open in a few months as a six-room bed and breakfast. "*Nobody's Inn*" will keep *me* occupied, as long as I keep *it* occupied. After buying the mansion, paying serious dollars for the renovation. (I needed to give the termites some fresh wood to chew on), I topped off Grace Alice and Brody's trust fund and then sent half the remaining balance to Karen. After that, I sent a cashier's check for almost all the rest to the Church on the Way in Melbourne. Pastor David will be able to rescue a lot more fallen angels with a couple of million in the kitty. He doesn't know where it came from, but he probably guessed, and I'm good with that. Someday I'll head back up to Melbourne and share a five-cent bowl of bean soup with him at Meg O'Malley's.

Walking away from that treasure was the best thing I've ever done. I hope it causes him less grief than it caused me.

Rescues? Rio and I managed to get thirty-six girls away from the bad guys. Some repatriated to their home countries with a little nest egg to help them get started in real life. Many chose to stay in America and start over. A few, from what I hear, alas, fell back to the dark side. You can't win them all, but you always have to try.

Someday soon, I'll let the kids know I'm alive and kicking, quietly and without fanfare. I've finally managed to get the bad guys off my ass, and I don't want Brody and Grace to become targets after all this.

Speaking of the kids, Brody's working a pirate wreck off the coast of South Carolina. I hear he's well. Friends tell me he sleeps on shore every night and isn't lonely if you get my drift. Grace Alice is enjoying her trust fund, living among the pines in Washington State, working on her Bachelor's degree in music with an eye on a

Masters. The first member of my family to be college-educated.

Daddy's proud.

For the first time in a long time, I feel alive. If I want to eat, I have to make that little B&B profitable. In the meantime, I guess I can survive on shrimp, fish, and lobster, or, in hard times, grunts and grits and the occasional rum drink. I'm slowing down, but maybe there might be one or two adventures left in me. After all, adventure is my version *of Key West Normal,* and Key West's reality beats every place else's fiction.

I'm sure I'll think of something.

About the Author

Wayne Gales is a recognized award-winning author, chef, and resort marketing professional. A world traveler, former motorcycle racer, and active musician, Wayne has been a Florida resident since 1991. He discovered the magic of the Florida Keys while making visits to the islands on business. In his spare time, he poured over old microfilm in the Monroe County Library, tracking a Conch family heritage that goes back over ten generations. Gales finally moved to Key West and lived there for several years. During his final stay in Key West in the late nineties, he lived on a houseboat, closely following the storyline of his first novel Treasure Key. Today, Wayne is retired and lives in Melbourne, Florida with his wife Tina.

Also Available on Amazon By Wayne Gales

Treasure Key
Key West Camoflauge
Nobody's Inn Key West
Everybody's Bar in Key West
Southernmost Exposure
Southernmost Son
Bone Island Bodies
Once Upon a time in Key West
Living and Dying in Key West Time
The last three books available on Audible as a Trilogy

Cooking for the Hearing Impaired

Children's books, Illustrated by Lori Kus

We Wish to Fish
Sun, Sand, and the Salty Sea
Caught No Fish

Made in United States
Orlando, FL
27 May 2025

61630648R00164